ZION

The Long Road to Sanctification

Volume II   A Novel

Other Books by Authors

Larry Barkdull
  The Mourning Dove
  Praise to the Man
  The Touch of the Master's Hand
  Zion—Seeking the City of Enoch

Ron McMillan
  The Balancing Act: Mastering the Competing Demands of Leadership

Lance Richardson
  Knotted Gold
  They Saw Our Day—tape set

ZION

The Long Road to Sanctification

Volume II   A Novel

Larry Barkdull

Lance Richardson · Ron McMillan

Evans Book
Salt Lake City, Utah

Published by: Evans Book, Salt Lake City, Utah
                 801-975-1315

Cover Design by Douglass Cole of Cole Design, Orem, Utah
Edited by Paul Rawlins
Typography by SunriseBooks.com

Manufactured in the United States of America
10 9 8 7 6 5 4 3 2 1
Library of Congress Catalog Card Number: 00-133090
ISBN: 1-56684-652-8

To our parents
John and Doris, Mel and Dixie, Howard and Beverly

ෆ

Special thanks are extended to Ted Gibbons,
Larry Johnston, and Elizabeth Barkdull

This book and its predecessor are works of fiction. The content is the responsibility of the authors. Although the existence of Enoch and Zion can be documented, the authors have not tried to write a history book. Rather, the purpose of these works has been to *discover* the principles of Zion that Enoch taught and the people lived in order to establish the most successful of all societies. Multicultural and historical literature were consulted. Liberties were taken for the sake of creating a setting by which a story of Zion could be told. All said, the underlying intention for the authors' writing these books has been to foster an interest in Zion with the belief that such a society is in our future.

people and places

Abel
A son of Adam and Eve who was murdered by his brother Cain. Abel-worship, a sign of an apostate world, had crept into Dananite culture.

Abiah
(Ăb ī′ äh) Wife of Ebanel. Rabunel's mother who died in the drought when Rabunel was a child.

Adul
(Ăd ool′) Wife of Gensek from the land of Danan.

Anna
Wife of Enoch. She was born in the land of Cainan.

Asher
A Watcher from the land of Nod.

Azazel
(Āz ăz ĕl′) Chief of the Watchers and supreme leader of Nod.

Baruch
(Bäh rook′) Rabunel's former competitor in Shum. Father of Joshua. His wife Leah and daughter Rachel were killed in Shum. Also the name given to one of Micah's and Miriam's twin boys.

Benjamin
Eldest living child of Rabunel and Moriah. Married to Sarah. Father to Nathaniel, Dan, Deborah, who was named after his great-grandfather.

Cain
The wicked son of Adam and Eve who murdered his brother Abel by conspiracy and in the process founded a secret society called the Mahan. Later, he settled in the land of Nod.

Cainan
(Kān′ ăn) Not to be confused with Canaan. A land by the east sea founded by Enos, Adam's grandson, who named it for his son Cainan. The land where Enoch and Anna were born. The home of the patriarchs from Enos to Enoch, who described it as "a righteous land to this day."

Chaz
(Chăz) Prince of Shum, son of the king Mahijah. Formerly betrothed to Rabunel's daughter, Eve. Killed in the final battle of Shum.

Dan
Infant son of Benjamin and Sarah.

Danan   (Dăn´ ăn) A city of much poverty where the people
               lived in servitude to the people of Nod. Enoch and
               Joshua had great success in their missionary labors
               among the people of Danan or the Dananites.
Danbenihah   (Dăn bĕn ī´ häh) A former judge from the land of Abel.
Deborah   Infant daughter of Benjamin and Sarah.
Ebanel   (Ĕb ăn ĕl´) The righteous father of Rabunel. He was the
               son of Simeon, the Watcher. He died in Shum helping
               Rabunel and others escape. Also the name given to
               Joshua's and Eve's baby.
Enoch   The young prophet called by God and ordained by
               Adam to preach repentance and build a city of con-
               summate peace. He was born in the land of Cainan
               and was the son of Jared. He was the "seventh from
               Adam," and had the birthright. He established ZION
               when he was sixty-five. Being the great-grandfather of
               Noah, he is father to the human race.
Enos   The youngest son of Rabunel and Moriah who married
               Naomi.
Esther   A former slave girl who was ransomed by Enos.
Eve   The daughter of Rabunel and Moriah who married
               Joshua.
Gad   A leader of the army of Nod and the former captain of
               the Rahaj in Shum.
Gensek   (Gĕn´ sĕk) A prominent Dananite whom Joshua
               brought to the City of Enoch along with his family. The
               husband of Adul and father of Naomi.
Hanannihah   (Hăn ăn ī´ häh) A prominent city and crossroads of
               trade where Enoch preached. The land where Micah
               formerly managed mines.
Ishmael   A leader in the City of Enoch. Overseer of the
               Shepherds' Storehouse.
Jarom   (Jĕr´ um) An outpost near Nod where their army
               trained. The place that Moriah was taken hostage.

Jerel   (Jĕr ĕl′) Son of Rabunel and Moriah. He was killed by a bear during a trade trip with his father.

Joshua   Son of Baruch. Married Eve. Father to Seth and Ebanel, who was named after his great-grandfather. A successful missionary to the Dananites.

Mahijah   (Mäh hī′ jäh) The king of Shum.

Mahan   (Mäh hŏn′) Secret society first established by Cain to obtain power and wealth by conspiracy. Held together by priestcraft.

Melca   (Mĕl′ käh) Young daughter of Enoch and Anna.

Messiah   In the various books of Enoch, he is also called the Holy One, or the Elect One of God. It was understood that he would come to earth many years after the time of Enoch and atone for the sins of mankind. Enoch preached that he was the servant of the Messiah.

Micah   One of Enoch's first converts in Shum. A large, strong man and great leader in the City of Enoch. He married Miriam and had twin boys, whom he named after his two friends Baruch and Rabunel.

Miriam   Rabunel's niece, whom he adopted. Mother of Rachel and twin boys fathered by Micah: Baruch and Rabunel. A dedicated servant to the infirm of Danan.

Moriah   (Mōr ī′ äh) Wife of Rabunel. Mother of Jerel, Benjamin, Enos, and Eve.

Muriel   (Mūr ē êl′) A woman from the City of Enoch who died and was seen by Rabunel during his visit to the world of spirits.

Naomi   (Nā ō′ mē) Daughter of Gensek and Adul. She married Enos.

Nathaniel   Eldest son of Benjamin and Sarah.

Nod   The land that Cain settled. The Mahan and Watchers were headquartered there and marshaled a force bent on conquering the world. The people of Nod were the mortal enemies of the People of God.

Omar	The chief guard of the prison of Saad.
Omner	A neighboring community to the land of Sharon. Place where Baruch traded.
Rabunel	(Räh boon ĕl') Main character of the story. Grandson of Simeon, who is the leader of the Watchers; son of Ebanel, who died in Shum; husband of Moriah; father of Jerel, who died, Benjamin, Eve, and Enos. Rabunel is also the name given to one of Micah's and Miriam's twin boys.
Rachel	Daughter of Miriam who was fathered by the Watchers in Shum. She was delivered by Baruch, and became the granddaughter to Rabunel by adoption. Through her descendants a girl would be born who would marry Noah's son, Shem, thus preserving Rabunel's posterity on the earth.
Rahaj	(Räh häj') Militant, corrupt, police-like force that was subservient to the Watchers. The Rahaj was especially active in Shum.
Ramurah	(Rä mūr' äh) The first king of the land of Shum. Son of Shum. Father of Mahijah.
Rebekah	The young woman with whom Jerel fell in love in the world of spirits.
Reuben	Son of Ishmael who infiltrated the army of Nod and helped the people of the City of Enoch escape.
Saad	(Sähd) A city across the river and lying in the same valley as the Dananite camp. It was close enough to the City of Enoch to influence trade and entice worldly temptations among the People of God. Saad harbored the Mahan, Watchers, and some of the army of Nod. Initially shunned by the People of God, Saad was eventually embraced, which, in part, caused the downfall of the first City of Enoch.
Sarah	Wife of Benjamin. Mother of Nathaniel, Dan, and Deborah.

Sasha	Young Dananite girl who suffered from leprosy.
Seth	Joshua's and Eve's first son, named after Adam's son.
Sharon	A land adjacent to Shum whose people Shum considered to be enemies. It became the envy of Mahijah for its incredible wealth.
Shum	A land established after a global drought. It became a prosperous tent city under a king named Ramurah and later his son, Mahijah. It was the city where Rabunel, his family, and many others lived when Enoch was sent by God to preach repentance. It was destroyed because of its wickedness.
Simeon	Wicked grandfather of Rabunel. The leader of the Watchers and now a leader in Nod.
Watchers	False priests who had once been righteous and had officiated in the temples of Adam, learning much about God, then rebelled and followed Lucifer. Originating from the Mahan society that Cain established, they corrupted every truth to prosper themselves and get power over the people. They openly fought against God.
Zion	Individually and collectively the pure in heart, a person or people who is or are sacredly devoted to God. A name for God's holy city. A place so sanctified that God can dwell within it.

These all . . . confessed that they were strangers and pilgrims on the earth . . . But now they desire a better country, that is, an heavenly: wherefore God is not ashamed to be called their God: for he hath prepared for them a city.

Hebrews 11:13, 16

"All that is not given is lost."
—Hasari Pal

City of Joy

the mahan

ℭ

I am Rabunel. This story is mine. I lived it every part.

I broke into the darkness of night, fleeing like a fawn from danger. I plunged into a ravine; then, in full stride, I leapt to a craggy edge and clawed for the top. I heard the pounding of a horse's hooves behind me, fumes of hot air blowing from the animal's nostrils. The dark figure of a man shadowed me. Then another. Without warning, the first screamed and charged me. I cut to a clearing that narrowed as I raced through it. Although the night was moonless, I could distinguish the dim boundaries of the gulch tightening about me like a noose. A sharp thought knifed through my brain: I was being driven!

Then the horse was upon me. A hard blow to my shins sent me tumbling out of control. I hit the ground, rolling, crying out in pain. Someone dove on my back, a large man, thrusting his arms up under my shoulders, lacing his fingers behind my neck.

—You're a dead man! he breathed. You'll never get to Danan.

I smelled his sweat. A sliver of spittle leaked from his mouth when he cursed me. I struggled, but his weight and strength were twice mine. Quickly, the other horse's rider leapt from his mount and came to the side of the big man, sitting on my flailing legs and binding them with a rope. The big man rolled me to my back, straddled me, and pinned my shoulders to the ground with his knees while the other tied my hands over my head and gagged me with a rag. The two spoke in grunts or short phrases: *Ropes tight? Yes. Lift him up.*

I could recognize neither of them, not their voices nor their faces. They were hooded and seemed intent on disguising their speech. The large one hefted me onto his shoulder as easily as one might lift a sack of grain, then threw me, stomach down, over the sway of a horse's back. The steed went wide eyed and reared its head, stumbled, then found its footing. Within moments, the small man took the reins and led the horse and its load away at a quick clip.

☙

How long had I ridden belly-down over the horse? My stomach ached from the pounding. I tried to beg a reprieve through the gag, but I was answered with a rod across my back. I thought, *If I were a strong man like Micah, I would break these bands and free myself.* But I wasn't a strong man.

—If the Dananites join the City of Enoch, no army will be able to conquer them, said the small man.

—Too many people, the big man said. They are becoming too big. Is he conscious?

The small man stopped the horse and came around to check me. I closed my eyes. He lifted my head by the hair.

—Unconscious, I think.

The big man made a grunting sound and said, Lower your voice.

I sensed the jerk of the reigns and the horse stepped forward. I had left the City of Enoch earlier that evening on a journey to Danan. I had volunteered but still had felt reservations. Obviously, somebody didn't approve of my mission to proselytize the Dananites. Few issues had evoked more passion among the people of the City of Enoch.

We traveled a long distance in silence. My legs swung limply from one side of the horse while my arms, bound at the wrists, hung over my head as though I were reaching for the ground. My face pressed against the sweaty flesh of the horse's side, and I could hear the animal heaving as it plodded forward. I thought my ribs would break. The men began to converse again.

—Nothing short of killing him will stop him, said the big man.

—Simeon said to hold him.

The mention of my grandfather's name made me shudder. Our paths had diverged long ago, and I had hoped they would not cross again.

—Simeon is a fool, said the big man. He's sentimental. He will save his life because Rabunel is family. Better that we kill him. We're the ones taking the chance, not Simeon.

—You want to answer to Simeon? He said beat him and hold him.

—Too risky.

—We'll beat him like we planned, said the small man. Then it will be on Simeon's head whether or not Rabunel goes to Danan.

—Of all people, you know what that means.

—I know. Too many people. Too many.

—Rabunel will go to Danan, alright. Simeon is a fool.

—I've never taken a life, said the small man.

I sensed a pause, as though the big man was surprised.

—I'll do it, he said.

I tugged at the ropes that bound my hands and felt a knot give way. In the cloak of darkness I struggled until I felt some freedom in my hands. Soon, the big man ordered the small man to stop, then he pulled me from the horse, and dropped me on the ground.

—Beat him, but don't kill him, argued the small man.

I sensed silence as though the big man was making a decision.

—Dig out the opening to the pit! he said, finally. We'll beat him and leave him for Simeon. But it's a mistake.

I turned my head enough to see the small man retrieve a spade and began to dig.

The large man knelt beside me, grabbed me by the hair, and said, If it were my choice, this would be your grave!

Then, he doubled his fist and sunk it deep into my belly. I curled in pain. The air exploded from my lungs and I fought for breath. He hit me on the jaw—first on the right side, then on the left.

Suddenly, the small man said, It's open.

The big man stood and walked to the digging site. I groaned and rolled to my side to see the two standing over what appeared to be an opening. A night mist hovered about them like infernal apparitions rising from Hell and encircling them in eerie gloom. The small man picked up a stone and dropped it, and the two leaned forward as if listening for the sound of its striking ground. Momentarily alone, I struggled to slip my hands from the bands and, one freed, I quickly removed the rope at my feet.

I heard the big man say, It will have to do. Let's go get him.

As the two dark figures moved toward me, I lay still and groaned.

—Take his arms; I'll take his legs, said the big man.

That was my signal. When the big man reached down to grab my feet, I kicked hard and caught the big man in the thigh, sending him sprawling.

—You'll pay! he cried.

I jumped to my feet, pushed his startled partner out of the way, and leapt on the horse. The big man had recovered and rushed me.

—Stop him! he cried.

The small man scrambled to his feet. As he ran at me, I dug my heels into the horse's flanks and aimed the animal at him. The steed reared, and while I fought to keep my balance, the small man pulled me from the horse's back, and the animal ran off frightened into the night.

The big man raced to where I was lying, blade drawn, and he wrestled me to my back, then made as though he would run me through. I caught his arm with both hands and the small man tried to pull him back.

—If you kill him, Simeon will make us pay! The Mahan are not allowed failure.

—I don't care!

The small man grabbed him at the wrist.

—Think what you're doing!

I struggled to spit the rag from my mouth and cried, Don't kill me!

The big man clenched his teeth. His arms were tight and cordlike. Even struggling together, the small man and I hadn't the strength to stop him. Suddenly, he bore down with all his strength, and I felt the sharp edge of his blade slice into my side. The small man tugged at him to pull him back, and I cried out in agony. That the knife missed its aim seemed to infuriate the big man. He shoved the small man aside, cursing the knife, yanked it from my side, then poised to strike again. The small man seized him and pulled him off me. As they sprawled backward, I reached for the knife but hadn't the strength to remove it.

—Our brothers of the Mahan will kill us both, said the small man.

I rolled, tried to pull myself up, but fell to the earth. My head spun, the terrible pain in my side hindering my ability to think.

The big man sat up, breathing hard, and stared at me.

—He can recognize us, he said.

—No. We've worn the hoods.

Once again, I tried to rise to my knees, but I collapsed. They just stared at me like hunters watching their prey die. They went quiet as if contemplating my fate.

—I'll do it! the small man said finally.

The big man didn't move. As the small man rose to his feet and moved toward me, I pushed myself up on an arm, my wound bleeding through my tunic.

—Will you kill me? I whispered as he approached.

He answered by stepping behind me, taking me by the arm, and dragging me to the opening he had dug. He said nothing. My side pulsed in pain.

—Who are you? I asked.

His response was, I'm sorry to do this.

The small man stopped, stepped to where he could face me, and seemed to examine me. I tried to plead with my eyes.

—Is he dead? yelled the big man.

—Nearly.

—Get on with it.

The small man gave me a look that I thought spoke pity. Then he dragged me to the edge of the opening and dropped me into the pit.

coaxing the god of heaven here

C3

—Amazing what can happen in a year, Micah said to me.

His voice disturbed the calm of morning. I had risen early to wander the circumference of the City of Enoch and drink in its beauty. I finally ascended the Mount of Sanctuary—the hill where we had placed our tabernacle—to watch the sunrise. Micah's comment startled me. I looked up and gazed at the imposing figure of my friend.

—I came up here to be alone, I said, joking.

—You came up here to get out of working, he laughed.

I patted a place beside me, and the big man sat down. Micah had migrated to Shum from the frontier of Hanannihah. He was about my age, closing in on fifty. Born to be large, Micah had gained additional brawn by mining ores and overseeing rugged quarry men. Hard living had honed him in body and character. After losing his wife and children in the great drought, he migrated to Shum and immediately became a voice for Enoch, the young seer from Cainan. From the time Shum had fallen—three years hence—Micah had been our champion, upholding Enoch as our prophet, marshaling our defenses in times of trouble. Micah was a gifted orator. His command of the language astonished me, and his physical features demanded that he be heard—square jaw, thinning dark hair, deep-set black eyes. Micah stood a full head higher than me and was almost twice my girth.

We had only lived a few months in our old mountain home over-looking the valley of Shum when we were driven out by the army of Nod that invaded the land. They hunted and scourged us for two years as we were forced to live as nomads, constantly driven from place to place. Finally, after two years, Enoch led us into another mountain valley, where we had now lived for a year. We called our new home the City of Enoch. I was not alone in my hope that here we could live in peace forever.

—I love it too, said Micah.

—What?

—Sunrise on Mount of Sanctuary.

I looked up into the gray sky—neither night nor dawn—and watched, anticipating the colors of morning. Dew had gathered on everything awaiting the burning rays of the spring sun. The fragrance of freshly cut cedar, stacked for transport from the Mount of Sanctuary, drifted in on a slight breeze. I knew the patterns of day-break by heart—the song of the oriole, the rise of geese from glassy ponds, the click of waking insects. I folded my arms about my knees and gazed up at the milk-colored eastern sky, anticipating the sun's breaking over high, yawning peaks and washing over the City. As the first beacon of light touched the top of the temple that we were con-structing, it threw a long shadow the shape of the house of God, then, receding slowly from the City's western boundary, the sun painte houses, gardens, streets with the full spectrum of color. Situated exactly in the middle of the City in a great walled square, the temple served as the origin of streets that ran north to south and east to west. Recently, we had completed the temple's high, terraced walls that now shone in the morning sun as though they were illumined inter-nally, their rose reflection tinting the flowered temple grounds a soft pink.

—I'd like to build a home near yours in the City, if you could stand such an ornery neighbor.

—You'd be welcomed, I said.

I had built a home for my family in the eastern part of the City and another home on the Mount of Sanctuary adjacent to the tabernacle. I used the hillside home when I spent long days officiating in the tabernacle or when I wanted to retreat from City life. In my home in the City, I lived with my wife, Moriah, and our youngest children, Eve and Enos. Benjamin, my older son, had built a home nearby for his wife, Sarah, and their sons: Nathaniel, three, and one-year-old Dan.

From the Mount of Sanctuary, where Micah and I sat, we could see the entire valley. Enoch said it was a place that could be easily defended. A few pitiful attacks by Nod's army had proved him right. After pursuing us, attacking, then failing, they grew weary and departed, leaving only a clutch of spies to watch us for weaknesses. We let them watch. We were strong here.

The bowl-shaped valley was protected on all sides by steep, high mountains. A pass on the western side, above the tree line near the Mount of Sanctuary, led to a mountainous wilderness. Because of the harshness of the terrain, we only posted a few guards there, expecting that an enemy would think twice before attempting to scale our formidable peaks. A river, originating from a fresh water lake to the southwest, ran through the valley, eventually flowing under the City's western wall to make its way to the temple. We had planned the construction of the temple so that the river would gush from underneath it like a spring. As the river flowed out through the northeastern corner of the City, it meandered through the northern part of the valley and down through the northern pass. It was on the highest point of that pass that we constructed a watchtower the height of four men. Beyond the watchtower, we built a high, thick, gated wall guarded by thirty strong men. The river flowed underneath, making a formidable barrier. From the watchtower, we could enjoy a clear view of both our valley and the northern valley that lay beyond the narrow pass.

Beyond our mountain valley, Nod lay to the north; the land south was mostly uninhabited; and to the east lay the great sea.

When we first came to the valley, we settled into haphazard knots of tents pitched on muddy fields. Now, crisscrossing the City, hardened streets of clay and rock converged at right angles, squared to the temple, giving the community a look of symmetry. High, rock walls surrounded the City in a perfect square, with two thick, wooden gates on the eastern side. Rows of houses had now replaced tents. Most were covered with brushwood and pitch to keep out the weather. In warm months, we dried food on the roofs. The houses were made of white stone and wood—both considered gifts from God—and were unique from dwellings I had seen elsewhere. An exposed ridge near the Mount of Sanctuary held a cache of white stone in layers about the width of a man's palm. By striking the stone, one could easily break off blocks that could be stacked into sturdy walls. We discovered that by pulverizing the stone into powder, a strong mortar could be produced. The result was a gleaming, white city.

From where Micah and I sat, I noted neatly rowed gardens, ready for growing, adjacent to each home. Large, plowed farms, valleys of just-sprouting grain, and sapling orchards stretched out behind. Shepherds' flocks pastured in high places where new grass had erupted beneath yet snowy peaks. The deep, fresh-water lake collected melted snow and served as the repository for mountain streams and springs.

For the better part of a year, almost from the moment we had settled in the valley, I had worked on building the temple. Enoch had dedicated the place of its construction the day after we arrived. He had taken Baruch, my former competitor in Shum and now dear friend; his son Joshua, who was espoused to my daughter Eve; Ishmael, the great captain of Enoch's Camp and now keeper of the Storehouse; Micah; my son Benjamin; and me to what would become the perfect center of the City and declared it the place where we would erect a temple to our God. He had seen the temple in vision and was shown its intricate construction. Although I had little experience, I was chosen to form a plan and Micah was assigned as my master builder. I had relied on Enoch's vision and counsel to complete the task.

Simultaneous to announcing the construction of the temple, Enoch had chosen a flat, high spot on the western hillside for a tabernacle until the temple could be completed. Mount of Sanctuary became the name of the place, and I was to divide my time between overseeing the temple's construction and officiating in the tabernacle. What had been a portable holy place was now curtained off in a square of hallowed ground. We were anointed priests, and once ceremonially cleansed, we could then enter the tabernacle to offer sacrifices and administer covenants and ordinances to the worthy among our people.

—Sun's up, said Micah, looking back over his shoulder.

As he spoke, the City of Enoch emerged from the shadows of morning: hazy lines grew sharp, grays turned gold. Soon, the City awoke: men shooing drowsy cows into milking stalls, women beating dust from woven carpets, adolescents complaining about the earliness. I could make out distant songs of mothers going about morning chores. I knew what they would be wearing: durable clothing—modest tunics covered with robes, usually blue, falling in pleats over the neck and shoulders, held in place by a plaited cord. Simple leather sandals. Soon, I saw children burst into the crisp morning air, excited, their play obscuring every other sound. Women emerged from their houses, balancing jugs on their heads or shoulders. Soon the air would be charged with the fragrance of bread baking in outdoor ovens and bean and lentil stew simmering in earthen pots.

—Your aqueducts are working well, I noted to Micah.

—You did your share to construct them, he replied.

The idea was actually Ishmael's. While keeping the Storehouse, he had imagined a way to efficiently bring the water, which ran under the City wall, to the people within via the construction of aqueducts. Now fresh water coursed to every part of the City, appearing from a distance as a network of veins surging from the pulsing heart of the temple. Though I was a well-traveled man, I had never seen the

City's equal. Every part bespoke peace and beauty—a community rich and growing richer still, a city consecrated to God and reflecting its residents' covenants to help one another.

—I think we finally have a home, Micah said. We've gone from being a frightened muddle of refugees to a confident, prosperous city.

—In so little time and with so little to begin with, I added.

—It's oneness, he said. We could have accomplished nothing without being unified.

Micah was right. The people were productive and happy. Their needs and wants were supplied as though the earth itself insisted on lavishing upon them every comfort and abundance. Our happiness was a product of Enoch's genius, whose ability came from God. He administered to us a covenant: we would be called the People of God and worship him through a savior called the Messiah, or the Elect One, whom Enoch preached would one day come to save those who believed on his name. We were to remember the Messiah, to be considered part of his family, to keep his laws. As an evidence that we were willing to devote ourselves wholly to God, to carry one another's burdens, to live separate from the ways of the world, we gathered at the edge of the lake wearing white, and Enoch took each of us and immersed us in token of death of the old person of sin and raised us up in token of the resurrection of the new person born to God. Then he laid his hands upon us and promised us the Holy Spirit to sanctify us and to teach us the truth of all things. With the covenant as our society's foundation, Enoch set up a system of government unlike any I had known, an order based on the people's further covenanting for mutual protection and sharing their resources for the common good. He instituted the Law of the Shepherd whereby families were assigned care givers to watch over them—each family head being assigned another family or families to whom he ministered. I thought how much my father, Ebanel, would have enjoyed living here. I hoped that in death he had found the peace that he had sought so diligently in life.

As the City of Enoch grew golden in the morning light, Micah and I stood to make our way to the temple and begin our day's work. By midday, work on the temple would be in full motion. Although uncompleted, the rising temple stood elegantly in the center and high point of the City, its rose-colored framework stair-stepping toward heaven. Enoch called the temple the Mountain of the Lord, the place where man rises above the entrapments of this world to converse with God. Micah put his arm around my shoulder, smiled, and bid me a good day.

—Something extraordinary is going to happen today, he said. I feel it.

—You're a prophet now? I said, laughing.

—No, just his friend and servant.

The sun was fully visible now. I felt it wrap its warmth around my shoulders like a shawl. With cupped hands, I hooded my eyes and tried to peer up at it, but only for the flicker of a moment. Its brilliance blinded me, and I was forced to look down.

—That would be a goal, I said out loud, to look into the light and see without turning away.

ᨒ

Micah could not have known that the fulfillment of his prophecy would come in the form of Joshua's return from the land of Danan. Joshua had been sent there by Enoch to proselyte that people. He and my daughter Eve had postponed their marriage so that he could accept the prophet's charge. What had begun as a short mission had long. Through it all, Eve had been supportive and patient. Joshua had been sent to the Dananites once before. During the previous summer, he had converted and escaped with a small group of Dananites back to the City of Enoch. He had said they were fortunate for Nod did not allow defection. Joshua and his little band had seized an opportunity during a season of celebration when the men of Nod were drowning in wine. Once safe within the City of Enoch, Joshua reported that the guards of Nod would not make the same mistake again, and rescuing the remainder of the Dananites would prove challenging. Undeterred, Joshua left again for Danan that following autumn, and he had now returned with another group of Dananites, many in number. Their coming shook the very foundation of the City of Enoch. I remembered the day well.

I had spent the morning working on the temples lower face. Hot and sweaty, I gazed skyward. Warm, clear. I had just picked up a ladle of water when I heard the trumpet of a ram's horn from the direction of the watchtower in the narrow pass. Then Eve's cry.

—Joshua!

Ever apple cheeked and free spirited, my golden-haired daughter dropped a basket of wet clothes, ran the distance to where Joshua stood, and leapt into his arms. Joshua was not prepared for the assault. He swung her around until her tunic billowed; then they tumbled to the ground.

At the tumult, Moriah stepped into the frame of the doorway of our home. She wiped her hands on a cloth, then laid it aside, hooded her eyes with a hand and stepped into the morning light. From where I was working at the temple, I called to her and motioned northeastward. She first appeared puzzled, then smiled, threw her hands in the air, slapped them to her thighs, and hurried toward me. We were a slower pair than our daughter. Within moments we came huffing and found Joshua and Eve rolling on the ground and laughing like two silly children.

—Father! Mother! Joshua has returned! cried Eve.

Despite her resolve to be supportive while she waited, Eve had seemed lonely and distant lately, and to see her laughing again was a sight we had prayed for.

—I think you've put on some weight, Joshua joked with Eve.

—I have not! I think you've lost some muscle! she said, as if to sound insulted.

—I think you both look ridiculous, said Moriah.

I looked at Joshua and thought, *The boy has become a man.*

Joshua, once lean in frame, was the one who had added weight. Long ago he had lost the squeak in his voice, and the deep resonance of it now could draw one's ear as to a fluid melody. His native fair complexion appeared weathered. His mahogany-colored eyes gave him a kindly look. A man's copper stubble grew on his jaw. His long hair, now approaching a pleasant russet hue, had begun to thin on top as had Baruch's, his father's. In every way, time was molding Joshua to the form of his father—the color of his eyes, the tint of his skin, the tone of his voice, the similar mannerisms, the height, the weight— Joshua was uniquely Baruch's son. Looking at the young man, I began to feel old.

I reached out my hand to Joshua, but another hand found his first. A small, brown-skinned man, dressed in a red wrap and a black turban, stepped in front of me and lifted Joshua to his feet. The little man was smooth faced, with prominent cheek bones and deep-set black eyes, and thin to the point of appearing frail.

—My friend, Gensek, said Joshua, gesturing with a hand while he brushed himself off.

Gensek bowed.

—Welcome, I said. I know you, don't I?

—I have visited your city as an ambassador, he said.

—Yes. Ishmael showed you our Storehouse, Micah showed you our temple site. You are one of the few that Nod will let leave.

—Thanks to Joshua, I hope to never return, he said.

A slight, grave woman, whose face was partially covered by a scarf, stepped from behind Gensek. Five children gathered about her like chicks to a hen. The eldest, a beautiful, dark-eyed girl, stood nearest her mother, pressing two toddlers to her thighs.

Turning to Joshua I asked, Gensek's family?

Joshua nodded and said, These are Gensek's wife, Adul, and their five children.

Eve stood on her feet and brushed her skirts while Moriah picked grass from her hair.

I gestured toward the two women with me.

—My wife, Moriah, and my daughter, Eve, I said.

Another series of bows was exchanged.

—Do you un-der-stand our lang-uage? asked Eve, deliberately pronouncing each word. Of course the entire world spoke the language of Adam, but dialects had crept into nether regions of the land.

—We understand your language very well, said Gensek with a marked accent.

Eve reached for Joshua's arm with a look of embarrassment, and Moriah rolled her eyes at our daughter. Eve tipped her head and returned a tiny frown as if to say, I *didn't know!*

A small boy at the older girl's side began to fuss and she reached down to pick him up. Quickly, Joshua dropped Eve's arm and rushed to the girl's aid.

—Let me help, he said, lifting the child into his arms.

—Very gallant, Eve said, with a tone of irritation.

Moriah cleared her throat. Eve ignored the warning.

—You haven't introduced us. Eve nodded at the girl.

—Naomi, the girl answered in a quiet voice. I am the eldest child of Gensek and Adul.

Not tall by our standards, yet taller than her parents, Naomi was delicate boned, uncommon among the Dananite people. Her fingers were long and slender with transparent fingernails. She had a soft-looking complexion, her skin tone the color of bronze. She stood erect and dignified. Under a red veil, she wore her raven-black hair down, a cascade of dark tresses flowing to the small of her back, fluid and feathery. Her eyebrows, the same color as her hair, were thin and wispy, as were her long eyelashes. Her eyes were large and doe brown with eyelids that opened enough to give her a dreamy look. She smiled shyly, thin red lips touching gently, moist, suggesting the look of distance, too perfect to approach. She was a delicate willow, lacy, light, the kind of woman that jealous counterparts would label fragile, but that men would admire as ultimately feminine. Standing next to Moriah, I found myself making a conscious effort not to stare at Gensek's eldest daughter.

—You are very pretty, said Eve, with a hint of envy.

—We do not have the beauty of your people, said Naomi. Our Joshua has always said he could not wait to come home.

—Oh, you mustn't be modest, said Eve. I'm sure *our* Joshua was in good hands in Danan.

Moriah coughed loudly, and I ushered our guests toward a tour of the City.

ᙃ

That evening, Micah took me aside and asked, What has brought us to this?

—You mean all the Dananites? I asked.

—Of course. The City cannot absorb so many. There are hundreds. We haven't the means.

—We've brought in truth seekers before, even some from Danan.

—But not in these numbers, not of this type.

Micah was right on some points, but I did not agree with him that we could not assimilate the Dananites. We, as a people, understood faith and had witnessed the miracles of God time and time again. I believed we could accomplish anything that was counted the work of God.

—The Dananites are a strange lot, said Micah. They worship Abel, who was murdered by Cain.

—Joshua has been teaching them to worship the true God, I said.

—You know how well his other Dananites have been received, said Micah.

The Dananites had been welcomed into the City with mixed emotion. Over the years, the Dananites had developed a reputation as a dirty, lazy people, full of mischief, a race not to be trusted. Marriages with Dananites were unthinkable. Trade was tolerated because the Dananites tended toward being gullible. The Dananites' skin color was different from ours—a brownish hue, filthy looking to some. Because Dananites were short they appeared inferior to taller neighboring peoples. Danan was a mournful land, oppressed by our old enemies, the Watchers of Nod.

Our association with the Dananites had begun much earlier than Joshua's recent missionary *success*. After Enoch had settled us in our new mountain home, he left Micah and me in charge and departed for Cainan to retrieve Anna, his wife, and their daughter Melca, a spry red-headed waif who compensated for her diminutive size with a giant voice and an ample capacity for mischief—a continuing challenge for the man of God. I had known Anna and Melca for almost four years now. Anna was a young woman with boundless in energy and the kind of beauty women envied. She would maintain the visage of youth throughout her years. She was small, spry, light-haired—red-tinted in the right light—with a complexion the color of ivory, dimple cheeked, which gave her the appearance of a perpetual smile. On their return, Adam met them and blessed Enoch, confirming his calling and promising him that through his and Anna's seed would be born Noah and later the Messiah, the Deliverer and Savior of the world. Adam prophesied that through Enoch's ministry a city of holiness would rise—a great fortress of peace in a world suffocating from violence. The couple was then directed to go to Danan before returning to the City, where they would find an oppressed people hungry for the message of the Messiah. When Enoch returned to the City, he brought with him a small group of Dananites and called Joshua, Baruch's son, to go to Danan and teach the people there.

No one was prepared for Joshua's accomplishment. His dogged efforts were astonishing and now he had returned with a multitude: several thousand. Joshua's Dananites crowded the borders of the City, threatening to exhaust our resources and tax our tolerance. They came believing in Joshua's teaching, but not yet embracing our faith. Still, Joshua had extended them our hospitality.

—Enoch has called for the Fathers Council to meet, said Micah.

—You're going? I asked.

—I've been invited.

—Because you lost your family does not mean you are not a father, I said.

He didn't seem interested in my sympathy, but prodded me for information.

—How do you stand? he asked.

—They will be a challenge but we will manage.

—Manage? I've asked Ishmael how this will impact the Storehouse. Our resources will be depleted within months.

—We're going into the planting season. We'll give them lands to farm. We can help plow the fields for them, since they will be arriving weary.

—That takes manpower. Where will it come from? The temple workers? I've even heard Enoch say that more men are needed to go to Danan and bring more people.

—Your objection has nothing to do with their race or customs, does it?

Micah shot me a quick look.

—I'm sorry, I said. I know you are not a bigoted man. I don't have all the answers, but I know that those Dananites whom Joshua could not bring out are yet in slavery and will surely be punished because their brethren escaped. Would you have us leave them to be slaughtered?

Micah didn't offer an answer. We walked to the Fathers Council in silence until we arrived at a spherical stone enclave within the center court of the City. Two squarish, draped windows obscured onlookers' views, but allowed weak light to seep through and cast purple shadows on the floor. As I stepped into the doorway, Micah held me back with a hand and said, Our assignments in the City are hard enough. Bringing in the Dananites just makes everything harder.

Enoch convened the Fathers Council with a prayer to God. Then Joshua laid before us the plight of the Dananites and their subjugation by Nod, our old enemies.

—Nod has systematically pillaged the Dananite lands, he said. The Dananites were once a proud people, great warriors, strong and independent. But Nod killed their leaders and imposed upon them Nod's laws and way of life. Nod has made them as poor a people as I've ever seen. They slave for unfeeling taskmasters, never knowing if they will have enough to feed their children. Their women are bought and sold as chattel. Beauty is a curse to them. But when they are presented with the truth, their hearts are strong and they display incredible courage. Their dream is that the people of God will take them in and save them.

A great murmuring filled the Council House.

—The City of Enoch has finally enjoyed a season of peace, I heard some say.

—And our prosperity has excited the envy of our neighbors, said others. We could do without that kind of attention.

—What has that to do with the Dananites? asked shua.

—Greater numbers means more people to defend. Greater numbers draws more attention to us. More persecution. More danger.

Persecution had always been our companion. Like a pesky dog nipping at our heels, it seemed to follow us wherever we were forced to relocate. But in our new mountain valley we had discouraged attacks by smaller bands of marauders.

—You should have counseled with us before bringing a huge population of Dananites here, said Micah. The City's resources were already strained.

Some agreed with Micah. Enoch did not.

—The work of God is not always convenient, he said. We should not let our faith falter in times of plenty. Remember how we ourselves sought after God in times of peril. Did he not preserve us in our poverty? Can we shrink from rescuing his poor children from the hands of wicked men?

—A slaughter among the remaining Dananites is certain, added Joshua. There are Watchers in and about Danan. Even now many will perish if we do not go back to Danan and rescue the rest of the people.

—How many? asked Baruch.

—Maybe three thousand more.

—That would be an impossible number for us to absorb, said Micah. The Dananites are a poor people. How would we support them?

—We were poor when we came to these mountains, I said.

—Yes, said Micah, but the Dananites are ignorant and unskilled. We would have to carry them for years before they became productive. The timing of all this is critical to our survival.

—Would you have them die at the hands of their enemies? asked Joshua.

—I sense your zeal, said Micah. We want to reach out to all people, but we are not prepared.

Micah stood and paced in tight circles, his arms crossed. Then he stopped, pinched the bridge of his nose between thumb and forefinger and squeezed his eyes shut. I exchanged glances with Baruch, who raised an eyebrow. I dropped my eyes and brooded over a callused knuckle, waiting for Micah to speak.

—I am not insensitive to the Dananites' troubles, said Micah, softly. You all know me. Just like you, I have sacrificed everything for this people. I have worked beside you for three years. I have suffered hunger, thirst, persecution. There is nothing I have not sacrificed for our people. I do not speak against the Dananites. I voice my concern for the welfare of our people. Ask Ishmael if there is enough food or clothing in the Storehouse to support these people.

All eyes turned toward Ishmael, who had been leaning quietly against a wall. He straightened his tall body, squared his broad shoulders, and shook his head *no* in response to Micah's question.

—You see? said Micah. If we pursue this dangerous course, we will not only jeopardize our resources but compromise our defense. To support those Dananites who are already here and to bring more means taking men away from essential jobs of the community. Work on the temple would have to stop.

—Why stop building the temple? I asked.

—We wouldn't have enough men.

—What about the Dananites?

—Even for the most menial jobs they are unskilled.

For a long, uncomfortable time we remained quiet. Joshua's was the first voice to speak.

—We are divided, he said.

A thick silence settled on the Council. I surveyed the group. Most looked down. Finally someone said, We could settle them in the broad valley beyond the narrow pass. They would be close enough for us to help and still a community of their own.

Slowly, heads began to nod. I could tell from Joshua's expression that he was disappointed but resigned. The question still remained about bringing in the rest of the Dananites who were yet in bondage.

—What about Saad? someone asked.

A low murmur filled the room.

The city of Saad was an enigma. The place and its people were considered neither friend nor enemy. When we had settled in our mountain valley, our goal was to remain detached from the world, unsullied by its entrapments. The people of Nod and the Watchers had polluted the land to such a degree that mingling with them in any way meant defilement. Physical and spiritual separation were essential to our safety. In the mountains, we could protect ourselves. We cut a series of stairs and switchbacks into the rocky walls of the canyon leading to the City of Enoch. On a high point, we constructed our watchtower that provided us an unobstructed view of our valley, the canyon, and the valley of Saad. At the most narrow part of the canyon, we built a wall of hewn rocks four times the height of a man with gates of thick timber that could be locked and easily guarded, even against a superior force. Not that it was not tested. Over the years we had been dogged by a contingent from the army of Nod until, after repeated unsuccessful harassment, they retreated and mixed with the people of Saad.

Saad was made up of nomadic tribes of Cainic ancestry. They were idolaters, but they enjoyed great prosperity. When the Saadites had asked us to trade, we hesitated for a time, then accepted their invitation. As we began to venture into Saad's borders, the threats from what was left of Nod's army ended. We stopped thinking of the people of Saad as enemies, but we had no influence over them—none from Saad converted to the teachings of Enoch. But some of the Saadite ways did seem to be finding some converts within the City of Enoch. It was a trend that was troubling to some.

The consensus of the Council was that we would settle the Dananites in the opposite part of the broad valley from Saad where our guards on the high tower could observe both communities. Throughout much of the debate, Enoch had remained apparently detached from the conversation, sitting quietly with his hands placed softly on his knees. When I asked his opinion on the Dananites, he looked up, then retrained his eyes straight ahead, and said he was giving the matter serious thought. This was a man I had come to love. He was of average height, about as tall as me, erect in posture, broadly built. He seldom wore a head covering, but allowed his dark, wavy hair to fall just above his shoulders. His eyes were dark, either gray or green depending on the light. His skin was olive hued, like mine, his clothes plain colored and simple. The Watchers of Shum had labeled him a wild man. I laughed at that now. He was a genuinely mild person, even given to shyness. He still struggled with a childhood halt to his voice, a voice that grew sure and fluid when he spoke the words of God. Now, he moved easily among the people, engaging them in small talk, explaining deep doctrines, expressing interest in each individual. I loved listening to the tone of his voice, mild, reserved when speaking to individuals, articulate in front of groups. The people had come to know him as gentle, but counted on his strength in times of trial. He was as much a man as any I had ever known.

Soon, the Council divided into small groups to sort out the details of how to settle the Dananites. A low murmur of voices filled the room. The fire at the center made the room hot. Someone suggested that we should break, step outside where the air was less stultifying, then reassemble. But Enoch's voice brought us to silence.

—We must finish the temple, he said. It is the house of God, and God is our safety and strength. We also must bring in the Dananites. We must trust in God to preserve us as he has done in the past.

Those of us who were standing sat.

—We must go back to Danan to rescue the rest of the people, Enoch continued. This is the will of God.

He asked for our consent. Glances were exchanged and hands slowly rose.

—Who will go for us? he asked.

I sensed a thick uneasiness settle on those of us who sat in council. I looked straight ahead, avoiding eye contact with any in the room. Then I felt Enoch's gaze fall upon me. I knew my duty. I slowly stood.

—Send me, I said.

෬

The following morning I was to depart for Danan. I lay in my bed holding Moriah in my arms as the first gesture of daybreak touched the eastern mountains. Neither of us had slept much. Moriah had just drifted off, and I lay still so as to not disturb her. Years had not hardened her soft complexion, and her delicate features still inspired the envy of women her age. Her golden hair had resisted turning white. Over the last three years I had left her many times to serve missions. Each time it had grown harder to say good-bye. My departing for Danan would be the most difficult good-bye of all. My mission was not widely supported, and I had no idea how long I would be gone. I also had no idea that my supporting the prophet would have such a polarizing effect on the people. By the simple act of trying to do what was right I had offended some, but to what degree I could not fathom at the time. Both Moriah and I sensed danger in my journey.

As I was leaving the Fathers Council, Enoch had pulled me aside and said, You go first to Danan, then I will send others to help you.

The following day, as he and I had finished making plans for my journey, and after I had bid farewell to my family, Enoch walked me to the fringe of the City by the Mount of Sanctuary. Evening was near. I looked out over the community, took in a big breath, and let it out slowly.

—It's a bit of heaven. Isn't it? he said.

—Can there be heaven on earth? I asked.

My question involved a subject ever on his mind. He had spoken of it often. Today, he had hardly formed a phrase without yearning that his people might live so as to call down heaven here. I envisioned heaven as a place of consummate peace and happiness, a place where love reigns as naturally as does envy on the earth. But I could not imagine its existing here.

—Heaven can happen here, said Enoch.

I nodded, but doubted it. Since we had been driven from our mountain home above Shum I had experienced the worst side of humanity among our oppressors. If heaven could exist anywhere it would be the City of Enoch, but we had our problems. Enoch and I stood near the tabernacle and scanned the City. We still wore cloaks over our tunics to keep back the chill, coarse cloths for girdles, leather sandals, warm stockings. Spring had brought hope, but winter was a near memory. The smell of a midafternoon rain charged the air. Each night arrived a bit later now, mornings came a little earlier.

—Regardless of what others may say, Enoch said, the Dananites need us. Make your journey in haste and be careful. I fear that this has drawn the attention of our enemies.

Then he prayed for me and blessed me. Once more we surveyed the City.

—The most beautiful spot on earth, he said.

—Yes. Despite our challenges I'd choose to live here over any other place, I said.

—I have seen a vision of our future, he said. I see a place with no classes, no rich and no poor in its borders.

—Zion? I asked.

—Yes, Zion.

The word had not been used much. Enoch first used it to describe individuals—*Zion-like*, or *of Zion*. Now, he spoke of Zion the society.

—In vision, God has shown me a people who practice peace much as other nations study war, he continued. I have seen fathers coming together in council for the welfare of the community, then gathering their families to bless and teach them. I have seen mothers tutoring children in reading and writing, using the sacred words of God as their text. I have seen great places of learning where the arts and sciences are taught—knowledge that enlarges the mind, replaces ignorance, opens doors to the imagination. I have seen beauty everywhere—comeliness created as though to coax the God of heaven to reside among us.

Then Enoch paused, looked at me, and said, And he will come, Rabunel.

He said it as a declaration more than a wish.

—God? I asked.

—How could he not? When we have created it, Zion will be heaven on earth. He has commanded me to build it.

I envied Enoch's gift, but as much as I tried I could not see his Zion. I looked off, avoiding eye contact. Perhaps my years as a merchant had callused me to the spiritual things of life. I had made myself keen in working with men and could perceive their subtle communications of body: the raise of an eyebrow, an uncomfortable shift of weight, the nervous clearing of one's throat. I knew my trade, but I had given it all up when my greed had cost the life of my son, Jerel, and when I had later sacrificed everything to follow Enoch. Now, bidding good-bye to my friend of three years, I thought, *I shouldn't ask. Perhaps I am too presumptuous.*

Enoch seemed to perceive my conflict.

—How can I help you? he asked.

—I am a man with many weaknesses, I said, but if I could learn to see and hear as you do.

He smiled, bade me good journey, and said, You will.

Enoch embraced me then, and as I departed for Danan I pondered his promise. But how could I have known that my tutoring would begin by being attacked by the Mahan? How could I have known that I would be thrown into the darkness of the pit?

in the shadow of a great rock

ଔ

Whether it was night or day, I did not know. How long had I drifted in and out of consciousness? Hours? Days? Weeks? I remembered hitting the hard floor of the pit and reaching for the wound in my side. I had not dared to cry out. Why the small man had not killed me, I did not know. From deep in the belly of the cave, I had lain on my back and stared up at a dim opening through which the last sliver of moon squeezed while the Mahan who had abducted me sealed it shut. They appeared to stand the height of two men above me. As the final spade of earth covered the last fleck of light, I imagined I had gone blind. I lay still, shocked, solitary in the dark stillness. Only the sound of my labored breathing and the burning in my side proved that I yet had senses. I lay in the darkness. The lesion in my side throbbed.

I may bleed to death, I thought.

I tried ticking off time by the hard thumping of my heart. But I soon gave it up. With some effort, I made an agonizing attempt to roll to my knees. Straightening, I shook a fist at the black abyss above me then slumped back onto the cold floor. Grimacing, I groped for my side and touched a long, wet slit. With a hand, I tore at the hem of my tunic and jammed a piece of it into the wound. I felt my head go weak, and I fought for consciousness. The pain, I reminded myself, was my friend, for as long as I had it I knew I was alive.

One more feeble effort brought me to my feet. I teetered, instinctively reaching out for something to steady myself. I crept forward, the toes of my feet probing the ground, an outstretched arm groping for a wall, some defining edge, a boundary. Then I touched something—furry, like the back of a hairy man. My impulse was to recoil, but as I forced myself to explore further, a dim recognition settled on my brain.

—Moss, I said aloud.

I moved back and sat cross-legged on the cold floor. No movement of air. No sound. I saw nothing. I smelled the faint scent of blood and the dull odor of damp air. I touched thumb to forefinger to reassure myself that I still had sensation. What I did feel was fear, for the pit was dead, crypt-like, a hell more paralyzing than I had ever known. I was isolated. Alone.

—*How had I come to this?* I wondered. I had imagined the trajectory of my life aimed in an opposite destination.

As I sat in the darkness, I sensed the pupils of my eyes go wide straining to see. Starting at the temples, a dull ache migrated across my forehead and settled above the eyebrows. I realized how hard my eyes had been working to detect any glimmer of light. I squeezed them shut and found some relief. Then a trembling began in my hands. A chill entered my feet and began to crawl up my legs. I became conscious of my breathing—short, shallow. I was panicking! I was losing control.

I had thought I knew fright. Wasn't fright what I had experienced the night my son Jerel died, the night I was forced to save my life by gutting a bear and cowering in its belly? I answered my question by thinking, *Yes, that was fright. But, for all the fear I experienced then, my senses had not failed me. My mind did not reach out, as it does now, to detect something—a blink of light, a measure of sound, a sweet dash of odor—anything to remind me that I was alive.*

The throb in my side was a reminder that I was not completely devoid of my senses. I groaned. Again, the stillness answered me like an enemy who had severed my hearing and left me deaf.

—Is this what death is like? I thought. *Slipping from the body into blackness where existence is void and without feeling? Being, but incapable of doing?*

Despite my questioning I could not bring myself to accept it. I wanted to believe in Enoch's teaching: the kingdoms beyond this present state are glorious; man's destiny is more exalted than the mind can grasp.

Enoch had once asked me, Can you see, Rabunel? Can you see beyond the tedium of life's daily struggles? Can you see the grand purpose of your creation?

I could not. I had often pondered man's situation—his sojourn, what forces might predict his fate. I had wondered, *Why, if his destination is paradisiacal, is man's tendency to be natural, to set up camp in a world intended to be temporary? What rivets man's attention here? Fear? Undo attention to the details of living? Coveting that which is frivolous? A frenzied attempt to gather about him property for security? Is man's purpose not greater than this? Should not his reason for existence be more excellent?*

Enoch seemed to have a clear view of man's potential and his duty. When I had left him and departed for Danan, I had made my first night's camp with kindling and questions. Alone that night, I poked at the fire as if to probe answers from it. I was traveling to a land of despairing people to deliver a message of hope. But how deeply did I believe that message? Maybe Micah was right, maybe bringing back so many would jeopardize the City of Enoch. On the other hand, perhaps Enoch was right: do the correct thing and trust God to help.

I studied the fire and wondered how much I trusted. I wondered what spiritual well Enoch dipped from, and if I discovered it, could I quench my thirst? I envied Enoch's ability to see beyond life's troubles and wondered if I ever would. As the campfire dimmed, I was resolved on two points: I could not honestly teach what I did not understand, and I wanted to see as Enoch saw.

Then the Mahan attacked me.

In the blackness of the pit, the memory of my questioning offered a respite from the terror of my situation. I forced a loud laugh, and once more the growth on the walls absorbed the sound. When I opened my eyes I thought I saw lightening—quick spurts of light shooting through the dark.

—*Is this what happens when a man loses his mind?* I wondered. The idea of going insane evoked a glandular fear, and I lay back, pressed a hand into my side, and closed my eyes.

My mind began to conjure sounds, visual images, thoughts, any form of trickery to feed it. I thought I heard distant music. The vague apparition of a woman seemed to appear, flitting in and out of my gaze, her back toward me, rocking the form of a child. I thought I felt a cold gust of wind accompanying the delusion. The phantom woman hummed a haunting song that made my flesh go chill. Then she turned toward me, her eyes red with rage. As she glared at me, she held up the child, its eyes pasty white. Blind! Blind as I was! I pressed the heels of my hands into my eyes, trying to force the image out, but it would not go. Then I heard a voice say, *So, you thought you could fight the devil!* I drew my knees to my chest, folded my arms about them, and wept like a baby.

—*I am a dead man!* I thought.

Perhaps I fell unconscious. Maybe I slept. If there is no pain in death I was yet alive, for when I awoke the pain in my side was more pronounced and the beating of my heart labored.

—*Is this my grave?*

I stood on my feet and began to shout, O God, help me! Can you hear me?

Silence.

I tried to part my lips. A tacky adhesive had formed on the dry skin of my mouth. I reached with my tongue to wet them but it had no moisture either.

—*How long can a man live without water?*

My stomach was empty and ached. I began to tremble. Without the motion of atmosphere I felt I could not get air. The blackness seemed to tighten about me as though it were the strangling hands of an executioner.

I shouted in the direction of the sealed opening, I am dying! Help me!

I felt deserted, unguided, wasted. The image of a pocked globe came into my mind. It was misshapen and covered with fissures and craters. Around the sphere hung a dark shadow. It brooded and moved, constantly feeling for the pocks to exploit them and destroy the globe. Then I saw a light appear just above the surface of the sphere that seemed to act as a hedge against the bombardment of the shadow. Occasionally the light gave way and the shadow dipped into a cavity, causing the globe to shudder. Enoch taught that Satan ever stalks us, seeking ways to exploit our weaknesses. But God can use that opposition to reveal to us our flaws and help us fill the crevasses in our character. God withdraws momentarily, for our good, and allows Satan to afflict us. If we will receive the message that the affliction is intended to reveal, we will discover something about ourselves, and the sphere of our character will soon become round and smooth.

I shifted my body, trying to find a degree of comfort, but with each movement my wound pulsed to the cadence of my heart. My dry throat suffered for moisture. My stomach cramped for lack of food. I looked into the darkness toward a direction I imagined would be heaven's and cried, Do you know I am here?

Then I lay back and took in deep breaths.

—Perhaps, I thought, in future millennia, some unwitting soul will stumble upon this place, unearth the covering, and find lying on the floor a heap of bleached bones that once were the man Rabunel. How would the discoverer know that the man had married, that he had reared a family, that his kin had never known his fate. Then I wondered, Why does God not deliver me? He has saved me in times past. He has delivered the City of Enoch from vast armies. Can this trouble be more difficult for him? Am I forgotten? Is there consistency in the God of heaven? Does he save once on a whim then ignore future trouble?

I tortured myself with these thoughts. I remembered the question that had haunted me for such a long time and laughed out loud: *Can there be heaven on earth?* There could be Hell, I knew. Was heaven so far? Too far to hear? Too far to help? I remembered my conversation with Enoch the day I had departed the City.

—How can I help you? he had asked.

—To learn to see and hear as you do, I had answered.

—You will, he had said.

Allowing that hope to wash over me, I launched an audible prayer.

—Help me, I implored, my whole soul reaching out toward heaven.

At that moment, I sensed a voice speak to my mind, intelligent, fluid as running water, *Neither can the pit be so deep nor the abyss be so black that I cannot find thee.*

I thought I saw myself in an arid desert, barren of vegetation, devoid of moisture. I imagined I had tread its charred sand for days without respite. Then, when I was about to faint and perish, I spied a great rock rising from the sweltering wasteland that bid me forward. When I had dragged myself to it, I collapsed in its cool shadow until the sun that had beat upon me abated, and I lived.

I relaxed, lying back on the floor of the pit content, basking in the pleasant dream. I felt a calm sensation bathe me like a cool dip in a clear river. I felt free, light, unfettered. And when I had willed away all resistance, I closed my eyes.

a visit to zion

ଔ

At first, I imagined being surrounded by a thick darkness, as though it were a fog. As I groped to find an edge, I felt an overwhelming urgency to escape the blackness. I raised to my knees, then to my feet, and pushed forward, as though forging a deep stream against the current. Then I pressed through what I perceived to be a boundary into a realm of radiant light—palpable light, warm as that of a summer's day and suffused with feelings of love and peace. Wherever I was, conscious or unconscious, I sensed that the light pervaded everything, including my soul. I had the immediate sensation of completeness, and I drank the light into my being as a thirsty man will drain a cup.

Before me lay a grassy meadow, a verdant green unlike any green I had seen. Mounding clusters of flowers blossomed in infinite variety and vibrant hues. An assortment of lush foliage and trees—many of sorts I had never seen—speckled the meadow with colors of burgundy, yellow, purple, green, gold.

Above me, blues, pinks, and yellows converged into a breathtaking view. Although all was bright about me, I could clearly see stars and orbs of pale orange, brown, and red. The heavens looked close, beautiful, bright, defined. For one who had lived his life in a hurry, I felt at ease here, content to bask in the beauty, happy to soak in the peace. I found myself unprepared for the unspeakable sense of goodness in this place, as though all life here loved and accepted me unconditionally.

I began to walk through the meadow. An eagle drifted above me. I heard the sounds of birds and insects—some I knew, some I did not. I touched a flower and was amazed by the sense that I had communicated with it. Then I heard my name being spoken softly by a familiar voice.

—Rabunel.

In my life I had thought I understood the range of emotions—happiness, sorrow—but I had never known true joy until that moment. The voice was my father's, Ebanel. Dead three years, he now rushed toward me, vibrant, full of life, to embrace me. I could feel the strength in his arms and marveled that his body was tangible. It was the exact image of his physical body, except that he appeared younger, in his prime. He smiled at me, and I was immediately enveloped in his love. I knew that he was still my father, and I was his son. He was dressed in an exquisite white robe with the apparent texture of soft linen, brighter than I imagined anything on earth could be made to appear. It was open from his neck to the upper part of his chest and covered his body down to midcalf. On his feet he wore sandals. When he stepped toward me I had the sensation of my heart leaping in my breast. I gasped. When he kissed my neck, I melted and began to cry.

—Father, you are not dead!

—No, my son. I am very much alive.

—But how? I saw you killed by the Rahaj.

—They slew my body, but my spirit lives on.

I then realized that I was free of pain and fear. The memory of the dark pit and the excruciating pain of my wound had no more hold on me. I examined my side and noted smooth skin where a long gash had gaped open.

—Am I dead? I asked.

My father smiled and said, The death of the body is one thing. That which is uniquely you goes on forever.

Turning my palms up, I gazed at my hands. I viewed each finger, knuckle, fingernail. I felt astonishingly alive! Turning a slow circle, I took in every detail of each life form. Then, facing my father, I asked, Is this heaven?

—No. Heaven is where God resides. This is the world of spirits where we go after death and prepare to meet God. You would call it Paradise.

It was then I realized that he was communicating with me by thought—his mind to my mind. He had spoken to me with his mouth at first, but now his words came into my mind clearly and concisely, the kind of spiritual hearing Enoch had told me was possible. My father motioned me forward, and we walked along a stone pathway that led to the edge of the meadow.

—Ask your questions, he said. I am here to help you.

I felt reticent, as though what I wished to ask was presumptuous. My father seemed to perceive my thoughts.

—Yes, Rabunel. God exists.

—Here? I asked.

My father pointed to a glorious structure in the distance. It appeared to be made of glowing white marble. Its foundation was square and immense. From its base, the building rose to the height of an ancient pine, then stair-stepped, pyramid-like, another similar length, and rose again, tapering toward a top that I could not see.

—Although different in appearance, this temple is much like the one you and Enoch are building, said my father. That is where God visits his children.

Together, we walked toward it. A great field of green grass, flanked by lush shrubbery, trees, and flowers, lay in the foreground. People—tall, short, stocky, thin—wearing all manner of clothing filled the field. Some lay on the grass, apparently studying. Others stood in groups conversing. I perceived that all were engaged in learning and helping one other. Everywhere, everyone seemed busy.

—I had thought that upon dying one would enter a place of rest, I said.

—If by rest you mean to relax or do nothing, you will be disappointed here. I've never been so busy. But I also have no worries or stresses. My mind has been freed from these things. Here, I can assimilate knowledge at an incredible rate. I move about at will. I enjoy an unrestrained relationship with my Creator. My faith is perfect. That is the true meaning of rest. Being immersed in God's glory is rest.

To this point, I had observed only gentle people, those who apparently loved peace and embraced learning. From my experience on earth, I knew that a larger, more diverse group existed, and I could not imagine them in this world.

—Is this the place where all the dead come? I asked my father.

—Not all. Those who live here obeyed God's laws on earth and sought for peace.

He pointed toward the distant horizon. I saw a dark place, as though it were engulfed in the shadow of a storm. A great chasm lay before it, and I sensed a foreboding that bid me turn my face away and press my father no further on the subject.

—Look! my father said.

I saw people approaching the doors of the temple. Some stepped through, while others dropped their heads and walked away.

—The invitation is extended, said my father, but many shrink from the experience.

—Because of the guilt they feel?

—Yes. They still have things to work through. But mistakes can be resolved much more easily in the flesh.

—Why?

—How would you rectify stealing?

—Ask forgiveness, try to repair the damage.

—All possible in this world except for the last. How would you return that which you stole?

I realized I could not.

—Most people on earth do not comprehend the power of repentance, said my father. They come here so unprepared. If they only understood what precious time is given them to face and solve their problems.

—But can they solve them here?

—Yes. The power of the Messiah provides the opportunity. But repentance takes longer here.

My father's reference to the Messiah summoned a recollection of Enoch's teachings of the future prophet whose mission was to save the family of Adam from every condition that would keep them from the presence of God. From his earliest days as a teacher, Enoch described himself as the Messiah's servant on the Messiah's errand. His entire purpose had been to bring people to the Messiah so that they could experience his saving power.

—Nothing is harder than change, I said.

—True. But at some point we must face and solve everything.

—How?

—Through the gift of the Holy Spirit and the power of the Messiah. The Spirit reveals; the Messiah heals. There is a way of escape provided for every situation.

—I have wished to be saved from so many situations, I said. I know I have done things that are wrong, but beyond those, I have weaknesses that plague me, sicknesses. I have wanted to be saved from my enemies.

The look on my father's face said he understood. I paused and gazed at him.

—I want to understand life, but I admit that I don't, I said. I don't understand the reasons for pain, why the best people suffer, why the innocent hurt.

—A clarity comes, he said. Once here, I began to comprehend the purpose of my life and the reasons I'd experienced what I had. I came to feel deep gratitude, even for my former troubles and reverses. As my perspective expanded, I began to comprehend that it is in the depth of adversity where we learn lessons and that there is an end when the Messiah lifts you out. It is as though you rise from prisoner to prince.

Our conversation was interrupted by a rustling in the side brush. Immediately, a mighty bear sauntered into full view. My instinct was to run. I had backed off several paces when my father touched my arm.

—It's alright, he said. She won't hurt you.

My father stepped to the bear and began to scratch the beast behind its ears. The bear lifted her head, exposing her neck, and my father went to one knee and caressed the soft fur. As I watched them, my fear subsided. I sensed a thought from the bear's mind to mine as if to say: *I will not harm you.*

—All creatures are safe in God's kingdom, said my father, taking the bear's head in his hands and massaging its jowls. He took my hand and guided it to the beast's thick coat.

—Go ahead and pet her.

What I felt was love radiating from the mighty bear. She lay on her side as I stroked her coat, then rolled to her back as though she were inviting me to scratch her belly. I laughed out loud.

—I can't believe I'm doing this!

—She's someone you know, said my father. Do you remember her? You had an encounter with her on earth.

I stepped back and regarded the gentle creature. The sharp recollection of a bear's killing my son Jerel rushed through my mind. I remembered attacking the beast, thrusting my knife into its throat, making its carcass a shelter, making its skin a winter coat. I recalled eating its flesh while cursing the animal that had murdered my son. The bear looked up at me wistfully, its black eyes soft, full of love. She communicated the thought: *You frightened me. I knew no other way to protect myself.* I sensed her reaching out to me for understanding, and I felt my heart soften. *I do understand,* I tried to communicate, to make the mental effort to express my love for this wonderful creation of God. *You scared me, too, and I also knew no other way of protecting myself.*

At once, the bear turned its massive bulk toward the far end of the trail as though it had sensed something. I followed the bear's eyes and spied the figure of a man dressed in white approaching us. The bear bounded to its feet, like an eager puppy, and hurried off toward the man. He dropped to his knees playfully and let the bear pounce on him. Together, they rolled in the grass, the bear with the big, thick pads pawing the man, the man tousling the bear's ears and pounding its back. When the rollicking was over, the man stood, smoothed his robe, took the mane of the bear in his hand, and led it toward my father and me.

A thrill shot through me.

—Jerel! I cried.

I had yearned for this reunion since the moment I had placed my son's body in a stone grave. I had tried to imagine the emotions, what I would say and do. But now, standing face to face with my son, my reaction was to shrink. I remembered the reason for his death: my impatience to transport my newfound wealth back to Shum. All I could feel was regret. I gazed into Jerel's eyes and sensed a life lost, no chance to marry or have children, forfeited potential—I had cost him all that and more.

I fell on my knees, took the hem of his robe in my hands, and said, Please forgive me, son.

Jerel knelt.

—Let it be, he said. I'm happy here.

He reached out with a hand and touched my face, his eyes meeting mine. His look wrested all regret from my soul, and a rush of peace flowed through me with fluid warmth.

—I have someone to introduce you to, he said.

Before I could ask who, the bear nuzzled me and I fell into Jerel, knocking him over. My father began to laugh at the scene, then Jerel laughed, then I. The bear just yawned.

—Look, said Jerel, coming to an elbow.

A young woman had come near. She had clear, blue eyes, nearly transparent. Her skin was the color of pearl and her hair bronze. She had a dimple in her chin and stood just shorter than Jerel. She was petite but not frail, looking to be in her midtwenties, I judged.

—This is Rebekah, said Jerel, standing, stepping to her side, and taking her hand.

—I'm happy to. . .

—We've fallen in love, interrupted Jerel.

My jaw dropped.

—*Now* you tell me! laughed Rebekah, pinching Jerel's arm.

Jerel squirmed and said, She's a tease, but I love her anyway.

—You said I was too old, said Rebekah, wryly.

—You *are* too old, said Jerel. Then, leaning toward me, he whispered, She died a hundred and twenty-six years before I was born!

—That just makes me wiser! interrupted Rebekah.

My father raised his hand to stop the bantering and said, Rebekah took a bad fall in her eighth mortal year. Since she came here, she has worked tirelessly with children who have died and need comfort.

I took Rebekah's hand and said, I am so pleased to know you.

Then, I eyed my son playfully and whispered to Rebekah, I warn you, Jerel is a challenge. I couldn't teach him anything on earth.

Rebekah laughed and said, Well, I've got lots of time to train him.

My father put his hand on my shoulder and said, Jerel and I are so proud of the work you are doing with Enoch.

—You know?

—We've helped.

—You can leave this place?

—By permission.

—Everyone can?

—Only those who have assignments. Although the world of spirits is part of the earth where you dwell, there is a boundary that separates the two places. For most of those who live in this world of spirits, that veil is all they see. But it is possible to cross it and go back and forth.

Ebanel turned and pointed toward a grayish fog extending as far and high as I could see. It hung like a curtain I could not see the top of.

—We call it the veil, he said. It separates our two worlds. Those on earth cannot detect it with their coarse senses.

I noticed a group of people, dressed in white, that had gathered there. They stood in a semicircle and were squeezing one another's hands. I thought I recognized some of them.

—What are they doing? I asked my father.

—Just watch.

A hush came over the group. A moment later, an elderly woman walked through the veil. Shouts of joy and tears of happiness erupted as the greeters gathered around the woman and welcomed her. Her expression of bewilderment suddenly changed to elation as she recognized the people in the circle. She looked down at her legs, tried them as though she had not had their use for a long time, and smiled. Suddenly, a tall, gentle-looking man came through the crowd and said to her, *Welcome home, my love.* The love and relief I sensed from the couple overwhelmed me and I wept freely. I thought, *No matter what tragedies happen on earth, they don't matter. Ultimately God makes everything right.* At once, the woman turned back and said, *What about my son whom I've left behind on earth?* The people gathered around her and comforted her, and I was given to understand that she need not worry, for family ties continue, and she could turn her concerns over to a caring God.

—I never tire of the sight, my father said. Honorable people coming home, relieved from their trials, restored to those they love.

As the group ushered the woman away, they passed near us, and she fixed her eyes on me. She looked surprised at first; then a glimmer of recognition came to her face. She reached out and squeezed my hand.

—Good to see you, Rabunel, she said.

My surprise bound my tongue. The group moved on before I could respond. I turned to my father.

—I know that woman! Her name is Muriel. She came to live in the City of Enoch from the land of Sharon. She had been with us four months when her husband died. She had lost a leg to an accident. I remember her constant pain. Where are they taking her?

—To a sacred reunion.

—Will she be allowed to help her son on earth?

—If she is assigned to that work.

—Have you and Jerel helped me? I don't remember.

—It's not a spiritual skill you've developed, said may father. But we've visited you just the same. We've seen your trials and have helped. When you've offered prayers, we've offered prayers, and we've often been allowed to assist in answering those prayers.

I was astonished at the thought.

—There is so much I do not understand, I said.

—Family is the ultimate society of heaven, said my father. The love that binds us on earth never diminishes, but goes on and on. I am your father. I loved you on earth; I love you still. Being here changes nothing. If I can, I will always try to help you—and so will the father of us all. Make prayer a dialog between you and your father. Ask questions. Listen. Wait for an answer: thoughts, feelings. They will be accompanied by a feeling of love. Learn to trust those feelings and act upon them.

—Seek the gift of faith, added Jerel. It requires faith to trust feelings that touch your heart and mind. It requires greater faith to act upon them.

My father drew my attention toward a distant place. Muriel had joined with a larger congregation of people who were celebrating and feasting. Beyond my wonder at their sitting to eat as would we on earth, I was impressed that her family was immense—grandparents, great-grandparents, uncles, aunts, cousins, parents, her husband, a child who had died in infancy. The bonds of family had only been dimmed by Muriel's inability to *see* while she resided on earth.

I faced my father. Enoch has the gift of seeing and hearing, I said. I've never understood it.

—Spiritual communication is individual, he replied. You may have a thought enter your mind, something presses you toward an action. Maybe it will come as new knowledge, or perhaps a clarity of ideas. You may feel a sudden warmth that burns within your breast. Peace, clarity, love all accompany spiritual communication. Confusion, depression, a weighty dullness are not from God. He does not speak that way.

I gazed out at Muriel, then turned to Rebekah.

—Where is your family? I asked.

—I see them often, but we are all very busy. I have a special assignment to work with the little children who have come here having been sick or abused. Their trials are unique—more severe than children should have to bear. My companions and I comfort them and heal them.

—What a wonderful work, I said. But is there no way to stop the suffering in the world?

—We are never allowed to interrupt men's choices, she said, even if those choices mean temporary pain for another. It does not mean we do not weep for the abused. But we have learned to rely on the healing power of the Messiah, he who will save man from his sins, he who has infinite ability to dry all tears. We are here to help. When suffering children pass into this world, we help them deal with their trials. We encircle them in arms of love and help them through the healing process so that they can learn to give in return. They become some of the most giving and loving people in Paradise.

I gazed at Rebekah with deep admiration, wishing I knew her better. She was beautiful. She had woven her arm into Jerel's, and it was obvious to me that my son loved her dearly. I realized how much I had missed him. The peace and love I felt from my family here and from this place were sweeter than any I had known. I felt I was home. I belonged here. Then my thoughts turned to the work I had left behind, helping Enoch as he struggled to build a society of peace on earth. I thought of Moriah, my children, my grandchildren. I wanted desperately to share this experience with them. In the midst of my contemplations, I realized I had not given one moment's thought to my former trade, my merchandise, my worldly worries: relationships, finding enough food to eat, securing adequate shelter, combating sickness. But I felt a yearning to be back with my family on earth and to fulfill my life's mission.

My father took me by the hand and began to lead me forward. Rebekah took Jerel's hand, and together we followed a path that crested on a grass-covered hill. I was aware of how effortlessly we moved—more like gliding than walking. From the top of the hill, I observed a small valley that lay before us. At its center stood several gleaming buildings that had the appearance of light-colored polished marble. Several hundred people moved between the buildings in an open, market-like area. All seemed busy. Everyone seemed happy. I sensed that there was no selfishness there, no envy, no malice. I was struck that each person had arrived at the deep commitment to do good for the whole community. *They have become of one heart*, I thought, *just as Enoch has said we must become*. That *oneness* had neither stifled individuality nor repressed freedom of expression. The people were dressed differently, engaged in diverse activities, distinctive in every way, but obviously bound to each other by love and purpose. I remembered an old proverb: *That which is given must first be received. He who gives with pure intent is he who receives all that God has.*

As we moved among the people in the community, I listened carefully to their conversations. They spoke of their work, of what they were learning, of whom they were helping, of what assignments they had. I could have been standing in the marketplace of any number of cities I had visited on earth, except for the lack of envy, the feeling of abundant love and hope, the sense of purpose permeated a society where everyone seemed essential and appreciated. Each appeared to contribute to the society his own uniqueness, talent, personality. Some had gathered into groups and were laughing, joking, but not rudely. I sensed that humor was important here. As we walked among them, I felt no judgment, no avarice, but complete acceptance and sincere interest in my well-being. I perceived that each person realized his responsibility in bettering the whole society.

—Why can we not achieve this on earth? I asked my father.

—Pride, he said. Pride is the stumbling block of Zion.

—Pride?

—Pride is enmity towards God, man, and nature. Pride is the universal sin, the great vice.

Zion—the elusive term Enoch used and insisted be spoken reverently. I had not understood it. But now I saw a society of people at peace, busily working for the common good, individually progressing. And they were prospering. Family was the fundamental organization here. Husbands and wives loved each other. It was a society excelling in education, drawing down information as if from a library of truth linked to heaven. Truth had replaced ignorance. Peace had supplanted war. Beauty was the hallmark.

—Rabunel, do you know what you are seeing? asked my father.

—A society patterned after the heavenly city.

—The same society that Enoch is trying to create on earth.

—Zion?

—Yes.

—Is Zion a city?

—Zion is the pure in heart. Zion is a person, a family, a society. Zion in all its forms is characterized by love, service, being one in purpose with God. Look and see the future of Zion.

Suddenly, a grand vista burst upon my view. An ineffable light shone around me, the purest, brightest light I had ever seen. I beheld an immense city extending out to distant borders, thronged by myriad people from many nations. In the midst of the city stood a magnificent temple, which in magnitude and splendor was beyond anything I had known on earth. I gazed with wonder and astonishment. It was constructed of hewn stone, polished to a brilliant luster, adorned with large windows and carved door sills. The temple's foundations were of precious stones, its walls burnished gold, its window agates as clear as crystal. Its top was dazzlingly bright and seemed to mingle with the skies. A bright light arced over the temple, extending rays of glory in all colors of the rainbow.

—Zion's temple is the sanctuary of freedom, said my father, the palace of the great King, the center of Zion's government. Look and see the magnificence, the order, the glory of this kingdom.

Once more the vision increased in my mind, and I saw the gates to the temple, twelve in number, three on each side, defining the perimeter of the large square on which the temple stood. The gates were built into a strong wall of masonry enclosing the square and harboring the interior courtyard that was ornamented with walks, grass, flowers, shady groves of trees—the whole arranged in perfect taste with an elegance, neatness, and beauty that might well have compared to Eden.

—Enoch has spoken of Zion and its temple, I said, but I was never able to envision their existing on earth amidst all the evil and violence. Is it possible?

—God cannot lie, and he has promised Enoch of Zion's coming. But the people must desire and choose it. They must leave the world although they live in it.

—We've left it. We've lost our homes and been driven out.

—But many of your people have brought the world with them. Urgency has united you together more than love.

—It is true, I said sadly. I had thought that our people had chosen God long ago, but there are enemies among us. My life was threatened by the Mahan, who could only have come from the City. Only those in the City knew of my journey to Danan.

—And there are others. Many people in the City of Enoch still cling to their secret sins and soothe themselves by thinking that God does not know, or that if he does, a little sin will not matter.

His words struck like a stab to the heart. Beyond those who loved sin and hid it was an immense sea of humanity who went about daily doing the best they could, but falling victim to their own weak natures. I was one. How often had I cursed the weaknesses that lay just at the waterline of my life? When I tried to walk into the light I had but to turn to see my shadow, a dark image of myself, mocking my every move.

—How can a man know what sins he harbors? I asked. How can he break the chains of weaknesses that so easily bind him? How can he know what debilitating attitudes or characteristics he carries in his person that may have been passed down and imposed on him from former generations?

—It is possible, said my father, but this freedom comes ultimately as a gift from God after all you can do.

Jerel said, The key to receiving is asking. Ask God for his mercy. Mercy comes from only one source.

—The Messiah, I said.

—Yes, said my son. Once a man understands that, his whole being reaches out for mercy and relief.

—The process of sanctification, Jerel explained, begins with a man's heartfelt petition to God, his confession that his heart is broken by the weight of his sins and weaknesses. He is contrite, ready to learn and do what he must for mercy to claim him. He yearns to become a new creature and leave the old behind. The Holy Spirit begins to search the individual, revealing those things spiritual, mental, and physical that retard progression and presenting solutions as quickly as the individual can implement them.

—It seems a long, lonely process, I said.

—Often long, said my father, but it does not have to be lonely.

He bade me look more closely at the society we had entered. I saw men in authority teaching individuals saving principles, directing every person to the Messiah and God's plan of redemption for his children. I also saw women teaching and comforting. I perceived that they helped both by assignment and by charity.

—You can see, said my father, that no one in Zion is left alone. For every person, a system of support is created so that aid and encouragement are always close at hand. The beauty of the system is that the helped person soon becomes the helper. In this way Zion is created one individual at a time.

—But what is it that we are missing to create Zion on earth? I asked.

—Don't fall into the trap of looking beyond the mark, my father said. You have already received all you need to know. What is missing is your decision to do it. Zion is built by perfecting the basics: more faith, greater love for one another, truer service.

I remembered Enoch's prophecy: *God will come to live in Zion, Rabunel. How could he not? For Zion will be heaven on earth.* I stood silently for a long time regarding the people of the paradisiacal society. They seemed to be living lives of total fulfillment. Love radiated from each of them to everyone they met and to all God's creations. Every form of vegetation, each insect, every animal seemed to feel and emanate this love. Even the incredible beauty that graced this world seemed an exhibition of that love being returned. As I absorbed the feeling, I knew for certain that I wanted Zion to be my home forever.

—It is beautiful! I said.

—Yes, said my father.

He took me by the elbow.

—There is still someone who desires to see you.

I felt puzzled, but looked in the direction that he pointed. A young-looking, dark-haired woman was walking toward me. She appeared small and willowy like my daughter, Eve. At full stature she wouldn't have reached my shoulder. Her feet were bare, her complexion clear, alabaster, nearly transparent. Her eyes were green, her lips red. She walked briskly in a loose robe, robin-egg blue. Even at a distance I knew her. I felt the emotions of a child coming home.

—Mother! I breathed.

She ran to me and threw her arms around my neck.

—Cricket! she said.

I hadn't been called that since I was a child. I had only known her for a few years before she had perished in the great drought, but I remembered *Cricket,* and I remembered her kiss when she gave it.

—You've become a man, she said as she wept.

She took me by the shoulders with her two hands and looked up into my face.

—I have children and grandchildren now, I said.

She laughed and said, I know!

—Of course you know, I said.

—I love to hear you talk, she said. Say something else.

I couldn't think.

—You could only say a few words when I left you.

—You are so beautiful! I'd forgotten, I said, gazing upon her face.

—That's what I wanted to hear, she said.

—She loves flattery, laughed my father, kissing her on the forehead.

—Not true!

—Oh, Grandmother, you know it is! said Jerel.

After we enjoyed a laugh, I said, Now I feel complete.

—Can you remember how I came to call you Cricket? she asked me.

I shook my head.

—When you were a baby, just barely able to sit up, a cricket hopped onto your bare leg and frightened you. When I ran to see what had happened, I flicked the insect away, and you began to cry. I thought, *What a sensitive boy I have.* So I started calling you Cricket.

—The bug probably bit him, said Jerel, that's why he started to cry.

—I like the *sensitive boy* version, I laughed.

When my father had said, *Enough foolishness*, my mother took my arm with one hand, my father's with the other, and motioned Jerel and Rebekah to follow. She led the family toward the boundary of a meadow, the place where I had entered this paradisiacal world.

—Do I have to go back? I asked.

—It's your choice, said my father. There is a work for you there, if you will accept it.

—And my mother and brothers and sister need you, said Jerel.

I turned to my mother and said, Do you want me to leave?

—I want you to be happy, she said.

Happy? I looked all about me, surveying the incredible place once more, and tried to imagine leaving its love and peace for the sorrows of earth. I thought, *If this is a dream, I'd prefer to remain in it. What could possibly convince me to return?*

Softly, Jerel took the hem of my robe, and I suddenly found myself at my home in the City. I heard the sounds of chiseling and hammering as men worked on the temple. I surveyed the City and saw the people bustling about doing evening chores before the setting of the sun. A familiar voice caused me to pivot. It was Moriah's.

—*We should talk about this later,* she was saying to Enos.

My son was dressed in warm clothing and looked to be equipped for a journey.

—*I must find Father,* he said to her. *I have a feeling of foreboding.*

—*As do I,* she said, *but I can't let you go alone*

—*I'll be fine. I'll go over the high pass and check every byway and each outlying community.*

—*Why start out at night? Go in the morning and take other men with you.*

My son's look of determination seemed to soften at the tone of worry in my wife's voice. His body relaxed and he stepped forward to hug her.

—*As you wish, Mother,* he said.

Then I found myself with Eve and perceived her fear for my well-being. My thoughts of Benjamin, Sarah, and my grandchildren took me to their home in an instant. I watched them kneel together in prayer as Benjamin offered an emotional plea for my safety. As I stepped from their house, I saw Enoch and his wife, Anna, putting their daughter, Melca, to sleep, and I remembered the happiness I had known working by his side. I realized how much he still had to do and how much I loved him. Beside my love for my family on earth and what I perceived as my incomplete life's mission, nothing else mattered. Then I looked back at the paradisiacal world and began to mourn.

—I wish I could feel that peace always, l said.

—What is stopping you? my father asked.

—There are obvious differences between the two worlds.

—Do you suppose that peace comes only because of environment? Have you learned nothing?

What had I learned? I stared deeply into his face. My mother squeezed my hand. Jerel put his arm round my shoulder. Weren't these not still the people I had loved on earth? Didn't the love of family span the distance between life, death, and life?

—Look at us, my father said. It is true that we now exist as spirits, but some things remain the same. We still must develop faith; we must repent; we must make and keep covenants. How and what we choose still dictates our progression. We have the same consciousness, passions, feelings. We still must work through our problems. The primary difference between our two worlds is that those of us here have chosen to live a better way. It comes down to choice. If we can do it here, you can do it there.

I knew he was right. I suddenly sensed an incompleteness within me. I had not accomplished all I needed to on earth. That realization summoned within me both sadness and excitement.

I took my mother into my arms and said, I need to return. I'm not finished there. Saying good-bye to you is the hardest of all.

—I know. I love you . . . Cricket.

—We'll miss you, my father said, but we'll never be far away.

—You have been given a great gift, said Jerel. You've experienced Zion. You know it's possible, even in a wicked world. When you are converted, help those around you.

His comment astonished me.

—But I *am* converted, I said.

—You now know something about the destination of man, he said, but conversion comes from another source. Because a man believes or knows does not mean he has changed his actions.

—There is a burden in knowing, added my father. More than ever, you will be aware of and hate the pettiness and evils of the world. You will find yourself in the world but with your heart here.

In times of trial you may find yourself questioning why you made the decision to return to earth. The depth of your conversion will hold you on your course.

—Why? I asked.

—Because the sign of a man who is converted is his ability to yield his heart to God. If God has a work for you to do on earth, then you must discover it and sacrifice all you are and have to accomplish it. But in the process you may find yourself doubting both yourself and God.

—Do you have the courage? asked Jerel.

—I am ready to return, I said.

—I'll take you back, my father said.

I embraced each of my family. Then I took my father's hand, and we stepped forward into the veil.

for the first time, seeing

ᦤ

A sharp pain sliced through my side. My lungs fought to take in air. I opened my eyes but perceived only darkness. I was back in the pit, writhing in pain on its cold, hard floor. My spirit fought to maintain consciousness.

Maybe it was a dream, was my first thought. Then I paused, stared out, and thought, *It was not.*

Suddenly I thought I heard the sound of chopping, as though a tree were being split by an ax. My mind reeled, the agony pushing me toward insanity. Then a wedge of light sliced through the darkness, stabbing my eyes, blinding me. I thrust out my hand as though I were shielding my face from a fire and thought, *I must be dying.*

—Rabunel! a voice cried from above. Take the end of the rope and pull yourself up.

After so long in silence, the voice was deafening, and in reflex I shoved the heels of my hands into my ears.

—Rabunel! It is Micah!

I tried to answer, but only managed a groan.

—Shall I come down to help you?

I could not even achieve a meager, Yes.

Through blurred vision, I saw the shadowy figure of a man descend the rope with a torch clinched in his teeth. As he neared, I cowered as though he were an enemy, for as yet, my mind was dull.

—You are hurt, he said, crouching beside me.

Micah ran the light of the torch up and down my body, assessing the damage.

—I died, I murmured.

—No, you will not die, he said.

He had not understood me. Again, I tried to say, *I died*, but I could only mouth the words. Micah stood and said, I'll get you out.

I may have passed out. The next thing I remembered was my limp body being lifted and a rope being looped about my waist and up under my shoulders. Once more I moaned.

—I wish there were a painless way, he said.

That said, Micah laid me on my back and climbed the rope, saying, I'll draw you up with my horse.

A hot pang shot through my wound, and again I fell unconscious. A dream tortured me. I imagined having been dropped back into the pit, the opening sealed, and my being surrounded by darkness. I thought I saw my emaciated body lying pale, stomach distended, hollow eyed—a starved skeleton. I ran a dry tongue over my parched lips. They bled at the touch. I imagined rolling over and seeing myself lying in a pool of blood, life draining from my wound. An apparition appeared in the form of the large man of the Mahan. He said, *You want water?* and drug me to the edge of a river, took me by the nape of the neck, and forced my head under. I was startled from the dream by a big voice and a bigger hand holding my head.

—Rabunel, drink. Don't fight me.

It was Micah's voice that wakened me from the hallucination. He was pouring water into my mouth from a pouch. As I gazed into his eyes, a burst of understanding replaced panic, and I reached out to take his hand and guide the water to my mouth. When I began to choke, Micah pulled back the pouch, turned me on my side, and struck me on the back.

—Slowly, old friend, he said, pouring water into the cup of his hand and washing my face.

He reached into a bag, produced a loaf of bread, tore away a piece, and offered it to me. As I took the morsel, I began to sob, and Micah, stroking my head, said, I thought I'd never find you.

—Where am I?

—Near Saad. I'm taking you home.

—How long have I been gone? I asked in a whisper. Weeks? Months?

—Four days, he said.

Only four? was the last thing I remembered saying before I awoke in my own bed with Moriah tending me.

—Where is Micah? I asked my wife, when I later awoke.

She sitting at my side sponging my face with a wet cloth.

—Working at the temple, I suppose, she answered.

—How did he find me? How did he get me out?

—A map and a note were left at his home. He pulled you out.

—I must warn Enoch, I said, making a motion to rise.

The slightest movement came with great effort and sharp pain.

—You are going nowhere! said Moriah. Enoch will come. He's been here many times, but you've been sleeping.

—How long?

—Five days.

Four days in the pit, five days unconscious. I could not make sense of anything. I looked into Moriah's face then scanned the room. I was lying in my bed in my home on the hillside near the tabernacle. My children, grandchildren, and Joshua stood in the doorway of my room.

—We've stayed with you, Father, said Enos.

I motioned them to come near.

—I died, I said.

—Almost, said Benjamin.

—No. I actually *died*. I left my body. I saw my father, Ebanel. He showed me the heavenly city. I talked with Jerel.

Eve began to cry.

—He's still not well, Mother, she said.

Moriah held Eve, stroking her long hair.

—No, it's true. I remember, I said. I was in a place—Paradise.

I began to cough, and Moriah laid a hand on my head.

—Still hot, she said.

She looked into my eyes.

—You've been through a lot. Dreams can seem so real.

Maybe she was right. My head was pounding with as much pain as the wound in my side.

—Don't talk now, said Moriah.

I nodded and again slipped sleep. I awakened to the sight of Benjamin's face a palm's distance from mine.

—He's breathing and awake, he said to others in the room.

My family gathered round me. Eve took my hand. Moriah stroked my head.

—The fever has broken, she said. He will be alright.

I surveyed the worried faces of my family. Then I looked at Joshua.

—You believe me, don't you? I asked.

Joshua came close, sat on my bed.

—Believe you?

—About dying.

Eve began to cry again.

—Stress and pain can make you dream terrible things, Benjamin said.

—But this was wonderful, I said.

Joshua stared into my eyes.

—Is there a heaven? he asked finally.

—Oh, yes.

He studied me for a long moment, then said, I believe you had an experience.

—But he's delirious, said Eve.

—No, said Joshua. I think he's alright—more than alright.

Joshua turned back to me. Can you tell us about it?

I looked at my family, their weary faces, and said, Soon. Now, help me outside.

—You're not well, said Moriah.

—Well enough.

I gestured to Benjamin and Enos to help Joshua lift me. My sons shot glances at their mother who, relenting, returned a slight nod. Then, making a saddle of their arms, my sons lifted me, and Joshua steadied me from the back. They carried me outdoors, where Moriah brought some bedding and strung netting between two cottonwood trees, then said, Why don't we let him lie quietly for a while.

As my sons laid me in the cot, Benjamin whispered in my ear, Maybe you shouldn't say too much about dying until you feel better.

I responded with a smile. My mind was too occupied to debate. Something wonderful was happening. As we stepped from the house into the light, I tipped my face to the morning sun and let a bath of warm beams wash over my skin. I felt as though my whole being was being drawn out toward a reality foreign to me. As much as the pit's darkness had duped my senses, the sun's brightness now charged my body, the most minute part of it attracting, storing, emanating intelligence. I had the sense that the whole purpose of my physical creation was to be a receptacle and to emanate truth. I reached out with my mind to *feel*—truly feel. Marveling, I studied a leaf and pondered the threadlike veins that formed a webbed skeleton spreading out from the spine. I noticed that moisture, like tears of dew, had gathered as if in a cup. Pooled finally as a weighty drop, the bead slipped the distance of the spine to the long, tapered tip of the leaf, clung stubbornly, then dropped. It splashed where a colony of ants had constructed a kingdom by excavating bits of balled earth and transporting them to the surface. The dew drop must have seemed like a flood to the tiny creatures.

What had happened to me in the world of spirits had changed me. Everything within my gaze appeared vibrant. I wondered at the uniqueness of each creation, how nothing, not even two blades of grass, was duplicated. Looking closely, I concluded, one might detect within the architecture of each creation the signature of God. I felt as though I was seeing everything for the first time: distinct grains in wood, dusty sunlight filtering through young shoots of tree branches, motes of pollen settling on rose petals, the curve and texture of rocks, the smooth sheen of water at rest. I beheld it all. Nothing escaped my gaze. I soaked in all the world around me, welcoming each nuance of intelligence, my entire body a sponge, until my family returned and stood around me.

—I thought I would never see or hear again, I said reverently.

—We thought you would not recover, said Moriah.

—Enoch came and blessed you to live, Enos said.

—I don't remember, I said. I must tell him of my ordeal.

—Enoch has gone with Ishmael to oversee milling timber for the temple. But he will return soon.

—And will Micah come? I asked.

—He has visited you often.

—We have begun plowing and planting the land for the Dananites, Joshua said.

I looked at him incredulously.

—You plowed the fields? When did you find time?

—We, in the family, and some others who are sympathetic to the Dananites' plight—all of us took time to prepare the ground. Those poor people can't come here without hope of a harvest.

—Thank you, I said, reaching out and taking his hand. I was worried about how they would survive. Now I know they will.

—Do you know who abducted you? asked Benjamin.

—I don't know. There were two. They wore hoods. One had a familiar voice, but I couldn't place it. I think he saved my life. I heard them say *Mahan*.

At my mention of *Mahan*, Moriah grew pale.

—We have an enemy among us, she breathed.

Enos looked at his mother, then at me, and asked, *Mahan?*

—An ancient society, said Benjamin. Secret. It was established by Cain and his followers to murder Abel. Its purpose was to get gain.

—Like the Watchers? asked Joshua.

—Yes, I said, but the Mahan preceded them. The Watchers are now the more public part of the society.

—The Mahan are here? asked Eve.

No one answered. It seemed that no one dared believe it.

Joshua came near, lifted the dressing over my wound, then replaced it.

—You have become a threat to someone, he said.

We looked at each other, then out over the City as if our scanning might detect an adversary. Eve wondered if the assailants might not be from Saad. I said it was possible, but I doubted it. The words of the big man were still a fresh memory: *You'll never get to Danan!* Only someone from the City of Enoch could have known of my journey. Surveying the City, reviewing each home, each occupant, Moriah's terrible pronouncement rang true: There *was* an enemy in our midst. But who? An infiltrator from Saad? Someone who sympathized with the Watchers? It would be someone who worked alongside us, I assumed, one who worshiped with us, who shared our hospitality. Someone who had a secret life, one different from his public self.

—It could be anyone, said Joshua, quietly.

—Everyone has some hidden part of them that they keep tucked away, Benjamin said.

—Can someone be that good at concealing a secret life? said Eve, visibly disturbed.

—Who we are in public is not always our real self, I said. But that is not what I experienced in Paradise. . . .

Moriah gave me a worried look.

—I believe it is not possible to be dishonest there, I continued. People are known as they are.

—We should talk about this later, said Moriah, touching a finger to my lips.

—You said that same thing to Enos when you worried about his wanting to go off alone to find me, I said.

Moriah's face went ashen.

—How do you know that? asked Enos.

I, myself, was surprised by my words. I had not expected to say them. As I looked at my wife and son, obviously stunned, I proceeded slowly, saying to Enos, You said you would search the byways and check the outlying cities. Your mother said she would not let you go unless you went with other men.

—How did you hear us? breathed Moriah.

—I don't know. Suddenly I found myself listening to your conversation. After I had been stabbed and dropped into the pit, I expected to die. My pain was terrible, the darkness thick and deep. But then I thought I felt myself in another kind of darkness. I felt myself groping and struggling, and soon I stepped through something like a veil into a world of consummate peace and beauty. My father, Ebanel, was there. So was Jerel.

—Jerel! cried Moriah.

At saying his name, Moriah began to weep.

—I talked with him, I said. He is happy.

—Do you think you experienced heaven? asked Benjamin.

—No. I was in a world of spirits, a place between heaven and earth.

I looked at Eve who still appeared worried over my state of mind.

—There are flowers in colors and types that you cannot imagine, I said to her. My senses seemed heightened. I smelled fragrances beyond the ability of man. I saw and heard more clearly. Don't you believe me?

—I'm trying, said Eve.

—Run your hand over your arm, I said.

When she had, I said, The peace I felt there was as palpable as what you are feeling.

—In your state of mind, you could have dreamed it, she said.

—I know. But it seemed so real.

—Are there animals? interrupted my grandson, Nathaniel.

—Yes. All kinds—some I'd never known. They are at peace. They don't hunt one another. You can pet them and even talk to them.

—Talk to the animals? said Nathaniel.

He didn't give me time to answer, but was off chasing his dog and trying to communicate with it.

Sarah, Benjamin's wife, said to her husband, Nathaniel will pepper us with questions until we scream!

Benjamin nodded and laughed.

For the remainder of the day I tried to answer my family's questions, attempting to remember as much as I could. Then, late in the day, my eyes became heavy, and Moriah ordered everyone to let me rest. We could resume our conversation another day. That said, my sons helped me back inside the house and laid me on my bed. As Benjamin was turning to leave, I caught the sleeve of his tunic and said, All the time I was there, I kept wondering: if they can do it, why can't we?

—Do what? asked Benjamin.

—Make a heaven on earth.

Benjamin and Enos looked at each other, perplexed.

—Don't you see? I said, We never lose our personality; our consciousness and individuality continue on. Our strengths and weaknesses follow us. While I was in Paradise I was plagued with a question.

—What? asked Enos.

—Why can they achieve Zion and we can not?

I became weary, rolled to the side away from the wound, and closed my eyes. I recalled the day Enoch had asked me to go to Danan. That night, as I had departed the Fathers Council, I had come upon Micah and Ishmael discussing the prospect of absorbing the Dananites. I heard Micah saying, *I worry about so many Dananites arriving at our borders.* Ishmael said, *I've been asked to help the Dananites make their journey here. I am to follow Rabunel. I worry about*

*the management of the City in my absence. The man replacing me is a fine
person but has little experience.* Micah replied, *And my best men are being
taken from the temple to follow Rabunel to Danan.*

I seemed to have startled them when I came near.

—How can you doubt? I had asked. After so many evidences of
God's protecting and supplying us, why should he withhold his help
now?

I had not tried to hide my annoyance from them. For who they
were, Micah and Ishmael should have been more supportive. They
were mighty men in the City. Their influence was felt in every corner
of it. Ishmael was admired for his ability to bring organization to
chaos. Micah's stature as a leader was unquestioned. Because he was
a gifted orator, Enoch often placed him before the people to expound
on the doctrines of the Messiah. Micah had developed such a closeness with Enoch that I sometimes imagined mild envy among the pop-
ulace. Who wouldn't covet standing in the shadow of God's anointed?
Ishmael, Micah, Enoch, and I could have been brothers. I had
expected more loyalty, and their disparaging tone had angered me.

—You are a man of faith, Rabunel, Ishmael said to me. Your allegiance to the prophet is admirable, but. . .

—But aren't we allowed to think for ourselves? said Micah, interrupting Ishmael's thought. After all, does God bless the blind followers? As much I want to extend charity to the Dananites, doing so will
tax us to the point of ruin.

—Does my supporting Enoch diminish my ability to think for
myself? I asked. No one has taken from me the capacity to choose.
Enoch is a man of God, a man of vision. We know this from long experience. Would he attempt any undertaking without a clear directive
from God?

—His actions approach empire building, Ishmael said.

Micah quieted his companion by placing a finger on his arm.

—The Dananite issue is divisive, he said.

—To be sure, I said, taken aback by Ishmael's comment.

—It's fine to be visionary, Micah continued. But I still fear that more people coming to the City will overwhelm us and we will suffer.

—Perhaps, I said, but now that the decision is made, will you stand by Enoch?

Micah didn't have an answer.

—Ishmael? I asked.

He turned his head away. I suddenly felt very alone. I offered a good-bye, and they nodded. I left them, and as I did, I heard Micah and Ishmael resume their debate. I was too upset to go home, so I decided to roam the streets of the City to discover the attitude of the rest of the people.

The walk was one I had always enjoyed. These were people I had come to know and love. This time, however, my walk was a search more than a stroll. I felt a need to judge the people's response to the Dananites' coming and what measure of support they held for the prophet. I feared I knew, but I hoped it wasn't true. As I walked, some approached me saying, What say you, Rabunel? Must we crowd our children together to make room for the people of Danan?

In contrast to that question, I recalled the look of relief in Gensek's face when he and his family had arrived in the City, the hope in Adul's voice when she allowed herself to imagine a peaceful home for her children, the tears that welled in Naomi's eyes as she watched her little brothers and sisters eating warm bread, drinking milk, laughing. I remembered that Gensek had said, *I can work stables. I know how to clean up after livestock. Can I gain employment in the City doing that?*

Now, in the streets of the City of Enoch, I heard low grumbling: *Haven't we worked hard for what we have? The City looks and provides as it does because of our hard labor. Haven't we earned the right to be careful with what we have? Are we expected to just throw it all away?* Some forecasters agreed with Micah, predicting that the infusion of a large number of destitute people would drain the assets of the community and compromise us all. I heard other whisperings about the Dananites: a woman in a knot of weavers saying, *The ones I've seen have no concept of grooming.* Another replying, *Have you seen how they eat?* A third stating, *I know they are poor, so were we when we came to these mountains. But at least we had the initiative to work hard and make this place beautiful.* Congratulatory nods followed the comment, and I continued my walk, pondering what was happening.

The fact that the Dananites were markedly different from us, could not be dismissed. Their customs were different. They rose at a different hour of the morning, for example, and were used to working past the dinner hour. Their children ran free while ours were more disciplined. Domestic animals were treated like pets and allowed in their homes. They wore bright headpieces and clothing that seemed to some of the City overly colorful and gaudy. A language of classification had begun. Distinctions like *us* and *them* had entered the communal vocabulary. As a point of pride, we of the City liked to say that we were fellow citizens and often used the appellation *People of God* to single us out. Comparison had crept into public thinking: people were being measured by their perceived productivity, intelligence, lineage. I heard whispered suggestions that *if* the Dananites *had* to come, could we not segregate them in their own part of the City?

Furthermore, Joshua had become a topic. Some said he had assumed too much by thinking he could impose this burden upon the people of the City. He should have kept the Dananites outside, at least until additional lands could be prepared. *Where does he think the accommodations will come from? Let's just see if he can educate them.*

Zion was the word that rattled around in my brain. Were we *Zion?* Some people had begun using it as a label: *Zion* this, or *Zion* that. But I had never been comfortable with the casual references.

—Where is Zion? I'd once asked Enoch, doubting my ability to recognize it.

—In the heart, he'd said. Zion is the pure in heart. Separate, consecrated, sanctified, complete.

—It isn't here, I'd said, sadly.

—Not yet.

∽

I awoke from my remembering with the sun just breaking through a pink sky. It felt warm on my face. For the first time, I knew I would heal. What I had experienced, whether in or out of the body, was still fresh on my mind. Regardless of the circumstances by which it had come, I was grateful for it. I was changed. Nothing could deny me that or make the experience more real. I was a new person and had been set on a road and a destination I could not have dreamed, at that time, would lead to my greatest blessing—and my most difficult trial.

a soft word

୪

Recovery is a wearisome thing. The waiting is tedious at best. One must abide a *wellness* regime, postponing work, enduring pampered care, feeling as useful as a splint on a wooden leg. I supposed Moriah had sensed my impatience in mending and, suppressing her tendency to mother, allowed me time to range and think. Rebelling at convalescing, I spent my time becoming reacquainted with my family and catching up on the doings of the City. When I had regained a little strength, I occupied my mornings by going to the temple site. I monitored the construction and made the workers crazy with my fussiness. Looking out over the City, I memorized every home, every stable, every shop. I rediscovered each byway and thoroughfare. I saw farmers, shepherds, artisans, mothers, children. I considered the mentors who taught eager students. I watched smiths forge metal and craftsmen work wood. Sometimes I searched the direction of Saad and considered the danger. Other times I turned my head toward Danan and thought of the possibilities. When I returned my attention to the City I was glad I lived here. It was home, despite its flaws, and there were no better people under heaven.

Still, I was ever watchful for signs of the enemy, *my enemy*—a telltale gesture, a sudden contrary wind, a whisper of evidence, an impression, a hint, any glimmer of motion that might betray my foe.

A feeling of foreboding nagged at me—perhaps this was all too good to last. Moriah always said I tended toward the negative. *If Enoch is the prophet of God,* she said, *you are the prophet of woe.* I had once traded in a distant land in which the people's ancestors had constructed a massive structure to study the heavens. When I had visited the structure it lay in a heap of mismatched stones crumbling in the sand. The builders had overlooked minuscule cracks in the foundation that, over time, had widened and led to ruin.

Looking down on the community, day after day, alone with my thoughts, I thought I detected tiny fissures in the foundation of the City of Enoch. Beginning with my family, I noticed Enos's lack of interest in taking a wife and rearing a family. I had once suspected that he and Esther, the slave girl he had ransomed, would marry. But Enos was enamored with government and seemed to be intent on rising within the structure. Ego and ambition: a dangerous combination.

A visit with Benjamin caused me further concern. Benjamin was a spiritual leader in the City, widely sought out for his counsel. In private, however, he was overly strict with his family. If his wife, Sarah crossed him, he was quick to put her in her place. Over time, she had grown callused from the encounters. Now they bickered over trivial things. I had watched her go about her chores while tending Nathaniel, balancing little Dan on her hip, and toting a stomach full with number three. For a young woman, she looked old. Her eyes sagged like a hound's and appeared as tired and woeful. She could have used more help and less reproach. When I expressed my worry to Moriah, she shrugged off my words, saying, *It's a woman's lot.* I wondered why. If a woman gives all she has to her family, must she also sacrifice her dignity? Beasts of burden are groomed, well fed, given rest—should not a man's wife receive as much? Where is the kind word? The offer to share the load? The soft touch?

—Women make a vow of obedience to their husbands, said Moriah. Should we not do as we are told?

She spoke of our custom, that the man ruled in his family without being questioned by his wife or children. Being looked upon as lord, he could mete out punishment for disobedience without challenge. In extreme cases, this could include banishment or death. I was seen as weak among some of my male associates because I had treated Moriah differently in our marriage, and now Eve had seen her mother's freedom and had grown up speaking her mind.

—A woman need only be obedient to her husband as he follows the commandments of God, I said.

—You have always put my comfort first, she said. You've treated me as your equal, as your queen. Many men do not.

For me, my one true love was Moriah. Each morning of my recovery I had held her in my arms as if that day would be our last. I felt complete and often could not hold back the tears that feeling of wholeness brought. Nor could she. As couples grow older, I concluded, they gain a certain oneness. How I longed for Benjamin and Sarah to feel that harmony.

∽

I made an unannounced visit to their home.

—*Don't hurt Nathaniel!* were the words I heard as I arrived. The voice was Sarah's. *A boy must be taught,* I heard Benjamin say. The next sound was Nathaniel's—a yelp like a dog's when it is struck with a stick. *I'll be good! I'll be good!*

My heart broke.

I stood at the doorway and coughed.

—Father! said Benjamin, surprised, hurrying to wash the look of rage from his face. His was breathing hard, as though he had climbed a steep hill.

Nathaniel, sandy haired, stocky, milk cheeked, pulled free from his father's grip and ran to hide behind his mother.

—I've arrived at a bad time, I said.

—Nathaniel has been bad, said Benjamin, tipping his head toward the boy.

I looked at Nathaniel, visibly afraid, shaking, shoulders slumping.

—Perhaps he did a bad *thing*, I said.

The little boy, always wanting to be big, sobbed, unable to catch his breath, and was embarrassed by it. Sarah set Dan on the floor, knelt beside Nathaniel, and held him.

—Stop crying! said Benjamin curtly. I didn't hurt you.

Nathaniel cried more.

Turning to me, Benjamin said, He's got to learn.

Little Dan—named for my friend Danbenihah—began to cry, and Sarah, big with child, stood and lifted him as he buried his face in her shoulder. She said to Benjamin, Why do you torment them?

—This is not the time! said Benjamin.

Beginning to cry herself, Sarah said, You walk among the people as a man of God, but you cannot comfort your own family.

She left saying, I'm sorry, Father.

Then she carried her two sobbing children and her big belly from the room.

I said nothing. Benjamin appeared embarrassed.

—I'm sorry, Father, he said. It's hard raising a family.

—To be sure, I said.

—I love them, you know.

—I know.

Benjamin looked away, and I felt uncomfortable.

—I should go, I said.

—No, please don't. Lately, we've had a lot of challenges: health problems, my being away too much. Nathaniel is at an age . . .

—I remember, I said.

—Sarah is having a hard time and seems to snap a lot, he said. She just isn't the same woman I married. I don't know what to do. She can't seem to handle the children, so I've had to become the disciplinarian.

—A hard job, I said.

—Yes, I don't like it.

—Her job, I mean.

—Oh.

—Do you want counsel from an old man who has made too many mistakes?

Benjamin smiled and nodded.

—Your wife is a remarkable woman. You are used to her now, but can you remember how you felt about her when you were courting?

Benjamin smiled a tired smile.

—You could find no fault, I said. She was the most beautiful and wonderful woman you had ever known, and you were bound to love, support, and protect her all her life. Now three pregnancies later and years of hard living have changed her some. But can you still see the bride in your wife?

Benjamin seemed thoughtful. Tall and lean, he had always borne the visage of intelligence. He had dark eyes, dark hair, a pale, almost transparent complexion—a contrast that made him stand out. Over the years I had come to depend on Benjamin's ability to perceive the advantages and dangers in alliances. He sensed strategies—a gift that was as natural to him as sight or smell. His stubborn zeal, which he had inherited from my father, Ebanel, sometimes got in his way when dealing with others. But more often, Benjamin was sought out for his insights into relationships and for sorting out difficult situations. It was Benjamin who had warned against the dangers of dealing with Saad. His vocal opposition had made him unpopular with the Saadites and those of our people who were becoming rich from Saadite commerce.

—Enoch taught me something about marriage, I said. I'll share it with you, if you want.

—I'd like that.

—Since the earliest days we have been taught that man was created in the very image of God, and it was God who said, *It is not good for man to be alone.* By definition God is the only one who is truly *good*. Thus man could not be *good* or *Godlike* unless he became like him— a father. And *Father* is the title that most defines God and the name by which he desires to be known.

—And so he gave Eve to Adam, Benjamin said.

—Which, by interpretation, means *Mother of All Living*, I said.
Benjamin began to fidget.

—I have been taught these things from my youth, he said.

—Yes, but have you considered that the relationship of Adam
and Eve is a pattern? To you Sarah is like *Eve*, the mother of all living. From you two spring lives, endless posterity, just like Adam and
Eve. It is something that I learned from my experience in the pit.
Family is everything, and every wife, Sarah included, should be
extended profound respect, the same honor that Adam extended his
wife. Every wife should be treated as a queen.

Benjamin looked thoughtful.

—I've wondered about relationships when we leave this world, he
said.

—They go on and can be sweet. But the foundation is formed
here on earth.

Benjamin became quiet and dropped his eyes.

—You are right. I don't mean to belittle my wife, he said. And it's
true, I have forgotten how much I loved Sarah when we were first
married. Lately, when I could have been home I've chosen to be away
and left her with the burden of the family.

—You don't have to chastise yourself too much, I said. Most men
are guilty of neglect and insensitivity. Also, it's man's tendency to lead
by force rather than by love.

—I've not been a father. I've been a disciplinarian, he said.

—Both are needed, I said. Every time I thought I knew something
about parenting, another child came along with a totally different personality. Then came the rethinking, adjustments, new rules. When I
finally thought I understood what it meant to be a father, I was too
old—no more energy. Do you know what the secret is to living forever? Have no children!

We both laughed.

—You might be right, said Benjamin. I've noticed a few gray hairs.

—I've got a head full of them, and every gray hair came *after* you children! Do you remember how I struggled to raise you? That aged me.

—I got the switch a few times, said Benjamin, laughing. But I deserved it.

I became sober at his comment and put my hand on his knee.

—Be careful with physical punishment, I said. I made mistakes with you. I know that now. I was too harsh at times. I think I was more concerned about losing control than teaching you right from wrong. It's quick and easy to cause fear in a child. Patience, understanding, love are so much harder. I'm sorry I so often chose the quick and harsh way of disciplining. Had you been an adult, any other person, I would not have treated you that way. The hitting, humiliating, shaming was wrong, and I fear that I sent you into adulthood with a poor model.

—Now you're the one being hard on yourself, said Benjamin. I have a mind. I know right from wrong. You were a good father to me. I hope I can be as good to my children.

—I just pray you will look around you at other fine examples of fathers, I said. Watch what they do. Emulate the good. Discard the bad. Find your way to do this very difficult job of fathering.

—Because of the discord at home I've struggled lately in counseling others, he said.

—The Spirit is grieved with contention, I said. No man can live two lives, one spiritual and another abusive.

—But how does a man deal with a wife who is quick tongued? he asked.

—Love her. Help lift her burden. Let no concern come before her comfort and happiness. Ignore the largest flaw, and compliment the smallest good. Never give up. It is the soft word that turns away wrath.

I left with an appreciation that fatherhood never ends. I trusted my boy. I always had. Once presented with truth, he would consider, then embrace it—no matter the cost. As I made my way home, I wondered how I might become a better husband, myself.

too much love

 og

It was a day I could have done without.

I had regained much of my strength and was spending more and more time at the temple site. The wound in my side had nearly healed, the red scar fading now and becoming pale. That morning I had awakened early to watch the sunrise. I had spread a carpet on the dewy ground and wrapped myself in a blanket. Cross-legged, I sat and watched the colors of dawn. In my memory was last night's promise to help Moriah weed the garden before the day grew hot. The still of morning was broken by a deep voice.

—Good day, Rabunel.

The voice was Micah's. He said he hoped I was recovering well.

—I miss my work, but I love being with my family, I said.

—May I sit with you? he asked.

I patted a place near me. Micah squatted, adjusted himself, and began to fiddle with the nub of a stick, focusing his gaze upon it. The look of discomfort in his face was apparent.

—Looks like rain, I said, tipping my head, trying to ease him toward what he had to say.

—Clouds are too high.

His comment drew my attention to the gray sky overhead. Overcast. I had noticed dark clouds gather at the horizon and drift over the mountains from the west. I had not considered that they floated too high for precipitation.

—Smells like rain, I said.

Micah didn't answer, but thumbed the stick and studied the carpet.

—Have I thanked you for saving me? I asked.

—Yes. You're welcome.

—The inflammation is gone now, and my bruises . . .

—I have a purpose in coming, he interrupted me. His voice was a whisper.

I waited.

—Your niece, Miriam, is a beautiful young woman . . . and her child needs a father—those Watchers of Shum!—and I have been so long without a wife . . .

From the time my father, Ebanel, and I had found Miriam in hiding and had helped her to escape from Shum, she had been my daughter. Her child, Rachel, was almost three now—a mischievous tot, hard to keep track of, running, jumping, skinning knees and elbows, more a boy than a girl. She had her mother's fair skin, hazelnut hair, green eyes. Micah was correct in his assessment of Miriam's beauty. Three years from Shum had given her the look of a woman. She carried herself with the same grace as did Moriah and Eve. That a rollicking free spirit like Rachel could have sprung from her was amazing.

—You've been years alone, I said.

—Years, he repeated, wistfully.

I anticipated his saying more, but he had gone back to the stick.

—Your purpose is to ask for her hand? I asked.

—You are her father now.

—But you are old enough to be her father.

Micah turned toward me.

—But I have noted in Miriam a certain maturity. I would make her a good husband.

Micah's voice became awkward like a boy's. The mighty orator of the City of Enoch could not manage to express what he felt. I studied the yearning in my friend's face, a face that revealed grooves of age, marks like crow's feet at the eyes, eyebrows thick and graying. As my peer, I could not treat him as a young man seeking the hand of my daughter. I wondered, if I were to lose Moriah, how would I seek another's hand, being so long removed from courting skills.

—It is true I am Miriam's guardian, I said, but I would not presume to give her hand in marriage.

Micah's face sunk.

—However, I continued, I have no objection to your courting her. She can make her own decision.

At that moment, Moriah called for me from inside the house.

—I'd better go, I said. I promised her some time in the garden.

As I made a movement to rise, Micah stood first, lifted me to him, and smothered me with an embrace.

You will not be sorry, he said, hugging me.

I am sorry already, I thought, anticipating the trouble that usually accompanies matters of the heart. I had stepped into an emotional arena, and there was no escape.

Micah shook my hand vigorously and said, I will make you a good son . . . *Father*.

I was not comforted by the title. Moriah called again. I stood, gathered up the carpet, and went into the house.

—You have a visitor, she said, motioning.

I peered around the doorway and saw Baruch sitting, waiting. His posture was erect, his eyes forward, the fingers of his hands laced and placed neatly on his lap. His dress was formal, uncommon for a workday: white tunic and robe that hit his calves midway, sashed at the middle, a smartly pleated turban at his head, new leather sandals braided up above his ankles. The look on his face was sober and his coloring pale. When I stepped into the room, he looked up.

—Baruch, my friend. What an honor, I said.

Baruch stood and took my extended hand.

—Do you have a moment? he asked.

I glanced back at Moriah, who tipped her head toward the garden and seemed perturbed. Then I observed Baruch, who looked woeful. I nodded.

—May we step outside? he asked.

As we moved toward the doorway, Moriah handed me the carpet, raised an eyebrow, and tipped her head toward the unweeded garden. I took her gesture as a sign of disapproval and avoided eye contact. In the yard, Baruch took two corners of the carpet and helped me position and smooth it on a flat place. Then we sat. I waited. Baruch looked down and away and found a twig to roll between thumb and forefinger. After a long pause, I said, Do you think it will rain?

—Perhaps. There's a smell of moisture in the air.

—That's what I thought, I said, but maybe the clouds are too high.

Baruch did not look up, but said he had seen rain fall from higher ones. Then he became quiet again.

—Your work among the people is admirable, I said, reaching for conversation.

—Very kind for you to say so.

—I've heard your name spoken of . . .

—I have a reason in coming, he said, breaking in.

I waited.

—I have been so long without a wife, he began. Your niece, Miriam, is a beautiful young woman . . .

—And her child needs a father, I interrupted.

Baruch looked up.

—Yes, I suppose she does, he said. When we were in Shum, my family and I hid Miriam away. I loved her as a daughter then. But something wonderful happened when I helped her give birth to little Rachel . . . I don't see Miriam as a child now.

—Are you asking for her hand in marriage?

—You are her father now.

—But you are old enough to be her father!

—She is older than her years. I would be a good husband.

I gazed at Baruch. Here was another man sounding like a boy. The look on Baruch's face expressed the yearning he could not communicate. Years of living had sculpted a hard face, furrowed above the brow, graying at the temples, bald on top, a slight sag of flesh at the chin. His embarrassment was apparent. Only the deepest feelings could have brought him to this point, but he was as poor at courting as was Micah.

—As Miriam's guardian, I said, I would be pleased to have you court her. But the decision to marry must be hers.

Moriah called from the house. Her voice had a tone of impatience.

—I am coming, I shouted back to her.

I gestured toward the house, and Baruch smiled a knowing smile.

—We will talk again, I said, and I stood to fold the carpet.

Then Baruch embraced me long and hard, until I thought I would faint.

—You will not be sorry, he said as he left.

It's too late, I thought.

—Good-bye . . . *Father*.

Inside the house, Moriah greeted me with her back turned, stirring a pot with a wooden ladle, and mumbling something about *When there's work to be done*. . . . I started to say, *I'm sorry*, when she spun, waving the ladle. Hands on hips, lips pursed, she blew an wayward strand of hair from her eyes and said, *Are you aware of the time of day?*

I was about to say, *I couldn't help it*, when she pointed the ladle gardenward, reminding me that I had agreed to work with her today, and did I expect her to pull weeds alone—*again?* When I mentioned that it might rain, Moriah huffed out the door and passed Eve, who was entering the house.

—I'll never get married! Eve cried as she stomped past me, rushing toward her bed and collapsing upon it. I stood open-mouthed and watched her roll to her stomach, fold her arms over her head.

I thought, *This would be a good time for a long walk—alone!*

Then Eve repeated her *I'll-never-get-married* prophecy, with greater emphasis on *never*, and began to cry. I sat beside her and stroked her hair.

—Why would you say that?

I expected I would regret having asked the question. I glanced at Moriah in the garden. Eve cried harder.

—It's Joshua. Why does he have to act like that?

—Like what?

—Like a—*man!*

Until that moment, I had considered myself an adequate orator. I'd spent much of my life speaking to individuals and groups on topics ranging from trade to government. I had preached to diverse audiences far and wide, explaining difficult doctrines, and I had raised my voice in the councils of the City. But to Eve's indictment I had no reply.

—It's that Dananite family! she stated flatly, sitting up, drying her eyes, and setting her jaw. Joshua spends every minute doting over them. And I know why. It's that girl, Naomi.

—You think Joshua has feelings for her? I asked.

—Have you seen her? She's beautiful!

—Yes, but you have always had his heart.

Eve responded by flopping on her back, arms stretched wide, and blurting out something to the effect that she'd never had any luck with men, never would, and she might as well cut her hair off and get on with being a spinster since she was bound to be one anyway. I let the comment fall unanswered and gazed into the yard where Moriah was wrestling a stubborn, root-bound weed. She seemed to be losing. When I looked back at Eve, shaking, bawling, the heels of her hands dug into her eyes, I thought, *A long trip would be nice right now.*

—If Joshua has feelings for me, why doesn't he show them or at least say something?

—If it were only that easy, I said.

—Why?

—Saying and showing what you feel is more natural for women. *I love you* is hard to say for most men. I imagine from the time of Mother Eve, women have wished men could be more romantic.

—Joshua seems to have no problem showing his feelings for Naomi.

—Sounds like you're jealous.

Eve sat up and stiffened.

—I am not jealous! she said.

—Yes you are, and you're good at it.

The expression on Eve's face showed I had startled her. She paused, then seemed to weigh her words as she answered. I knew her feelings were deep. She and Joshua had postponed their wedding while he preached in outlying areas. Now, she thought, her reward was to lose him.

—I am only making an observation, she said. Joshua seems to have deep feelings for Naomi.

—You think he loves her? I asked.

—Yes.

I rubbed my chin.

—You're right, I said. He does love her.

—I don't want to be right!

Eve began to cry again, and I pulled her head to my shoulder.

—It's a different kind of love, I whispered.

She didn't understand.

—I'm sure what Joshua feels for Naomi—for all Gensek's family, for that matter—is not *romantic* love.

—What, then?

—Not all love is the same. The love I feel for you is not what I feel for your mother, but both types of love are as deep. When a young man teaches sacred truths and sacrifices himself, he changes. He is drawn out in concern for those he works with. And you must allow it. His experience will make him a better husband and father. What an advantage he has, going into marriage knowing how to deny himself and give of himself completely. The love Joshua feels for Gensek's family is real, but it is not the same love he feels for you.

—But he seems to be able to show love to them so easily, Eve said.

—Yes, just as a father is often able to show his love more to a small child than to an adolescent. His lack of skill does not mean he loves less.

As I said these things to my daughter, holding her in my arms, I realized that Eve was no longer a little girl, but a woman in every sense. Her entire being cried out to receive and give love. I remembered her as a little girl, freckled nose, knotted hair, silly laugh. How had that bud of a girl blossomed into a woman? I could not recall the moment—a child one instant, a young woman the next. As a young woman, Eve had tried on one love interest then another as easily as changing clothes. Love was a transient thing then, appearing, then fading, then appearing again, a reflection cast onto a pool of water, materializing, then ebbing with any contrary ripple. Somewhere along the journey to adulthood, Eve had discovered that she wanted more—a mature love, a devoted, grounded, lasting love. But the little-girl part of her still clung to the thrill of infatuation and the terror of rivalry.

—Joshua is not very romantic, she said.

—No, I agreed, so you'll have to be patient. You'll have to teach him that he is safe when he expresses his deep feelings.

—What about Naomi?

—Allow him to love her as a friend. Don't forget that he was her teacher. He gave her a gift that required his personal sacrifice and investment. You would never want to take that from him. Trust him, Eve. He is enough of a man to know what he feels.

Once more, my eyes wandered from the house to the yard where my wife labored in the garden. Eve and I sat in a shadowed room, and I wondered if Moriah could see us. Even if she could, I doubted she would agree that I was doing something productive.

—I'd better go help your mother, I said.

—She'll be angry with you? asked Eve.

—She'll pretend to be. Your mother has always loved me in spite of my shortcomings.

Eve and I shared a laugh. Then she dried her tears, and I walked her to the door.

At the doorway Eve called out, Do you want something cool to drink, Mother?

—I want help! Moriah shouted back.

—You're in trouble, Eve said to me.

I took a deep breath and said, I know.

—It's my fault, Eve called out to her mother, I needed to talk to Father.

—Oh, never mind, muttered Moriah. I'll manage. I always do.

Eve turned to me again and said, I'd better walk out there with you!

When we came to the garden, I grabbed a spade and began to whack at weeds, checking Moriah for signs of forgiveness. Eve smiled wryly, and I shook my head. The warning went unheeded. Eve went to her mother, put her arm around her, and squeezed. Moriah straightened and made her face go more stern. Then Eve began to giggle. So did I, snickering at first, turning away to stifle it, then giggling when I could no longer stand it

—I'm not amused, said Moriah.

Eve tried to respond, but the words got caught in her laughter.

—You really shouldn't, I started to say. But I couldn't make my face go stern. I began to laugh more and turned to beat at a tough root.

—It's not nice to laugh, said Moriah. I've been working out in the sun while you two . . .

But she couldn't finish. Her voice cracked, and she swallowed a chuckle.

—What was that? Eve teased her mother. Did I hear you laugh?

—No.

—Sounded like a laugh to me, I said.

Moriah shook her head violently. But the expression on her face was beginning to approach surrender, and that drew from Eve the sound of s-s-s-s through her teeth.

Moriah said, That's not ladylike . . .

But that's all she got out. I started shaking, trying to stifle the laughter.

Eve said, Your eyes are watering, Father.

None of us could hold back. I whooped; Eve bawled; Moriah sat in the dirt and hooted.

I hugged Eve, dried my eyes, and tried for a tone of seriousness.

—Eve, I said, when I married your mother I thought I could never know more happiness. Then you children came, and the boundaries of my joy increased. Now, the most perfect joy I can imagine is being a couple with children, especially when those children have chosen to do right. That's what Joshua feels for you. He loves Gensek and his family differently. He has introduced them to the idea of spiritual life, and they have embraced it. Be patient with him while he adjusts to being home.

Moriah said to Eve, I don't know what you two have been talking about, but I've noticed Ishmael's son, young Reuben, watching you when you walk through the City.

—Reuben! He's all muscle and no brain! He just wants advice about Esther. He thinks I can help him.

It was Reuben who discovered the intrigue of Simeon and Gad when we were delivered from Shum. Bronze-skinned, with dark, deep-set eyes, Reuben was the image of his father, except that he had inherited his mother's short, lean stature. Still, he was an athletic, sinewy young man built for speed. He wore his dark hair long, slicked back over his head, to his shoulders. His sculptured face revealed high cheek bones, muscled jaw, square chin with a deep cleft. Two years Eve's senior and unattached, Reuben was *eligible*, and that fact had not escaped the attention of the City's young women. It was whispered that she who won Reuben's heart would be *lucky*. To Eve's comment about Reuben's physical-over-mental prowess I bit my tongue.

I knew she was wrong. Ishmael's son was often called upon to use his interpersonal skills to settle disputes, and his understanding of the law gave him the aura of being wise.

—Reuben is interested in Enos's Esther? asked Moriah.

—She *was* Enos's Esther when he bought her away from the caravan owners, said Eve.

—What has changed? I asked.

—Enos acts just like a *man*, Eve said. He's always off trying to make a name for himself, and he has neglected Esther.

—Now Reuben wants to court her? asked Moriah.

Although surprised by Eve's comment, I could blame neither Reuben nor any young man for being drawn to Esther. Her smooth, olive complexion, long, black hair, mahogany-colored eyes, slender frame, red lips, and the way she carried herself gave her a regal look. Furthermore, Esther had become an asset to the City. Gentle, soft-spoken, caring, she had a gift for comforting the sick and the patience to do it.

—He hasn't started courting her yet, said Eve. That's what I mean about more brawn than brain. But Esther and Reuben have become friends. I think Esther's heart is still with Enos, if he were smart enough to notice. But he is gone, mostly, and Reuben is always around.

—I always thought that Esther would be part of our family, I said. I'm going to find Enos and have a talk with him.

—You shouldn't talk love with people, said Moriah. It will only lead to trouble.

—You may be right, I said, but if there ever was a day for it . . .

And I left off finishing my thought to find my son. The weeds in the garden lived to see another day.

ॐ

I found Enos on an errand for Micah.

—May I walk with you? I asked him.

—Of course.

My youngest son had always boasted a brawny build, but his light complexion and little-boy face kept him looking young. He was cheery in disposition and ambitious by nature. In recent years his shoulders had broadened, and he carried himself with the demeanor of self-assurance. During his teen years he passed his parents and siblings in height and was growing taller still.

—I have heard *interesting* news, I began.

He did not slow his gait at my comment, but said, Tell me.

—I have a question, I said.

—Ask me.

—Very well. Are you willing to lose Esther to another?

Enos stopped.

—Lose her?

—Yes. She is being pursued by another.

—Who?

—Reuben, for one.

Enos stared at me blankly for a moment, blinked, and said softly, Reuben is a good man. He would make a good husband . . .

—That is what you have to say?

Enos cast his eyes skyward, seeming to be searching for an answer.

—I am fond of Esther . . . , he began.

—*Fond?*

—She is very sweet and pretty . . .

—But—

—But I don't want to get married.

—To Esther?

—To anyone. I have things I want to do first.

From the time Enos was a youngster, he had been enamored with law, the workings of government, the inner circles of power. Jerel had followed artistic pursuits. Benjamin had once gravitated to the profession of the Watchers. But Enos was the one who had followed me to Shum's council and begged me for information on the happenings. In the beginning I had considered his interest a positive thing, but as

he grew older and joined the Rahaj, his interest became an obsession—not a yearning to serve, but a compulsion to command.

—You are making a mistake, I said.

—Esther and I have an understanding, he said. We have a deep
affection for each other, but I allow her to explore her interests and
she allows me mine.

—You are guessing about her feelings, I said.

Enos looked puzzled.

—She wants a husband, someone to care for her.

—I care for her.

—Enough to marry her?

Enos became silent.

—I've pried, I said. I'm sorry. I wanted to warn you, and now I've
butted in. I just wanted to tell you that you might spend your entire
life climbing what you think is the mountain of achievement only to
discover when you arrive that you are standing on the wrong peak.

—You want me to marry Esther?

—I want you to think about your life, what's important. When
you begin to lose important relationships you should reevaluate your
life. Marry whom you will. It's your choice. But don't marry a career.
Happiness has never come that way. That was so obvious to me in the
world of spirits. There were no politicians there. Only families were of
ultimate importance.

ॐ

When I returned home, I slumped on my bed, exhausted. Moriah
brought me a cup of water and sat beside me.

—What's the matter? she asked.

—Too much love, I answered.

—Not toward me, she said.

I raised myself to an elbow and looked into her eyes. I suddenly
felt sheepish.

—I've been taking care of all the love problems except the one in my own home. Haven't I?

Moriah smiled and stroked my head.

—I've been neglecting you, I said.

Moriah said, Come and kiss me.

—Kiss you? Why?

—I just want to know if you remember how.

a marriage in zion

CB

—Rabunel! Come and see!

Moriah's voice roused me from my evening meal. I had been reclining on a carpet, dipping a crust of bread when she summoned me. When I stood to come near, she motioned me to be quiet and cracked the curtain so I could see. In the front of our home Joshua and Eve were standing hand in hand.

—I can't hear them, I said.

—Shhh! He's saying he's always loved her, even from the time they were children.

—What's she saying?

—She's saying that she feels the same. Now he's asking if she's over losing Chaz. She's nodding and asking if he has feelings for Naomi. He's saying he's fond of her and her family, but that's all.

Joshua and Eve walked to the shade of a tree, and Eve leaned up against the trunk. Joshua took both her hands and looked down at the ground. She stared at his face. Soon he raised his eyes to meet hers and asked, Will you be my wife?

When Eve said yes, Moriah and I burst from the house and rushed to embrace them. So did Enos and Benjamin and Sarah, who had been watching from other secret places. The couple looked surprised and embarrassed. Joshua said, Well, we won't have to spend too much time announcing our betrothal.

Thereafter, plans for the marriage were brisk. The couple had known each other for such a long time and they had waited for this moment for so long, there seemed to be little reason for waiting. And so the preparations began.

—If only we could be married in the temple, said Eve.

—Only if you want to wait another year, I said.

—It will take that long?

—Probably. But we'll make a beautiful bower for your wedding.

—And the wedding feast?

—One that the City of Enoch will not soon forget.

Eve threw her arms around my neck and squeezed hard.

—I love you, Father, she said.

—It's hard letting you go.

ɞ

Eve and Joshua planned their marriage like two giddy children. None of us could stand to be around them. The day of their wedding came with a flurry of events, and Moriah and I were too tired to think about how we would miss our Eve. That night, as Moriah fitted Eve into her wedding robes, Eve asked, Why does the bride braid her hair with precious stones?

Moriah looked to me for help, and I said, I think the bride's total attire suggests that she is becoming a queen.

—Joshua will become your king, said Moriah. When Enoch declares you husband and wife, you will start your own kingdom— endless lives springing from you down through the ages.

—That's why Joshua will be wearing a crown? Eve asked.

—Both of you will be wearing royal clothing to signify your ruling and reigning over your kingdom forever.

When Moriah placed the last jewel in Eve's hair and smoothed the sheer veil over her face, she said, You are the most beautiful bride I've seen.

Eve hugged her and said, Mother, I'm scared.

—I know, Moriah said. But you're marrying a good man, and you've both kept yourselves clean for this special occasion.

I gazed upon my daughter and a flood of memories raced through my mind: the little waif with constant skinned knees; the girl who presented me with a wild flower bouquet each time I returned from a journey; the one who cried in sympathy with each person she saw hurting. How could I give her away? Then again, how could I not? Moriah was right. Eve made a beautiful bride. She had spent the day being ceremonially washed, dressed in royal robes, her hair braided with precious stones, a fine veil covering her face.

We hadn't time to say more. By tradition, a friend of the bridegroom arrived to fetch Eve from our home. Thus the wedding procession began. Soon, Joshua joined the throng, wearing fine robes, jewelry, a crown. Suddenly, it was as though all the houses in the City of Enoch emptied and filled the streets. The people were singing, dancing, making merry. Eve began to dance and laugh. When we arrived at Joshua's home, Enoch was waiting for them under a canopy. He blessed Eve, saying, *Our sister, may you increase to thousands upon thousands; may your offspring possess the gates of their enemies.* Then Eve removed the veil from her face, placed it upon Joshua's shoulder, and declared, *The government shall be upon his shoulder.*

I felt Moriah squeeze my hand in both of hers as Enoch administered the covenants of marriage. I looked out over the audience and saw Benjamin and Sarah holding each other, Sarah crying. Enos stood with Naomi, his arm around her shoulder. Micah sidled up alongside Miriam and lifted Rachel into his arms. Baruch, the groom's father, stood silently alone, and I could only imagine how much he missed having Leah at his side.

A great shout interrupted my thoughts, and suddenly Joshua was twirling Eve around and around. We ate. We drank. We danced and sang. We made merry. Joshua and Eve presided over the feast like a king and queen. They were in their own home. They were happy. It was all a father could hope for his daughter. And as I'd promised her, the celebration was one that the City of Enoch would not soon forget.

six months of change

൙

The memory of the attack by the Mahan was still fresh in my mind although six months had come and gone. I'd detected no further evidence of them and wondered if I had suffered only an incidental attack. I tried to convince myself that the danger was past. Summer had become autumn; autumn had brought harvest; harvest brought celebration. When I looked at the scar in my side now, it was a thick white line, and I moved about with the vigor of youth. In the air, warm-weather birds were flocking and flying south as days were becoming chill, short, gray. Soon, men would begin to prepare for spring planting by dunging the tired soil with plow and ox. Women would start to cool vegetables in dugouts, dry fruits and meat, tailor winter clothing. Children still groaned about chores and preferred to romp in red and yellow leaves. Yet, of all autumn's events, the one most anticipated was the completion of the temple.

When I was not working on the temple, I spent much time writing about my extraordinary visit to the world of spirits. Those close to me, my family and friends, now believed I had truly had the experience. I spoke of it when asked by someone sincere, but otherwise I kept my what had happened sacred.

It was Enoch who told me, You should write your experience.

Enoch was a writer, recording the great knowledge he had received from God. He had been shown the heavens and endless creations of God. He had been shown this earth, the purpose for which it was made and the end thereof. Many of these things he wrote in his books and kept them hidden from the world.

—The spirit of man has a great capacity to learn, he said. Man's body has a great capacity to act. The coupling of spirit and body is marvelous for acquiring knowledge and acting upon it. It is an act of faith to ask God for knowledge. By asking you acknowledge that he is the fountain of truth that you wish to draw upon. Asking is spiritual in nature. Writing is physical. You should learn to write down what you learn. It is an act of faith. There is power in it.

Although I had an immediate desire to experiment upon his suggestion, I doubted my ability to ask and receive. Then, after several days of contemplation, I retreated to the hills one quiet morning with a determination to make an attempt. I couldn't have been more astonished by the results.

—Before you ask, Enoch had instructed me, pray to God, then study the words of the prophets. You will feel the Spirit as it confirms the truth of those words, and soon you will be able to discern when the Holy Spirit is with you. Then ask your question. You may feel a calmness. Perhaps a soft thought will come to your mind. As best you can, try to write down the impressions that come to you.

In the solitude of a thicket of aspens I found myself alone and at peace. A cool breeze washed through the thinning branches, causing orange leaves to shimmer and sound like the flow of a river. Songbirds chirped warnings as I walked on a carpet of leaves. A busy squirrel stopped short, stood on hind legs, eyed me, then scurried into the safety of underbrush. I soon found a large altar-shaped stone and knelt beside it.

—O God, in the name of the Messiah, guide me as I study, I prayed.

I knew the power of the name *Messiah* from Enoch's teachings.

I positioned myself for comfort, leaning my back against the stone and rolling out a scroll of the words of the patriarchs: Adam, Seth, Enos, and others. Their words were profound, deep, gathered together as witness to their authors' individual knowledge of God. *How had they come to that intelligence?* I wondered. *How did they become who they are?* As I questioned, a sweet stillness settled upon me, and an impression came to my mind, one that I attempted to write:

Obedience is the first law of heaven. Sometimes obedience to God's laws is seen as limiting. Men often see only the rules without perceiving the blessings in living them. It is pride that leads men to accuse God of yoking them with myriad laws, thinking that he does so to reduce or eliminate man's freedom. Untrue. To a child, a father might impose the rule of avoiding a treacherous cliff. The child might complain that the father's law is unduly rigid. But should the child venture too close to the cliff's edge and fall, he will not avoid the consequence of disobeying his father's rule. Ignoring or breaking the laws of God leads to peril. Adhering to them leads to safety and liberation. Because God's laws are governed by truth and are eternal, the blessings and penalties of those laws are eternal. God lives within law, and he has infinite power and perfect happiness. He reveals laws and conditions to man that he might be emancipated, not limited. Obedience always involves sacrifice—the forfeiture of something highly valued for something considered of greater value. When men choose to obey a law of God, they are effectively sacrificing their way in favor of making a choice of greater value—God's way. Then the blessings for obedience flow as they always do with every right choice; hence comes the saying: sacrifice brings forth the blessings of heaven. As you learn to sacrifice alternative choices to be obedient to God's laws, you will align yourself with his will. It is his will that you become as happy as you can be. You will quickly discover that you have forfeited nothing. That is the law and the promise of obedience.

I stopped and wondered if I these were just my thoughts? Perhaps I was making this up. Then the thoughts came into my mind, *When the Spirit speaks it is soft and often evokes strong emotion, a warm feeling in the bosom, a sense of elation, an immediate clarity of thought. You must be careful to not deny the true source of inspiration when it comes. When men claim it as their own, the Holy Spirit withdraws, and access to spiritual things becomes very difficult. Remember, love and righteousness invite spiritual communication. Fear, doubt, sin drive it away. Be aware of sudden strokes of ideas. Look to your heart. Do you notice the swelling motions in your soul that the Spirit brings?*

My understanding of prayer suddenly felt inadequate. I began to search my mind for clarity. The thought came to me, *You are trying too hard. The central difficulty in prayer arises from your forgetting that God is your father and you are his son. Remembering that relationship prompts your prayers to become natural. Prayer should be an act in which the will of the Father and the will of you, his child, are united. Your faith should be centered on the fact that God knows your request before you ask it, and he already intends to grant a blessing, if what you ask is a righteous request and according to his will. But you ask amiss if your prayer is focused on changing his mind. Rather, you should put your energy into discovering what he wants for you. Then you can ask in faith, and you will receive.*

Departing the aspen grove that day, I realized that I had experienced something extraordinary. I felt lifted, inspired. Spiritual communication could be a part of me now. I had discovered that learning to ask correctly can unlock doors of truth.

ᛒ

Completing the temple of God had occupied the community's thought for the past months. Its construction had been the focal point of daily life since we had settled in the mountain valley, and building it had required the labor of every able man, woman, and child. We had been promised that it would be God's house, the place where his worthy children could enter and commune with him, the place where we would be blessed with knowledge and power.

To construct the temple we had quarried a cache of rose-colored stone in the nearby mountains. The river that flowed from the lake provided a route to float the hewn stones to the construction site.

In addition, we lived in an area surrounded by splendid forests of cedar and fir. Hardwoods could be found at a distance.

Enoch had taken me into the high mountains to seek God's direction for the pattern of the temple's construction. As the Seer plead for inspiration, he said he beheld a vision of the structure come into full view. He asked, *Do you see it?* I answered that I did not. Enoch said he saw it appearing at a distance, and when he had taken a long look at the temple's exterior, the building seemed to come right over him so that he could see inside and view the intricate details. I sketched as best I could what he was describing, and he later confirmed the accuracy of my rendition.

Now, nearly completed, the edifice I saw before me was becoming what Enoch said he had seen in vision. The temple was broad based, as wide as it was long, terraced on its face, reaching for heaven as it narrowed toward its tapered top. It was set on a hill, a high point in the City, to represent the first solid earth that emerged from the waters of chaos on the morn of creation, the navel or center of the earth. In the early morning it glowed the color of rose. It was truly the Mountain of the Lord, a great altar lifted up off the earth, like a knot binding earth to heaven.

As completion drew near, the pace of construction seemed to quicken. A feeling of excited anticipation permeated the City. When the temple was completed, Enoch would set a day of dedication and celebration. We would come dressed in white, fasting, contrite of heart, praying that both we and our offering would be accepted. On the day of dedication, we would rise early. I could imagine the soft light of autumn breaking over the eastern mountains. We would come to the temple singing. Enoch would offer a prayer. We would shout Hosanna! And the heavens would envelop us in the arms of acceptance. No sacrifice was too great for building the temple. We would spare neither the best materials nor the finest craftsmen. The dedication would be glorious.

During the months of summer and into fall, Anna, Enoch's wife, by her own initiative, had beautified the temple's outer courts as she had the City. Flowers, foliage, shrubbery, walkways—Anna worked nature as musicians work their instruments or as artists work their paints. As much as she had an eye for beauty, she had a way with animals. She could coax a squirrel to feed from her hand, or talk a fox from its burrow, or urge a robin to perch on her shoulder. Few understood her ability, although some attempted to duplicate it. Somehow Anna had been born to cool the enmity between animals and men and turn back time to the gentle days of Eden. Almost single-handedly, Anna had changed our attitudes toward animals—we saw them as neither enemies nor chattel, but as friends deserving of our kindness and care. By Anna's urging, others had helped beautify both the City and the temple grounds. The result was art. Now, flower gardens donned the temple area, trees shaded incoming thoroughfares, shrubbery bordered the outer courtyard, vines climbed trellised entrances, decorative stones marked walkways. Anna had designed areas that were set apart for quiet meditation and paths that encouraged pensive strolls. Through Anna's example, both the City of Enoch and its temple were beautiful.

As much as we anticipated the incredible outpouring of heaven's blessings, we also felt the powerful draw of the world in which we resided. During the previous six months, Saad had grown in numbers and influence. Our once independent city had become dependent on trading with Saad for our livelihood. With little wonder, those who frequented Saad returned to the City of Enoch with diverse ideas, and strange attitudes began to permeate our society. The City of Enoch began to feel the effects. Consecrated offerings that were intended to stock the Shepherd's Storehouse were now dwindling, and the poorer among us had begun to suffer. Lavish clothing was appearing, art and entertainment were moving from sacred to common; there were more divorces, and children seemed less likely to honor their parents. We, who were leaders, marveled that those who had experienced such great blessings could turn so quickly from them.

Over the months that I had convalesced, some things in my own family had changed and others had not. Miriam, for example, was still romanced by both Micah and Baruch, but she showed little interest in either. Micah had been the more aggressive in his pursuit, which had turned his courting into an item of discussion. Baruch's pursuit, on the other hand, was quieter.

Other love interests intrigued me. Moriah had happened upon Enos and Naomi and heard her scolding him, saying, *You think because I'm Dananite and quiet by nature that I'm subservient and will put up with being second priority to your obsessions. When you've re-thought them, come and visit me.* I told Moriah that she shouldn't snoop. She said she wasn't. I asked her what she thought Naomi had meant. She said she didn't know, but hadn't I noticed that Enos was growing less interested in Esther and more interested in Naomi? And was it just her imagination, or did Esther seem awfully discouraged lately? I decided to ask fewer questions.

Benjamin and Sarah, on the other hand, had cultivated a beautiful closeness. Because of Sarah's difficult pregnancy, she had needed to lie quietly to prevent the child's early birth. Benjamin had been the one to step forward and help. Although he had received offers of assistance, he had mostly refused, saying that he savored the opportunity to reestablish his relationships with his wife and children. He delegated responsibilities to take care of things at home. Finally, a little girl was born—a bit early by the midwives' calculations. But she was healthy and fat, with dark eyes and hair, plus strong lungs. *Deborah* was certain to be spoiled by her equally loud brothers and two parents who loved each other. Benjamin had told me that the entire experience had taught him patience and had given him a greater appreciation for his wife's hard job—one more difficult than he had supposed.

Joshua had returned to Danan with Enos to bring the people out. They contrived a covert plan that called for arming the Dananites and being ready to flea at a moment's notice. When the time finally arrived, Joshua fled south with the main body of the Dananites while Enos implemented a diversion from the north that suggested an enemy attack. It left the army of Nod stymied and confused, unable to react, and soon the Dananites were safe within the mountains.

The Dananites had lived in terrible conditions: filth, hopelessness, privation. Why the army of Nod had treated them so and kept them in bondage, Joshua could not ascertain. They had no possessions worthy of envy; they were ignorant, gross in common social graces. Malnourished, the Dananites could only manage a meager labor. Joshua surmised that the purpose for Nod's oppression was that the scant effort put forth by a poor Dananite was more than his lazy taskmaster's. So, Joshua brought them out and gave them the hope of a new start with the fellowship and protection of the People of God.

Of the maladies that had beset the Dananites, perhaps the worst was leprosy. Several hundred Dananites suffered from it. When Joshua settled the new group with the rest of their people in the broad valley, he hoped for the City's charity to care for them—at a distance. I had my doubts. But a remarkable thing happened: upon learning of their brethren's plight, the few Dananites who yet lived in the City left to help those in the broad valley. We, in the City, gathered wholesome food, warm clothing, herbs for medicines, tenting material and sent it regularly to the Dananite camp.

Enoch had made the trip often. On one such journey of mercy, I accompanied him.

THE WRITINGS OF RABUNEL

My subsequent attempts at prayer had resulted in varying degrees of failure, I thought, until one morning when I had truly set aside the cares of the world and removed myself to commune with God. I petitioned the God of Heaven in the name of the Messiah. Then I listened, aching for that quiet communication that Enoch had said was the voice of the Holy Spirit. I hoped I would receive a message that would put me on a course of progression. I was not disappointed.

Rabunel, you must learn how to ask and receive.

The key to asking is invoking the name of the Messiah.

The key to receiving is asking.

If you accept the fact that God is perfect, then you must accept the fact that perfect generosity is one of his attributes. He is generous to those who come unto him. Asking is a pure act of faith—you recognize your dependence on God, the giver of all that is good. Asking is a heavenly principle that you will exercise throughout eternity. To expect that you can tap the treasures of heaven without permission is presumptuous. You must ask permission of the higher kingdom to draw upon its infinite resources, and then you may learn and progress as much as you desire. Learning to ask begins now while you are in the flesh. You must learn the language of asking, of petitioning God for everything—for you are nothing without him. The moment you begin to think that you prosper because of your genius or that you conquer because of your strength, you are doomed. Review the words of the prophets. Is not asking how they received every blessing? Is asking not how they became men of God? You see, asking is the key to receiving; it always has been, and always shall be so.

the lepers of danan

 os

The day Enoch and I set out for the camp of the Dananites was clear and cool. An autumn rain had washed the air and left it clean. I had brought an extra wrap for chilly times. I wore it now. On the way, we spoke of simple things.

—Tell me of your family, he said.

—Moriah spends her time spoiling the grandchildren, I said.

—How many now?

—Benjamin and Sarah have three: Nathaniel, Dan, Deborah is the baby.

—Quite a brood!

—Yes, I'm glad they are Benjamin's and Sarah's!

—You're not too old to have more.

—Too old in some ways!

I tipped my head to reveal graying hair and a thinning crown. He nodded and smiled. Enoch was still a young man, not yet thirty. At twenty-five he had come to Shum at the command of God, leaving his new bride in his homeland Cainan. A significant sacrifice, I had thought, for Cainan was a land of righteousness, and Enoch had left it on an errand for God to teach a wicked world the way of peace. Even as a lad in Cainan he had learned to despise the evils ways of the outside world and had given himself to serving God in the temple.

In that holy place, removing himself from the profane world, he consecrated his life to the work of God, praying before him, receiving
instruction, understanding, and wisdom. At Shum, prepared for his
ministry, Enoch taught us of the Messiah and the principles of true
living. We who followed Enoch did so by sacrificing all that we had.
We suffered persecution and escaped with our lives only by the intervention of God.

—What of your son Enos? he asked, moving to a different topic.

—The most eligible male in the City, I said.

—He's found no one?

—We had hoped Esther, but . . .

—Oh yes, the slave girl for whom Enos paid the ransom.

—Yes. She loves him still, but Enos seems in such a hurry to
accomplish things. Big things. He's always been ambitious, and I
worry about his choice of priorities.

—He had better worry about Esther, said Enoch. She is beautiful
and won't remain single for long.

—You sound like Moriah, I said.

Enoch shot me a questioning glance, and I waved off my comment.

—Eve is happy in her marriage to Joshua, I said.

—Baruch's son has a great future, said Enoch. He has much to do
in God's service.

—Joshua seems to have no qualms about shaking up the old
guard, I said, hoping to evoke Enoch's opinion about those who had
opposed Joshua's efforts with the Dananites. But Enoch only nodded
and appeared unruffled by my remark. I reminded myself that he was
not given to criticism. *It and other vices were of this world,* he liked to
say. *One should weigh his thoughts and actions against this question: Does
what I think or do have the power to hold me captive?*

While the Dananite situation was still a hot subject, the contro-
versy had not stifled the City's rallying to the Dananites' aid. Supplies
flowed steadily.

—Leprosy is a heartbreaking disease, I told him as we traveled. The rulers of Shum shunned lepers and drove them out. I really only observed the infirm at a distance. The first time I saw leprosy up close was among the Dananites.

—I have herbs to help them, Enoch said as we mounted a ridge overlooking the Dananite camp.

The area in which they had pitched their tents and constructed crude homes was in the broad valley that opened from the narrow pass leading to the valley of the City of Enoch. This broad valley was tapered on the north and south like a boat's bow and stern. The river that ran through the valley of the City of Enoch and out through the pass turned southward, when it spilled into the broad valley, and served as a natural division between the Dananite camp and the city of Saad, which lay at the base of the western mountains. The valley's shape lent itself to trapping smoke from cooking fires. A gray haze hung over the Dananites like a shroud. From where we stood, the people's movements appeared slow and tired. The scene brought to mind what we had felt when we had been driven from our homes and settled anew, only to be forced out again. Like the Dananites, our women bore children along the way, carried our sick in litters, buried our dead in rude graves. I observed that the Dananites had scrounged what materials they could to construct coarse lodgings. I doubted that the feeble structures would withstand the coming winter. There was no pattern to how the Dananites had placed their dwellings. It seemed that shanties had been thrown up wherever one had had a notion with no regard for organization. The scene was depravation only one step above what the Dananites had fled.

They had come from a sweltering, insect-infected land prone to outbreaks of disease. Leprosy was one of the worst, and the Dananites had brought it with them. I'd heard speculation that the leprosy had been introduced to the Dananites by herdsmen from the south countries who drove livestock through Danan and were known to carry the malady. Whatever its origin, leprosy had entered the community and had indiscriminately afflicted male, female, old, and young.

—I'm afraid of leprosy, I told Enoch as we led our supply-laden animals into camp. I had seen the effects of the disease, how it slowly disfigured and ate up its victims, how it left them alive in a dead body. I feared going near the infirm, breathing their air, looking upon their faces.

—Focus on the shame they feel to be seen how they are, said Enoch. Then you will feel only pity.

When we entered the Dananite camp, we followed a crooked, muddy path that led to a secluded area on the fringes of the settle-ment. The people seemed to brighten when they saw the Seer. That he had ministered among them before was evident. He took their hands, embraced them, stopped to talk, knew their names. Joshua had preceded us, bringing skins of deer, bear, and cattle. The Dananites had tailored the skins for clothing or hung them over wooden frameworks to warm their dwellings. Such places were scarce, and necessity demanded that they be shared by multiple families. Joshua had returned to the City of Enoch to petition more hides.

—I had no idea, I said, commenting on the condition of the people.

—Few do, said Enoch. Our people have been generous with their means, but few have left the comfort of the City to venture here.

When we arrived at the corner of the camp, we found Miriam, who had set up a modest infirmary. She had scrounged wood for its frame, and Joshua had helped stretch skins over its walls. The result was a poorly lit, rickety shack, barely adequate to discourage rain from seeping in. Of Miriam, Enoch said, *She has a keen concept of Zion.* I soon discovered why.

I had known Miriam since she was a child. She had been my daughter since Shum. But, when I saw her rushing from one sick per-son to another, applying compresses and ointments, offering soothing words, it was as though I was seeing her for the first time. Miriam was small with a creamy complexion, blue oval eyes, and soft raven hair braided to her waist. She frowned when she was busy, which was most of the time, and I guessed her expression would incline many to stay away from her. As a sign of fatigue she pinched the bridge of her nose between thumb and forefinger. Observing her hurried pace, I imagined that she had never learned to walk, that she had just skipped that phase and moved right on to running. She hustled about at a frantic clip, communicating in one-word commands and offering abbreviated sentences when cornered for conversation.

She had a hug for me when she first saw me. Then, stepping back, she eyed the supplies, slapped her cheeks with both hands, and smothered Enoch with an embrace. The assault knocked him backwards, but when he had recovered, he wrapped his arms about her waist and gave her a spin. They both began to laugh.

—You look well, said Enoch.

—You know better than to lie, she said.

She stepped back, smoothed her hair and tunic, mimicking a woman of culture and grooming. Then she fixed her eyes on me and said, Don't tell Aunt Moriah how you found me.

I promised. Miriam seemed much more sensitive about her appearance than she needed to be—in my opinion. Though it was true that her hands were rough from hard work, and her nails had dirt under them. Her eyes had dark shadows beneath them.

—Are you getting enough sleep? I asked.

—It's a luxury, she said.

—Are you eating?

—When I get a break.

—You need help, I said.

—I have help.

She pointed at a distance where I spied a familiar imposing figure.

—Micah is here?

—For the last fourteen days.

—I thought he had gone to the temple quarry.

—No. He's been here. And what a help he's been.

I glanced at Enoch, who raised an eyebrow.

—Is something wrong? asked Miriam.

—Come with me and let me show you what we brought you, said
Enoch, not answering her question.

Immediately, the frown returned to Miriam's face, and her eyes
grew attentive. I sensed that lighthearted moments for her were few.
A tug at the girdle of my robe drew my attention to a small girl standing near my side. I supposed her to be about eight. The sores about
her lips and cheeks were evidence of the malady that had deformed
her. She didn't speak, but pulled at me. I took her gesture to mean
that I should follow. Her hand was swollen, a thick lump. Only a finger and the thumb seemed to work. I felt a twinge of panic as she
reached for my hand, and I forced myself to not recoil. The girl's face
was swollen and discolored, spotted, white, pasty. Miriam called back
to me, *Her name is Sasha. Take her hand. You'll be alright. She wants to
show you around.* I attempted to bury my fears, see past the festering
lesions, ignore the acrid smell of disease. I took Sasha's hand and let
her lead me into the infirmary.

Sasha's leprosy was mild compared to the others who lay inside.
The skin of a doe served as a door. I parted it and peered inside. Dim
light filtered in through cracks in the infirmary's wooden walls. Gray
motes of dust hovered in the rays. The animal hides that served as a
ceiling sagged and gave off a gamey odor. The floor was hard earth on
the well-traveled parts, with matted grass in the corners and under litters. Low moaning. Sobbing. Sasha pulled my hand, and I ducked to
enter. Adults gasped and hid their faces. Sick children just stared.
Some of the patients were naked; others were covered loosely with
light material. The air was hot, trapped, without movement, thick
with the scent of illness. Night would come cold and afflict the
invalids. I hesitated, weighing whether or not to retreat. I was not
comfortable around sick people. In our marriage Moriah was the one
who tolerated the children's retching and fevers. I usually gave my
compassion but not my help. Now, my heart went out to the miser-
able who lay in Miriam's infirmary of lepers.

The doorway flap fell slack behind me, shutting out the sunlight.
When my eyes adjusted to the dim light I found that I stood in a

square room lined on its sides by twenty litters holding patients. Those who fared the best ministered to those too sick to help them- selves. As Sasha and I walked among them, some looked up, nodded, then went back to their work. I glanced down at Sasha, her eyes wide and moist. She motioned me forward and stepped out, tugging at my hand. In a corner of the infirmary she stopped, dropped my hand, and went to sit at the side of an old man. He lay on hard boards with a few blankets as cushions. He writhed back and forth, moaning, his eyes inflamed, sore to look at, one white and dead.

—Go back! he cried as we approached.

He covered his face with a forearm and waved me away. Sasha stroked his face. Soon he relaxed and fell asleep.

—Who is he? I asked Sasha.

—He's her grandfather, came a woman's voice, answering for the girl.

I swung around to see who had spoken. A young woman with a partly veiled face, hairless, red, inflamed eyes, motioned toward Sasha and said, She can talk, but she doesn't. She cries, though.

I turned and stared at Sasha's grandfather.

—He won't suffer much longer, said the woman.

—He's dying?

She didn't have to answer. Sasha lay the sleeping old man's arms at his side and stood. As I surveyed the diseased body, I wondered how he had lived as long as he had. His hands and feet were scarred, from burns, I surmised, since leprosy can make its victims susceptible to injury without feeling in the extremities. One leg appeared to be paralyzed, as he did not move it. The old man's body was covered with patchy spots, and his skin was swollen, lumpy in places, thick like a woodsman's calluses, raw at the earlobes. His face was deeply lined with sores about the mouth, red eyelids, no eyebrows. His hands were clawlike, disfigured from the muscles wasting away.

—How long does he have? I asked the woman.

If Sasha heard she didn't let on.

—A week. Maybe two.

—Is there nothing to be done?

—If he dies, it's God's will.

I marveled at her statement but did not comment. It sounded as though she had reconciled herself, yielding to a higher, unrevealed power—one that acted with cold uncertainty. I felt a hollowness form inside me. I could not bring myself to believe in a God who purposelessly *causes* suffering. My God was a god of mercy, the mercy I had felt in my paradisiacal experience, palpable mercy as real to the senses as a breath of wind brushing against the skin. I believed in a God who *allows* difficulties in order to strengthen his children's characters and to help them focus on him as their only means of support. I believed in a God who tries his children for an ultimate good beyond my ability to measure. I believed in a God who eventually dries all tears and who visits his children in their troubles. I believed in a God who helps lift his children's burdens as an example of charity to convince them in whom they can trust. As I scanned the pitiful infirmary congested with lepers, I felt compassion. That they were suffering was a verity, but I could not clearly ascribe their afflictions to God.

As Sasha and I left the infirmary, she stopped at the doorway and looked back at her grandfather. I looked out into the court and saw Enoch and Miriam unloading supplies. Micah had joined them. I went to help.

—Get that sack, said Miriam.

I obeyed.

—I'm surprised to see you here, I said, turning to Micah. Why the change of heart?

—I've never been against the Dananites, he said.

He lifted a sack of grain and walked with me.

—You seemed to side against Enoch, I said.

—You misunderstood. I know Enoch wants the best for the Dananites. So do I. But we disagree on the method. I still stand by my opinion. I believe what is happening now is the best: the Dananites should remain outside the City where we can help them along. To move them to the City would be a disaster.

Micah's influence on the Dananites was apparent. In addition to helping in the infirmary, he had begun to fortify the Dananite camp. A small army of Nod had followed them to discover the route of their escape. Their guards had milled about the fringes of the land until they settled in Saad. The Dananites feared them. Micah had organized a militia to fortify the camp with bulwarks of timber and mounded earth, then sent a portentous message to the commander of the army of Nod, informing him that the Dananites harbored lepers. For the moment, the strategy had worked. The image of leprosy could conjure fear in the most hardened of adversaries. Evidently the army of Nod was no different. Leprosy was a line they were unwilling to cross.

—What about leaving your work at the temple? I asked Micah.

—There wasn't use in staying.

—Why?

—You know what happened. When Joshua brought the Dananites to this valley, Enoch sent many of my workers to come here and help. To continue working on the temple would have been futile.

—Those men came here on a temporary basis, I said. Most are back in the City now. The work on the temple needs to go forward. You are the master builder. How can the work go on without you?

We deposited our sacks and began to walk back toward Enoch and Miriam.

—I have my reasons for being here, he said.

—And I am still Miriam's guardian, I said, raising my voice to one of authority.

Micah stopped short and stared at me. His face hardened momentarily at my comment. I knew he felt urgency in winning Miriam's hand. His move to the Dananite camp was disturbing but predictable. Both of us knew that with Baruch in the distant City, Micah would encounter no proximate competition for Miriam's affections. The look in his face softened. His shoulders relaxed. With a sweep of his hand he said, Look about you. The Dananites are being cared for. They have a defense. There is the beginning of order. You judge me too harshly, old friend.

He didn't wait for my answer. I wasn't sure I had one, only an uneasy feeling deep in my stomach. I felt torn between the obvious good work Micah was doing here and his leaving his assigned duty at the temple. I chastised myself for questioning his motive, but it seemed clear. I forced myself to remember the wonderful moments of friendship we had shared over the years. Besides Enoch, hadn't Micah been my longtime confidant? Hadn't we stood together in the councils? Hadn't we labored side by side caring for the poor, constructing homes, implementing the system of Shepherds, ministering among the people? Hadn't he been my companion on numerous occasions as we traveled to distant lands to declare the word of God? Most recently, wasn't it Micah who had pulled me from the pit and saved my life? But I shuddered when I thought about his opposing Enoch in the Council, and I wondered what was happening to this man I had grown to love.

As Micah and I approached Enoch and Miriam, I said to Miriam, You have some pretty sick people in your infirmary.

She nodded, then pointed to another sack she wanted me to carry.

I gestured toward Sasha and asked Enoch, Can you heal her?

Miriam stopped short and looked at Enoch. He continued to work, but the expression in his face said he was contemplating an answer.

—You ask as though the power is mine, he said.

—Can God heal her through you? I asked, rephrasing.

Once the words escaped my mouth I realized I had answered my own question.

Micah stepped forward, as did Miriam. It was a question that had troubled people since Adam. Why were some people healed instantly by the power, others over time, others not at all? God could not change. He was not a God of favorites—healing one and ignoring another. His power remained the same today as it had been in former days. Righteous men, such as Enoch, had the authority to act in God's name. Was healing, then, a strict function of the recipient's faith? What if the recipient were unconscious or hadn't the mental faculties to put forth the effort? What if those close to the infirm, who prayed for him, hadn't the depth of belief to aid the process?

Enoch said to me, If I answer *yes*, what would you have me do?

—I know what I would do, said Miriam, interrupting, motioning toward the infirmary.

I knew what her gesture meant and felt myself agreeing with her. I, too, would heal them all.

—When I had my experience in Paradise, I felt healed, I said, softly. What a relief to be free of suffering! I thought I saw people come into that sphere, having just left their sick bodies, jumping, running, shouting. In my mind, I could see the pain they had left behind: the paralysis, the maladies, the withered limbs, the broken bodies. I wondered then, *Is death the only road to healing? The only relief?*

—As a boy I spoke with a stammer, Enoch said. I lived with the mocking and disdain of people. My handicap caused me to withdraw. Then, my father, Jared, took me aside and, without mentioning the disability, began to teach me the words of God as an exercise. He had me recite those words. The repetition smoothed my speech, and my understanding of the ways of God increased. I discovered that my father knew God and loved him. I discovered that the words of God had meaning to him. I began to ponder what I was reciting. Slowly my weakness began to give way. The more I spoke the words of God, the more my voice became fluid. Thoughts came to my mind. I was able to give them expression. More important, my relationship with God was growing. The words I had learned spoke of his perfections and attributes. Soon I ceased to fear men, and I centered my confidence in God. I knew I could ask of him and receive. If you, Rabunel, had come to me as a boy and offered to heal me, I would have begged you to take my problem away. But now, as a man looking back, I realize that I needed my affliction. It helped me define the path that led me to God. Every person needs to find God, and I've observed that God is most often found in hardship rather than in comfort. If you had come to me in my youth and healed me then, you would have taken away my blessings and opportunities. In your charity, would you have healed me of my blessings?

—You found a purpose in adversity, I said, but so many suffer ignorantly.

—Adversity is useless unless one finds meaning. But that understanding comes by asking God and allowing him to heal you how he will. Healing comes in many ways. We restrict him too much.

—I don't care about all that, said Miriam. If I could, I would make them all well.

Her voice was sharp, her eyes moist. Her frown had deepened. She had been lining a shelf with herbs and balms. She riveted her attention on the shelf and avoided eye contact. Micah took a step toward her, but she moved away. Enoch and I exchanged glances; then he went to her and placed a hand on her shoulder. She shrugged it away and hid her face.

—I don't care what anyone says, she said, I would heal them all, every one.

—But you are, said Enoch, turning her to him, holding her as her body shook.

She buried her head in his chest and sobbed. I felt my eyes fill with tears and looked for a task to perform away from the moment. Then Enoch said, You are as good a friend to these people as they have ever had.

The subject was dropped. Enoch led Miriam toward the infirmary and began to explain a combination of herbs that would make a soothing balm. He could have healed Sasha. I knew it. I had seen him perform such miracles in the past. Why this was not such a time, I could only surmise, was because he recognized that the power was God's, and he was merely a steward. He hadn't yet received permission. Less spiritually mature, I felt helpless. The lepers' suffering was more than my sensibilities could endure. Left up to me, I would have healed them, just as Miriam had wished.

—Do you understand human suffering? asked Micah.

—No, I answered honestly.

—Do you think it was sin that brought leprosy upon them?

—No. These people have lived the best lives they could with the information they had.

—Perhaps disease is merely part of life, one of the perils of living in a dangerous world.

I answered perhaps, but I didn't know. Both Micah and I sat on a log and watched Enoch and Miriam treat a few lepers who lay in the warm sun outside the infirmary. They applied balm, cooled parched lips with water, massaged aching limbs, offered words of comfort. I thought, *I don't know why people must suffer, except that God, as our father, must cry as much as we parents do for our hurting children. As one who has all power, he must have amazing vision and self-control not to take away the pain immediately.* Observation had taught me that suffering comes by the hands of wicked men, by our own wrong choices, or by living in a hazardous world.

When Enoch and Miriam stepped inside the infirmary, Micah and I stood and followed. At the bed of Sasha's grandfather, Enoch sat and stroked the old man's head.

—Do you know of the Messiah? Enoch asked him.

The old man shook his head.

—He will come in time's meridian to save all mankind.

—From sin? asked the old man.

—Yes. And their sicknesses and afflictions.

—Pain?

—Yes. He will suffer so that he can comprehend the entire human experience.

—Why?

—So that he can help those who believe on him through every difficulty.

—Is he God?

—He is his son.

—God would allow his son to suffer?

—The Messiah voluntarily gives his life. There can be no greater gift than self. Only through suffering can he feel and overcome everything. He will bear the consequences of our mistakes. He will suffer each of our indignities, our sorrows, our infirmities so that he may be filled with mercy for those who believe on his name and come to him to be healed.

—For all?

—And for each of us individually. If you were the only person who ever lived on this earth, he would give his life for you.

—Why?

—Because of his infinite love.

—How is it done?

—The Messiah is the only one who will ever live on this earth with the power to both suffer and overcome. In the overcoming he will gain *keys* of deliverance. He saves us from all the consequences of our mistakes, the punishments that must be exacted for our sins, the pains we suffer in this world, so he is our Savior. He delivers us from bondage of every kind, so he is our Deliverer. He redeems us from Adam's and Eve's initial transgression and provides the resurrection as the way of escape, so he is our Redeemer. He mediates our individual cases with God, the great judge, to appease the demands of justice, so he is our Mediator and Advocate. He administers the covenant by which we can overcome the world, so he is the Messenger of the Covenant. His words are the true source of peace, so he is called the Prince of Peace. He our counselor, the King of Glory, the Bright and Morning Star, the Anointed One; he lives in the heavens and will condescend to live among men to suffer their indignation and to die at their hands. He will conquer all enemies: the grave, our weaknesses, our sins. He is mighty to save.

—What must I do?

—Ask God in the name of the Messiah for a blessing.

The old man became quiet and stared at the ceiling. After a long moment, he whispered, The Messiah will suffer for leprosy?

—Yes, said Enoch.

—I wish he were here.

—He has all power, even now. We can draw upon that power as though his sacrifice had already been made.

—Can he heal me?

—Will you believe me if I tell you?

—I will believe all the words you will speak.

—Will you allow God to direct a healing for you through Messiah according to *his* will?

—Yes.

—Then you shall be healed, said Enoch.

The old man closed his eyes and whispered, O God, apply for me the healing power of the Messiah.

The Prophet stood and stepped to where he could lay his hands on the old man's head. Before he spoke the words of the blessing, he said, We never make heroes of those who have never faced afflictions. You, my brother, are a hero. Sasha will be healed, marry, grow old, and become the mother of many nations. She will always remember your example.

That said, Enoch motioned Micah and me to join him. We laid our hands gently on the old man's head, and Enoch pronounced the words of blessing in the name of the Messiah. As he spoke, I felt the old man relax as his spirit slipped from his body. And as he died, in that very instant, I thought I heard a shout of joy.

Later that day, as Enoch and I finished our work among the people, we returned to the infirmary and saw Miriam holding Sasha on her knee, applying salve to sores around her mouth. Micah walked toward us and smiled at the sight.

—She's a most remarkable woman, he said.

—Yes, said Enoch, she's doing an incredible work here. As much as suffering has a sanctifying effect, so does ministering.

—I'm building an addition to the infirmary, said Micah, pointing to a distant spot.

—It is also a good work, said Enoch, and much needed.

—Thank you, said Micah.

—But is it the *right* good work?

Micah gazed into the prophet's eyes, and his face flushed.

—Th-the sun is setting, Micah said, stammering. I have rounds.

When Micah departed, Enoch looked at me and said, The road to sanctification is long, and few have the courage to travel it.

THE WRITINGS OF RABUNEL

One evening, as I removed myself to a quiet place aside from the Dananite camp, I prayed, pondered, and wrote down this information.

Listen, my son Rabunel, and I will tell you of love. Have you considered the condition of the place in which you live? The natural order of everything in your world is to decompose to its elementary state. Thus, all that you see around you is destined to fail. Only that of a higher order can endure. So it is with love. Physical love, not balanced with spiritual love, will fade and die. The only love that endures is the kind called charity, for that is the pure love of the Messiah.

Charity is patient;
Charity is kind;
Charity is not envious;
Charity is not proud;
Charity is not selfish or filled with conceit;
Charity is not provoked to anger;
Charity will not accuse or criticize;
Charity finds no satisfaction in iniquity, but loves righteousness;
Charity bears its burdens without complaint;
Charity is filled with belief and hope;
Charity rejoices in good;
Charity endures all things with hope for tomorrow.

My son, you may speak your beliefs and even go through some of the motions. But without charity you are nothing. Remember: all things of this world must fail, including worldly love. But charity, the love that belongs to a higher order, will never fail. Therefore, pray unto God with all your heart that you may be filled with this *love.*

the fragrance of flowers

CB

—Pull the ropes tighter! The tent is going to sag!

Eve, since she had married Joshua, had learned to assert herself. Her belly had swollen and nausea had become her companion. She had lost patience for imperfection and had no problem stating it.

Her condition drew from her heightened emotions and observations. On the one hand, she could be seen pinching her plumping hips and growling; on the other hand, she could be caught admiring her newly full figure. Joshua seemed perplexed with the whole process. He'd said he'd lost his wife and wondered who the woman was that he lived with. *Why does she cry for no reason? And what is this obsession with artichokes in the middle of the night?* Recently, Eve had felt a small motion in her low abdomen. It caused her to straighten and cry out for joy. She had grabbed Joshua's hand and placed it flat on her belly. A week's trying was required for him to *feel* the growing child. It was the only show of affection that he was allowed, he complained, for when he would try to kiss her, Eve would turn her head and offer a cheek, saying, *Kissing makes me gag.*

—If the baby is a boy, he will be worked to death, said her brother Enos, as he helped Joshua stake the tent.

Enos had bared his chest in the hot sun, pectorals flexing as he worked. He gripped a wooden stake in a sweaty hand and drove the shaft into the earth with a stone mallet. The muscles in his back and arms were sinewy and rippled beneath the tight skin. Naomi, the beauty from Danan, stood near him and seemed fascinated.

Eve reacted to Enos's comment with a glare, but before she could answer Benjamin interrupted with, It is a fact of life!

—What is? asked Sarah, feeding baby Deborah, a modest blanket thrown over her shoulder to cover the child.

—After a man is married he is condemned to a lifetime of hard work! replied Benjamin.

—By his wife's nagging, you're implying, said Sarah.

—You said it, not me.

Benjamin winked at Enos and went to help Joshua pull the slack from the rope.

—And women have it easy, I suppose! said Sarah with a tone of sarcasm.

The other women nodded. As if cued, they put their hands on their hips.

—Men do everything halfway and call it good enough, said Sarah. We women like things done right.

—You mean you like things *perfect*! said Benjamin.

—I don't think women know what *perfect* means, said Joshua.

—I know what it means, said Benjamin.

—Here it comes, said Sarah to the women.

—*Perfect* is what your wife tells you it is, he said.

His comment was met by a round of female groans. To make matters worse Joshua added, As *long as your wife has the prerogative to change her mind.*

—Mother, are you listening to this? Eve said to Moriah. I don't remember Father complaining when you asked him to help.

—Where were you when you were growing up? replied Moriah.

—Batting her eyes at every boy who passed by! said Enos.

—I did not! said Eve.

—Yes, you did! said Joshua, pulling at a rope, gritting his teeth. You were trying to make me jealous!

—I was n—

—I've always tried to be helpful around the house! I interrupted.

—When it was convenient, said Moriah

My wife smiled mischievously and said, No work would ever get done if it weren't for women.

—Amen! said Naomi, who knelt next to Enos and pointed out why the stake he'd planted wouldn't hold. Gensek's daughter had relocated to the camp along with our family to help her fellow Dananites. Or so she said. Her shadowing Enos wherever he went caused Moriah and me to speculate as to her true purpose in being here. We had given up on any relationship developing between Enos and Esther. He hardly mentioned her. Naomi, on the other hand, seemed to intrigue him. For now, he seemed less inclined to pursue leadership and office, apparently content to spend his time with the maiden from Danan.

—Now *you're* sounding like a wife! said Enos to Naomi.

Suddenly the bantering stopped, and all eyes shot to Naomi, who had gone red faced at Enos's comment. After a long, uncomfortable moment, my little grandson Nathaniel asked his mother, *Is Naomi going to marry Enos?*

Sarah shushed her son; Benjamin coughed loudly; the rest of us leaned forward to hear her answer. It didn't come, but Miriam's voice did as she came hustling toward us.

—It's not straight! she yelled at Joshua.

—What do you mean *not straight?* he answered, dropping the rope and standing.

With one eye closed, Miriam stretched out her arm and drew a bead utilizing the nib of her thumb. She repeated the act in the opposite direction, then clipped off how she expected the row of Dananite tents to run.

—More orders! sighed Benjamin.

Naomi's expression turned to relief as the subject was changed.

—Is there something you and I should talk about? I whispered to Enos.

—Later!

When my family had arrived in the Dananite camp, we had set about re-staking the tents and defining pathways in an attempt to give the area a look of symmetry.

—Why do you bother re-staking the tents if you don't make the lines straight? said Miriam, a challenging tone in her voice.

The women smiled and nodded.

—How straight can straight be? asked Enos. His hands had now gone to his hips.

—Straight!

Benjamin murmured, It's that *perfection* thing again!

Our goal in reorganizing the camp was to follow the model we had used for survival after escaping Shum. That same pattern had sustained us during the subsequent years of wandering in the wilderness. With the help of my sons and Joshua, I had organized the Dananite camp into lots, assigning a Shepherd—a title given because it typified one who cares and serves—over each. The Shepherd's *Lot* contained twenty to fifty families. Shepherds served purely out of love, without monetary compensation. They reported to me and a Fathers Council that enacted laws for the camp after a confirming vote from the people. The overriding social goal was order. Shepherds were to see that individual needs were met, to ensure that no one was forgotten or lost. In the Fathers Council we endeavored to promote education, individual industry, and self-sufficiency, knowing that these would help pull the people out of their poverty. Shepherds assessed the special needs of their people. For the most destitute and needy, Shepherds could draw upon the resources of a common storehouse of supplies. Notwithstanding the fact that the Dananites were poor, we found that by inventorying and combining resources, most needs could be met.

Following Enoch's pattern, and having been called by him to administer a covenant among the people, I bade them to live in the society for the mutual aid of each other. When I called them together I said, People of Danan, by the grace of God you have escaped your enemies and have come to this valley. You know the goodness of God and that you owe your very lives to him, and all he asks in return is that you obey his commandments and serve one another. Will you now make a covenant with him that you will be <u>one</u> people, that you will be called the children of God, that you will bear one another's burdens, and mourn with those who mourn, and comfort those who need comfort? Will you always strive to serve God and keep his commandments?

As if with one voice the people cried that they would make and keep this covenant.

An outgrowth of the covenant was to build a support system about each person. I called it the Law of the Shepherd and instituted it by saying to the people, Every family of Danan deserves to be watched over. Therefore, let the Shepherds assign Teachers to visit every family regularly. Let the Teachers instruct their assigned families how to pray and to care for one another. Let them strengthen the weak, assure that iniquity is checked, see that the people do their duty and that they are filled with charity. Will you support the Shepherds and do this service?

Again, the people promised that they would. By Enoch's instructions, I knew that the success of the community hinged on this critical mechanism of service. With Moriah's example of service, the women of Danan were asked to give physical aid and comfort to one another. Thus, every able person, male and female, served in the society, and every individual person received care. Within a very short time, we experienced incredible results: people ceased to go hungry; the burden of administering to the infirm was shared; housing was constructed for all. By covenant, the people donated part of their time to their community. Special assignments were given to those with singular skills: hunters brought food for the coming winter; farmers harvested the crops we had planted for them and prepared the ground for spring planting; tent makers sewed; seamstresses made clothing; tool makers crafted tools. When more skilled people were needed for particular tasks, we trained individuals.

Observing the blossoming Dananite camp, I thought, *It is amazing what a people can accomplish when they decide to serve one another without selfishness or fear.* An efficient camp began to emerge. Sicknesses, including leprosy, began to abate due to the aptitude of skilled people and effective care and treatments. Sasha's skin appeared clear, her scars fading, her energy returning. More astonishingly, the Dananites, who had once wallowed in hopelessness and poverty, were now happy, industrious, prospering—to the point of drawing the attention of the army of Nod, which continued to shadow them from the city of Saad.

I had once spoken with Enoch about the incredible change that had come over Miriam as she had found herself in service.

—She still has her weaknesses, I had said, but they are becoming lost in the bright light of her efforts.

We had shared this conversation as we traveled together from Danan back to the City. I was rehearsing to him the character traits in Miriam that I had observed and envied.

—Would that all could try as hard as Miriam, Enoch said. Hers is a life characteristic of those who are trying with all their souls to be sanctified.

His use of the word *sanctified* conjured up in my mind an ideal that seemed distant and unattainable to me. Enoch often used *sanctified* or *sanctification* in connection with Zion. *Sanctification* was as difficult a concept for me as was *Zion*, close but seemingly out of reach. Enoch's teachings concerning the terms remained basic and consistent. Maybe I had expected a profound piece of information to drop from his lips, an extraordinary announcement of a pattern, a key, a map, a formula, something divinely complex. But as the years passed, Enoch continually emphasized the basic doctrines that he ascribed as being the Messiah's: *Zion is the pure in heart. The pure in heart are sanctified by obedience to the commandments of God and yielding their hearts to him. Obedience requires sacrifice. Zion is achieved through perfecting the fundamentals.*

—There is a cycle, he told me. If you stay within it and do not look beyond it, the cycle will lead you toward sanctification, cause you to progress, open the opportunity for perfection.

—A cycle? I had asked.

—Faith, repentance, covenant making, confirmation of the Holy Spirit: Zion begins with these four, he said.

The terms were familiar enough, but I had not thought of them as sequential.

—Faith is the correct action, that which grows from a hope, belief, or knowledge that is true. Faith in the Messiah begins the cycle. The correct action of faith is *repentance*, meaning to change, or improve. Repentance leads one to make or renew covenants with God. Covenants allow one to draw down the blessings of God and make possible access to the resources of God's kingdom. As covenants are made or renewed, the Holy Spirit confirms that action, which increases one's faith in God—and the cycle begins again. Faith, repentance, covenant making, spiritual confirmation—cycling onward toward perfection.

—Sanctification comes this way? I asked.

—As does Zion, said Enoch. Miriam's selfless acts of service are manifestations of her faith.

—If only I were conversant enough with the subjects to teach them to my family, I said. I feel it is my responsibility as a father.

—Words are often forgotten, he said. Better to teach by example.

I had my wish soon enough. Later that day Enoch asked me to take my family to the camp of the Dananites to live among them and to serve and organize them.

∞

Moriah and I made evenings our time to gather the family together and talk of the day. Since we all had varying responsibilities and only worked together on occasion, evenings became our time to relax, enjoy each other, and recount the experiences that were clearly changing us. On one such occasion, our family had surrounded a night fire, and Miriam came close. She was the last to sit. I gave her a quick glance.

Her little girl, Rachel, snuggled up next to her, laid her head against Miriam's shoulder, and warmed a hand, holding it palm-out to the fire. Miriam reached for a bowl of beans and carrots and quietly ate. Then, when the conversation lulled, she set aside her bowl and said, I did something remarkable today—something I thought I would never do.

She stared into the flames. The night air was cool, and we had bundled ourselves in blankets. Summer insects had mostly disappeared. The sweet scent of freshly cut alfalfa lingered on a soft breeze. The distant sounds of mothers humming their young ones to sleep drifted over the camp. The night sky was clear, with an orange harvest moon that had risen round and full. Stretching out across the wide heavens, stars appeared in a wash of light. I located two stars that formed the edge of what appeared to be a giant ladle and drew an imaginary line northward to a lone star. As a boy, I had learned that it would be there night after night, no matter the season or how the heavens revolved.

Naomi asked Miriam, What did you do? Naomi had sat next to Enos and taken his hand.

—I set the leg of a small dog, said Miriam.

—The dog belonged to a little girl, added Rachel.

—You helped your mother with the dog? Enos asked her.

—Yes. I cried, though.

—I was helping the orphans when I heard Rachel say that she had seen a little girl crying, said Miriam. The girl's dog had been yapping at a cart and had fallen under a wheel. Rachel saw it happen. She came and fetched me. We found the little girl sitting in the street, crying, holding her lame dog. The poor little animal was yelping, and when I touched the break it tried to bite me. But after I stroked its head, the dog let me move the limb.

—The girl was afraid her dog would die, said Rachel.

—Yes, Miriam said to Rachel, but you held her hand while I set the dog's leg.

—How did you do it? asked Sarah.

—I've seen limbs set on people. I tied the dog down, then gently pulled on the leg until the bones aligned.

—The dog didn't cry out and try to get free? I asked.

—Yes. But I was able to hold it until I finished. Then I made a splint and handed the animal back to the little girl.

—She must have been relieved, Enos said.

—She was so happy, said Rachel.

—Was she smiling? I asked her.

—Yes, and she was happy in her eyes, Rachel replied.

—I know that look, said Benjamin. Today I was digging a well and heard two children squabbling. When I went to see what the trouble was, I could see that they had been given charge of washing the family's clothing. The littlest boy had dropped his bundle of clothes in the mud.

—They had already washed the clothes and were returning home? asked Sarah.

—That's right. His older brother was pretty upset. I knelt by the little boy, picked up his clothes, then walked both brothers back down to the river and helped them scrub out the mud. I guess they were grateful because they took me home to meet their mother. She was lying in bed with a newborn baby. The family lived in a patchwork tent that was a shambles inside. When I asked her if she had family to help, she said because they were so poor, her husband had taken work in Saad. She had no help because her parents were dead. I organized her boys with chores while I made the family dinner; then I made sure her Shepherd was aware of her situation.

—I wish I could get you to do that at *our* home, said Sarah, laughing.

Moriah said, When you do things at home it's called work; when you do things for someone else it's called kindness.

My wife shot me a glance when she said it.

—You're insinuating something, I said.

Moriah laughed.

—Am I supposed to take your comment personally? I asked.

Moriah laughed more and said, You should know.

—Very well, I replied defensively. Today I taught a group of women how to make mushroom sauce.

—You? chirped Eve.

—Yes, me!

—You're a disaster at cooking!

—I am not!

—You can't boil water!

When she started laughing, everybody—one by one—started enumerating the times I had burned dinner.

—I can cook as well as anyone! I said.

—You must be kidding! Moriah retorted.

More laughing.

—Have your fun at my expense if you must, I said with a ho-hum tone. But I actually *did* teach some women to make mushroom sauce. I know how. I heard two women complaining about how weary they were of preparing the same meal night after night. So I thought I would be nice and show them how to prepare mushrooms for flavor.

—That was nice, said Moriah.

I squinted my eyes at her and raised an eyebrow, sensing a slight condescending inflection in her voice.

Joshua whispered to Eve so all could hear, I'll bet he taught them how to make *toadstool sauce!*

After another round of hooting, I said I didn't need to stay where I wasn't wanted, which brought another series of belly laughs, and Eve patted me on the back and told me to stay put while she told what had happened to her that day.

Eve had grown plump in recent weeks, bulging with her baby and looking uncomfortable. Each day, Joshua urged her to slow down, but she insisted on helping her Dananite friends.

—Down by the river, she began, there are some tents where several widows live. A few are very old, but they want to help in the community. A while back they decided to make blankets for the poor. One old woman's hands were gnarled, and I could see that she was having a difficult time pushing her needle through the stiff fabric of the blanket. When I asked if I could help, she looked startled, then relieved. For the rest of the afternoon I pushed the needle as she pulled it through. We made a good team. I learned about her husband, who had died trying to defend Danan from the people of Nod. She told me about her sons and daughters and grandchildren who live in the camp, but are often too busy to come and visit her. I learned that she loves to grow flowers. I'm wearing one of her flowers in my hair. I would never have come to know her had I not noticed her need. Now she is a dear friend.

I glanced at Naomi, who seemed contemplative. The Dananites were her people, and I could sense that she was grateful for the service our family was rendering in the camp.

—What about you, Naomi? I asked.

She shook her head shyly.

—I don't think she'll tell you what she did today, said Enos.

—Won't you tell us? I asked.

Again, she shook her head and said, You all have such nice stories.

—You're being modest, Enos said to her.

—Why don't you tell us? said Eve to Enos.

Enos gave Naomi a questioning look, and she returned her consent with a tiny shrug.

—Naomi and I were helping Miriam at the infirmary, Enos began. When we ran out of clean linen for bandages, Naomi offered to run and fetch some more. I went with her. Before long we happened on an old, blind man who was struggling to find his way to the river to bathe. Naomi took him by the hand and led him to a calm, shallow place, and helped him in.

—It wasn't much, said Naomi.

—It was very kind, said Enos. The old fellow was so worried about being modest. Naomi and I held up a blanket so he could bathe without being seen. When he was finished, we helped him into his clothes and led him back to his tent.

—I thought I would be embarrassed, but the whole experience was beautiful, said Naomi. Later I picked some flowers and gave them to him.

She put a hand to her nose, drew in the aroma, and paused.

—Did you know that when you give flowers the fragrance stays on your hands all day?

I gazed at my family, happy faced, obviously fulfilled, each one having offered that day some measure of compassion. Once more I wondered, *Can there be heaven on earth?* And I answered my question, *Yes!* I remembered Enoch's having said, *The principle of giving is a pillar of heaven. We should be anxious to give what we have. It comes back to us many fold.*

Thereafter, news of our work in the valley of Danan began to spread to the City of Enoch, and more people began arriving to help. As contagious as had been the diseases that had plagued the Dananites was the spirit of service that now consumed those who had come to help. The care givers seemed to feel something they had forgotten—the joy that comes from the simple act of giving of one's self. Giving was transforming my family. Giving was elevating the Dananites. Giving was changing many of the City of Enoch.

THE WRITINGS OF RABUNEL

In mighty prayer I sought insight from God, a mystery—the way to recognize a righteous person. I wrote down my impressions.

A righteous person neither aspires to the honors of men nor seeks to amass worldly things. Rather, he cherishes the esteem of God. For strength, he binds himself to the powers of heaven, knowing that those powers can only be controlled by righteousness. He does not conceal, minimize, or excuse his sins. He does not pamper his pride, pursue vain ambitions, seek to manipulate or control others in any degree of unrighteousness. A righteous person does not compel in order to lead. He does not insist on domination. His is the quiet act of loving service. He is gentle. He encourages those who are struggling and weak with meekness and genuine love, demonstrating patience and rejoicing in minute steps of progression. A righteous person is kind. He embraces pure knowledge from God, which enlarges the soul without pride or pretense. He stands firm and defends the truth at all times. When he reproves sinful acts, he does so with absolute love, and then only when directed by the Holy Spirit, so that his reprimand does not discourage. A righteous person is charitable toward his family and strangers. Virtue ever fills his thoughts. He knows his standing before God—neither considering himself below others, which is self-pity, nor appraising himself as above others, which is pride. With this honesty and divine assurance, he has the confidence to stand in the presence of God and not shrink. The sublime doctrines of godliness distill upon him until he is saturated in truth. The Holy Spirit is his constant companion. A righteous person will advance the cause of truth. He remains in the sure path and is not moved to the right or to the left. As evidence of his righteousness, all good things flow unto him naturally without being compelled. As for his trials, the Lord will prepare for him a way of escape, including the hearts of his enemies being turned to him or their being moved out of his way. He finds no lasting charm in the things of this world. His movement is away and up. My son, seek these attributes in your life. This is the character of those who are truly Zion.

a fallen prophet

CR

—Rabunel, said Enoch, assemble the people that I may speak with them tonight.

His voice held a measure of urgency.

—Is it Saad? I ventured.

He nodded and said, Our people don't see the danger.

At dusk, all the people gathered at the center of the City on the temple grounds. The Dananites also came. We were instructed organize ourselves by families within the Shepherds' Lots. Men lit torches along the perimeter of our meeting place. Autumn was turning quickly to winter. A light breeze made the night air feel particularly chill. The smell of fallen leaves had given way to the flat smell of cold. Skies were gray now and were regularly depositing snow on the high peak, sometimes in the valley. As I blew into my hands, my breath formed a cloud that dissipated into the dark of night. Winter was coming. Nothing could stop that. The Dananites would suffer more than we. Beyond being more prepared, we in the City were less subject to the strong winds that blew down from the high mountains and out over the plain. Soon, the river would freeze, and we would obtain drinking water by chipping and melting chunks of ice. All of us—the people of the City and the Dananites—would while away the cold months huddled around home fires—in tents for the Dananites—

only braving the harsh elements to feed animals or fetch supplies we had tucked away. It was not a time of year I enjoyed. The sun would seldom show its face, and when it did, the slant of its rays would not warm. The moods of many would turn melancholy. Winter would task the Shepherds and Teachers. It would take more effort to watch over the people and care for their needs.

Enoch stood before his people and greeted us. Bundled about his tunic was a heavy coat of skins. His head was covered with a fur hat. I glanced at his wife, Anna, who had wrapped Melca in her arms. The little girl complained of the cold, and Anna rubbed the tot's arms and tucked her head in her lap. When Enoch stood, the crowd quieted. His voice was strong.

—When we came to these mountains, we found relief from the persecutions we had suffered. We knew that God had preserved us to live in this safe place. We have been able to defend ourselves from enemies who yet seek our blood. But there is a more dangerous enemy than the one we see lurking at the passes with swords—it is the enemy of pride that threatens us most.

I glanced around at perplexed expressions. Benjamin and Sarah sat near Moriah and me. They each held a son. My entire family was close. I balanced my baby granddaughter, Deborah, on my knee. She snuggled into my shoulder, and Moriah smoothed the hair at the back of her head. Micah sat with Miriam and Rachel. Baruch looked on, but sat with his son, Joshua, who was with Eve. Naomi had snuggled up to Enos, but her father, Gensek, and the rest of her family was near by. I looked out beyond our family and saw Ishmael and his son, Reuben.

—*Good people,* I thought, *all of them.*

I knew we had problems in the City of Enoch and among the Dananites, but I had overlooked most frailties in an effort to detect my mortal enemy, the Mahan. Struck with Enoch's pronouncement, I wondered if I were guilty of pride and what it was doing to me.

—Pride precedes destruction, Enoch continued. Pride is enmity towards God, man, and nature. Pride is competitive. It makes every person an adversary. It elevates itself by pushing others down. Pride is comparing. It gets no pleasure from having, only from having more than another. Pride is willful, not submissive. Pride is jealous—when it has, it looks down in disdain; when it has not, it looks up in envy. It is ever coveting and never satisfied. Pride feeds on flattery. It readily detects faults in others, but never in itself. It despises authority, feigns obedience, wallows in conceit, indulges in self-pity. Pride is self-seeking. By pride comes contention. It is easily offended. Pride leads to a lust for self-justified power, resulting in the abuse of the meek. Pride withholds forgiveness to defend its injured feelings, keeping the would-be repentant in bondage. Pride deadens feelings toward God, halts progression, divides people by rank. Pride retards unity and love. Pride is the universal sin, the great vice.

The stumbling block of Zion, I remembered my father saying.

—Look about you, said Enoch. Look at this beautiful city. But beyond the comfortable white stone homes, it is much as any other community. What were we commanded to do when we arrived here? What work did God give us with the promise that obedience to his command would separate us as a truly distinct people? What did he say would be our safety?

I heard a low murmur among the people. I sensed a communal fidgeting.

Enoch cried, Where is his home? Where shall we go to commune with him? Is it vain discourse when we congratulate ourselves on being called the people of God? How can he come when we have not obeyed him?

After a terrible pause, Enoch cried, Where is the temple to our God?

I had known silence. I had known it acutely in the belly of the pit. But I had never known the thick silence of guilt until that night. Eyes fell before Enoch's gaze. No one spoke. No one moved.

Enoch said, We have found other causes more important than fulfilling this commandment. Our stone masons venture to Saad to trade. How long will heaven withhold judgment when we fail to do what we are told? I fear that if we had built it, we would now look upon it, in the pride of our hearts, as only a beautiful ornament, an architectural wonder beyond any known in the world. But would we hunger and thirst to purify ourselves so that we might enter it and receive intelligence from our God there? Would we reverence it as the consummate symbol of our faith? Would we regard it as the preeminent place of learning and power? Would we sanctify ourselves to be worthy of having the house of God in our midst—the place where he would make his abode with a people who loved and served him?

Enoch plead with us to look into our lives and remember why we had come to this valley—to be distinct from the world, to live in peace, and to love one another. We had slackened in our efforts to finish the temple and gone after Saad. Why were we so intrigued with it? Did we need their commerce? No. Were we adopting their lifestyle? Yes.

—If you tempt the tiger it will devour you, Enoch said.

He ended his words by imploring us to regroup and look forward to the sanctifying principles that would be disseminated in the temple and to rededicate ourselves to the temple's completion. He said he must leave immediately for Hannanihah, for there was a group of people there who had requested that he teach them. He expected to be away for seven days. I, Rabunel, would stand in his stead, and Micah would assist me. Then Enoch began to weep.

—What I say to you I would say to my children, he said. It is the only desire of my soul that you should be caught up into the arms of safety of your God. But I fear that in our disobedience we have exposed ourselves to the full fury of our enemies.

He wept more, then said, I fear for the Dananites. I adjure you of the City of Enoch to check your pride and open your homes and bring them in. I plead with you Dananites to set aside old feelings and come into the borders of the City for your protection.

Eve leaned over and whispered to me, Are we in danger, Father?

—I fear it is so, I answered.

—Is the danger from pride or potential war?

I answered that I didn't know, but following the prophet had always kept us from harm.

—What shall we do? she asked.

—Tonight, you and the family will go back with the Dananites. Tomorrow, you will start preparing them for the move.

—And you?

—I will stay here to reorganize the work on the temple and map out plans for the influx of people.

—Some of the Dananites still harbor feelings about they way they've been looked down on by the people in the City. I fear many won't come.

—Benjamin will be in charge, I said. It will be his responsibility to teach the Shepherds how to persuade their people.

—Do you think we can do all this?

—We must.

&

The next morning, after I had seen Enoch on his journey, I met Micah at the temple. When I greeted him I was surprised to hear him grumble something about being publicly humiliated.

—We were all chastised for taking the temple's construction too lightly, I said.

—But it was obvious that Enoch aimed his comments at me, he said. Everyone could sense it.

—We of the Council often debate until we reach a consensus, I said.

Micah, then, began to defend himself by saying, I went to the Dananite camp, didn't I? Then I helped build them an infirmary and a defense system. But was I thanked?

—I truly think you are being overly sensitive, I said. If you are questioning Enoch's motives, you should express your feelings to him.

—Of course that isn't possible, since he left for Hannanihah this morning. No, I'll just work here at the temple and try to do what I'm told.

He turned away with a set of the temple's construction plans and seemed to study them. His face was drawn, his eyes hooded and dark. The corners of his mouth turned down, and the furrows of his forehead seemed forced and deep. He would not look at me.

—I've never seen you like this, I said. You are one of my dearest friends. What has happened.

Micah didn't immediately answer but continued to stare at the plans.

—Miriam has consented to be my wife, he said without looking up.

I took a tiny step back, then stopped. I considered my answer for a long moment. Then, attempting to choose my words carefully, I said, I'm happy for you both.

He didn't react.

I cautiously added, Of course, as her guardian I would have appreciated being *asked* for her hand in marriage.

—We plan to marry immediately, he said, as if he had hadn't heard me.

—I see, I said.

Micah turned to me then, his face red, his jaw firm.

—I don't think you do see, he said. You are content to follow Enoch like a mindless sheep. You know as well as I that despite our best efforts—mine included—the supplies of the City have sunk to critical levels because of the Dananites. I predicted as much, but when Enoch spoke, all followed him without regard to the consequences. Then, there's the issue of the temple. Enoch accuses us of being proud. Of course, he was directing his public chastisement at me.

—It's not true, I said.

Again, Micah continued his railing as if he hadn't heard me.

—None of what has happened has to do with pride. The reason we haven't finished the temple is because Enoch sent away my best workers on missions to bring in even more people. If he has his way, this valley will be filled with refugees, and we will all starve. He has never considered my counsel, and he has made it impossible for me to do the work. What good works I do go unnoticed, and I am publicly castigated.

I was too astonished to be angry. In the years I had known Micah, I had never seen the expression that enveloped his face. His stance was foreign to me. It was as though his entire countenance had fallen. We stood face to face and stared at one another.

—This is not worthy of you, I said. You are better than this. We have been friends—brothers. Why did you not come to me about Miriam?

—I did not ask you for Miriam's hand because you would have consulted Enoch. With the way he obviously feels about me, he would have denied the marriage. So, we *will* be married, and perhaps we will move away from the City for a time. I can no longer follow a prophet who has fallen.

I was more than stunned. I could not believe what I was hearing. I could not believe that a man—one of my dearest friends—was telling me, not asking me for my permission, that he was going to marry my niece. I could not believe that my sweet Miriam would marry without my consent. I could not believe that she would marry a man who was so bitter against the Prophet. The unsettling sense of woe I felt at the moment Micah turned from me and walked away was to prove only the beginning of trouble.

a house divided

ℭ

Gensek stood on a platform in the center of the Dananite camp and spoke. A large crowd had assembled. I lingered at the fringe and listened.

—Why should we Dananites go into the City where we are not wanted? he said.

—We should stay here in the valley where we can remain a distinct people, came a voice of assent.

—That is right, said Gensek. There is no future for us in the City of Enoch.

—But we are open for attack here, one man argued.

—Not so, said Gensek. Haven't we worked hard to build up our defenses?

—But Enoch has warned us to flea to the City, someone cried.

—To live where? said Gensek. In the houses of people who have never accepted us? To eat *their* food? To live off *their* charity?

—Better to live with them than to die, came a dissenting voice.

—I'd rather die with my dignity than to become a ward of the people of the City, countered Gensek.

I stepped through the crowd toward Gensek's platform and cried out to the people, You may debate this issue all the remainder of this day, even this week, and it will not change the fact that the Prophet, whom we have trusted, has given us a directive. We must put aside our feelings and obey him, or calamity lies at the door.

—Well spoken for one who is not of our race, said Gensek.

I felt the people near me move back. A low murmur rolled through the assembly. Others, having heard the dispute, began to arrive. My family came, as did Micah and Miriam. One man stepped to my side and said, This man and his family have made their home with us. Who has served us more? I will take issue with anyone who attacks his good name.

Benjamin stepped forward, then, with Joshua and a group of five Shepherds. He said, The Dananites are a free people by the efforts of Enoch and Joshua. Who can deny this? The Shepherds are agreed on this. Follow them and get yourselves to the City of Enoch.

Gensek shouted above Benjamin's voice, We are only trading one form of slavery for another.

—The self-pity of the poor. The pride of the minority, came a man's voice.

Heads turned to see who had said the words. All eyes fell upon Micah. Miriam, standing at his side, pulled a shawl tightly around her shoulders and dropped her head. Gensek shook a finger at Micah and said to the people, You see? We are nothing to them.

Micah waved off Gensek's comment, turned, and walked away. Miriam was left standing with little Rachel holding her hand. I searched for Enos and Naomi. Gensek's daughter had veiled her face, for shame I supposed, and was being led quietly away by my son. Joshua took Eve and Moriah and said to me, I'll get them away. Meet us at our tent.

Soon the crowd dispersed. Some whispered that they must hurry to gather their belongings; others mingled about in groups, continuing the debate. I felt alone, betrayed by Gensek. He yet stood on the platform talking to a handful of sympathizers. When he looked up, our eyes met. He straightened.

—Why? I asked him.

Gensek became silent, looking hard. When he had glared at me a long, cold moment, he shifted back to the group and conversed with them as if I were not there. Dejected, I turned away and saw Miriam. When I started toward her, she patted Rachel and the little girl skipped away. Then she drew in a deep breath, adjusted her face to a look of courage, and offered her cheek when I came to kiss her. Tears formed in her eyes.

—I've always wanted your happiness, I began.

Miriam interrupted me by putting up a hand.

—I'm married, she said.

I could not speak.

—I married Micah.

—I-I wish you joy, I stammered, struggling for something to say.

—He will be a good father to Rachel.

I nodded. Miriam paused, tears overflowing. Her voice broke as she said, He will provide for us and protect us.

—I know, I said, taking her into my arms.

Her whole body shook. I waited for her to speak.

—I'm sorry I didn't tell you, she said finally, pulling back, drying her eyes. Can you forgive me?

—Of course.

I took Miriam in my arms and let her cry again.

—I'm carrying Micah's baby, she whispered.

I tried not to act stunned.

—I hope you both will be happy, I said, urging myself to a posture of acceptance.

She did not answer.

—I wish I could have witnessed your marriage, I added. I had always hoped that Enoch would have performed it.

—We were married by a priest, she said.

I stared at her.

—A priest? Where?

She looked down.

—Saad, she whispered.

—In Saad? Who?

—I'd rather not say.

℘

In the City of Enoch, Ishmael was busy issuing essentials from the Shepherds' Storehouse. I had traveled to the City to help the people assimilate the coming influx of Dananites. Ishmael appeared disgruntled, his face hard lined, his brow furrowed. When I approached him, he was heaving sacks of grain onto carts.

—Get back! he yelled at a man who had stepped between him and a cart.

A sack nicked the man's shoulder and hit the ground near the cart. A blur of dust billowed up.

—Sorry, said the man.

—You pick it up. I won't.

Ishmael returned to throwing sacks in the rhythm of bailing water from a sinking boat. The man retrieved the sack, a rip seeping grain. Quietly, he angled away. Without breaking his cadence, Ishmael acknowledged me with, Don't get me started.

—I've only come to help, I said.

—Don't need any.

I glanced at the enormous pile of grain sacks and the lone, sweating Ishmael. He was a big man, certainly large enough to do the job. But I wondered why he would want to. Stubborn, I supposed.

—You won't let me help you?

Ishmael stopped, shoved the heal of his hand into the small of his back, and pushed himself erect.

—This is your doing, he said.

—Mine?

—Yours and Enoch's. Have either of you taken the time to see what is happening in the City? There is no order here. We are crushed together like sheep in a pen. No one has ever wanted the

Dananites here. Now they will be living in our homes—two, three families, maybe more.

—For safety, I said. It's temporary until we can build them homes.

—It's an excuse. You and Enoch have always wanted to assimilate them into the City. Now you've found a way to force them upon us.

—Not true!

—It *is* true. Look at those of them that have already come. Look at the people of the City. Are any of us happier? Are we more safe? Even the Dananites do not agree with this move.

—Most have come without complaint, I said.

—Many remain in the camp—as they should, said Ishmael. They were once supporting themselves with some of our help. They could have continued, and they could have defended themselves against any *supposed* enemy.

—Supposed?

—Saad. When have they ever been a threat? It's all an effort by Enoch to whip us into a lather and finally have his way to get the Dananites here. But under what pretense?

—Part of the army of Nod resides in Saad, I said. There are Watchers in Saad.

—Harmless, said Ishmael. They make noise. They always have. Why the sudden urgency?

I did not know, but knew that Enoch must have a reason.

—Why are you bitter? I asked.

—I resent having this situation imposed upon me, he said.

—But you've always stood by the Prophet, I said.

—I don't know what I believe anymore, said Ishmael. For me the cause is gone. It's all work now, drudgery mostly. I see things like this—he swept his hand out over the City—the congestion, the confusion, the hardship, and I wonder what can be the purpose. I sometimes think Enoch is delusional.

I first felt anger, then profound sadness.

—You've been one of my dearest friends, I said. What has changed?

Ishmael returned to throwing sacks. I departed without an answer. I walked to a place where I could be alone and survey the City. I observed a people in transition. Many seemed to be trying to make the best of a difficult situation. Some seemed upset. No one appeared to understand what we were preparing for. I heard words of anger: parents and children, husbands and wives, neighbors. The Dananites, who were arriving, seemed dejected. Theirs had been a long trail of affliction. Having escaped Danan, where they were in bondage and poverty, they had temporarily prospered in a new home, only to be asked to leave and accept mercy from those who had resisted accepting them. In a like disposition, many of the people of the City of Enoch appeared to be acting only out of begrudged duty, apparently resentful for the inconvenience.

Within the week, I sent word to Benjamin to urge the remainder of the Dananites to come into the City as Enoch had directed. My family came alone. Benjamin could not persuade the remaining Dananites to leave their camp, so he was forced to gather our family and to abandon those whom we had loved and served.

—The Dananites who have stayed are re-fortifying and say they feel safe in their valley, Benjamin told me.

The thought struck me, *They're making a mistake.* But I kept my feelings to myself. Being a leader among the people and a last firm support for the Prophet, I staggered under the weight, for as yet I carried the burden alone. I only hoped that Enoch would return to us soon from Hannanihah.

THE WRITINGS OF RABUNEL

After making a last plea to the Dananites asking them to reconsider relocating to the City of Enoch, after begging the people of the City to be charitable without offense, and after feeling the resistance from both groups, I retired from them all to commune with God. I poured out my soul in agony of spirit and soon felt comfort come to my mind.

Be of good cheer, Zion will come in your day. But not until your people's wilderness experience is complete. Not until the fulfillment of division, that essential step in the process of creation. This journey is neither one you can interrupt nor alter. When your people are proven, when they truly desire it, they will pray for Zion, and Zion will be established among them, the holy abode of God and the Messiah forever. You see, Zion already exists. You are mistaken to think you can establish it alone. You labor to build up the kingdom of God on the earth in preparation for Zion, but it is ultimately God who establishes Zion among his people. Your task is to qualify the people. Remember: Zion comes from above, not from below. It does not emerge from any earthly government or institution. It is not of this world and must remain separate. Zion must remain pure forever. As you assist my servant Enoch in preparing a people for Zion's establishment, you will feel the fierce pull of the world to hold you back, but your movement must be away. The world will fight to keep you, then to destroy you. But God will strengthen you, and, as you progress, he will fight your battles for you. Those who contend against Zion will be turned against each other—one person will fight against another, nation will fight against nation. Then, in the midst of the contention, God will grant you, Enoch, and those righteous men who follow after you a season to gather the righteous from the grasp of disaster, for the floods must surely come and wash clean a corrupted world. You will gather the meek followers of the Messiah to the safety of Zion. Among the wicked, Zion will be seen as terrible, for it cannot be destroyed or entered by the unrighteous.

What the world does not comprehend is that it is the spirit of the Messiah that gives and upholds life, even to temporarily protecting the wicked from the full consequences of their evil. But the Messiah's spirit will not always strive with man. At a future date, when the world is fully ripe in wickedness, the Messiah will withdraw his spirit, and the adversary, even Satan, will immediately seize the opportunity to rush in and fill the void, assuming full power over his own kingdom. Then, even the wicked will be amazed and quake with fear, for few have ever felt the adversary's awesome, devastating power. They will be alarmed to find that Satan will not uphold his children—not one. In his reign of blood and horror, those who have served him will cry out for the mountains to cover them. So great will be the destruction, that men's hearts will fail them. Everything of this world, which the wicked have known and trusted, will collapse, and Satan will laugh them to scorn. He will crush them in his hand and they will have no power to resist. They will cry out to God, but he will not hear them. Then, they will curse him for not delivering them, but he will give them over to their father, the devil. Everything will begin to fail: governments, institutions, associations, possessions, riches, every single person and thing that is not of a heavenly nature. But Zion will always stand steady and unaffected, and by and by the Messiah will raise it high into heaven from whence it came.

a distant purpose

CB

A trumpet sounded from the watchtower high on in the narrow pass. People began running through the streets of the City crying, The army of Nod is upon us! Micah rushed past me then, hurrying toward the tower.

—What is happening? I called out to him.

—Assemble the guard in the City and send them to tower wall, he shouted back.

—I will!

I found Enos and Benjamin at my house. The sun was setting pale orange in a gray, winter sky. A stiff breeze stung my ears. I pulled my cloak about me. Moriah was standing at the doorway conversing with my sons in a rapid cadence. I could see the concern in their faces.

—Are we under attack? asked Enos, when I approached them.

—I don't know. Can you summon the guard?

—Yes.

—Arm them all. Leave a contingent to keep order and lead the rest to the wall.

As Enos hurried off toward the City, I turned to Benjamin.

—I must go to the tower, I said. Will you take charge of the City?

—I will.

Moriah and I stood together and watched our sons hurry away. She said nothing, but her eyes spoke her worry. I squeezed her hand.

—They will be fine, I said.

Moriah did not seem assured.

—Are we at war? she asked.

—I'll know more when I go to the tower. In the meantime, stay here.

As I started to leave, I stopped and turned back. Moriah wrapped her arms around my waist and buried her head in my shoulder.

—Maybe you should gather Sarah and the children to Joshua and Eve's house. I'll either come or send for you there.

She backed away and nodded. Her eyes were wide, her face pale. I forced a smile, kissed her on the forehead, and made for the watch-tower.

A swarm of nervous guards and people had converged about the base of the tower where a frenzied discussion was taking place.

—Do you think we will stand and fight? some were asking, gazing up at the tower.

—No. There are too many of them, others answered. We should escape while we can.

—It is the Dananites who are still in their camp who are in the real trouble, someone said.

I pushed through the crowd, making my way toward the tower. I heard my name whispered by those who recognized me. I tried to pay no attention, but blew into my hands and reached out to take a rung to climb the tower. Suddenly, a woman grabbed my tunic at the waist and said, *You think we'll die?* I patted her hand, assuring her that we'd been protected before.

When I had counted thirty rungs, I felt the big hand of Micah reach down and pull me up on top of the tower.

—Look! he said, pointing toward the Dananite valley.

A light fog had crept out over the low hills. Saad, on the far side of the river, was mostly obscured from view. A crisp mist had frozen and drifted in the air like fine snow. When people spoke, a thin cloud formed about their words. The dim flicker of fires outlined the border of the Dananite camp, illumining the fog with an eerie glow and giving off enough light to see that the camp was under siege by an enormous army. The few Dananites that had remained were huddled in the center of their camp behind a bulwark of timbers. At the mouth of the pass, another part of the army, substantial but not as large, was making camp. They were close enough for us to hear their savage oaths and plans to destroy us.

—The Dananites will be annihilated, came a voice at my back.

I turned to face Ishmael. I looked up at the tall man. His nose was red. His eyes were watering from the cold.

—We must send help, said another voice.

It was Gensek's. He walked toward me and stood next to Ishmael, coming to his shoulder. I was surprised to see the three of them standing together, since Micah and Gensek had recently seemed at odds with each other. I was more amazed that any of them were speaking civilly to me at all. I attributed it to the urgency of the moment.

—Our guards could not push through the army at the mouth of the pass to help the Dananites, said Micah.

—Whose army is it? I asked, pointing at the outfitted men that filled the valley.

—The army of Nod, we think, said Ishmael.

—But where did they come from? I asked. Our guards have never reported so many.

—There has been some recent movement along the borders of Saad, said Micah. A large caravan traveled by.

—Your guards didn't investigate? I asked.

Micah's face went blank, and I left off challenging him.

—The Dananites in the valley will be slaughtered, said Ishmael, his tone even.

—You were the one opposed to bringing them into the City! I said.

He said nothing in response. I turned to Gensek.

—These are your own people, I said. You publicly opposed Enoch when he warned us to bring them in.

—Enoch didn't make himself clear, said Gensek.

I could not hide my ire. I forced myself to say no more.

Then Micah said, What good can placing blame do now? If we cannot help the Dananites, we have no choice except to turn our attentions to the City.

I nodded and pivoted away from the three men. I assumed that they understood my disgust with each of their actions, or lack of action, and they soon descended the tower. I heard the people pepper them with questions. I heard Micah order that the guards on the wall be tripled and extra bracing placed against the gates.

Soon, I was standing alone atop the tower. I wrapped my hands around the cold railing and became statuelike, gazing out over the darkening valley. Where there should have been a moon, the sky was black. The fog rolled in, ebbing in spots long enough to see scant movements of men. Occasionally, I heard voices, but they were muffled and faint. Those of our people who had earlier congregated at the wall had now been ordered to their homes, and only the guards remained. I stood silently as the night grew long and deep, staring, listening, reaching out with my senses for any hint of activity. Then, by the end of the first watch, I saw movement, as though the ring of fire was tightening like a noose around the Dananite camp. Two, maybe three torches shot through the air toward a rampart the Dananites had thrown up for defense. By the end of the second watch I began to hear shrieks of terror. The bulwark was suddenly ablaze. Shadowy figures bolted from behind it, silhouetted by the flames. I saw raised swords, flashing in the glint of the fire. Slumping bodies.

I stood alone in silent vigil, a solitary sentinel observing the extinction of those who had been too wise to be warned. I had loved them with a father's love. I had served them long. If I could have, I would have shaken them to break them loose from their pride. I wondered if it would have mattered. I felt too cold and too sad to cry. I tarried on the tower, frozen to my post, long into the night, a helpless observer. By the third watch, the Dananite camp was silent. The bulwark that had been built to hold back the enemy smoldered, sending a white line of smoke into the bleak, foggy night. The torches that had encircled the camp had now gathered into a tight clutch that was leaving the camp and advancing toward the mouth of the pass. I felt numb.

The hint of morning clipped the eastern mountains, and a dim light, the color of cream, blurred the sky. I sensed that my eyes were wide and dry, and it occurred to me that I had not blinked for a long time. The sound of feet climbing the rungs of the tower struck my ears. I did not move; I had no energy to turn. Soon, a hand touched my shoulder.

—Rabunel?

—Yes, I am here.

—You have remained all night?

—They are dead, I answered. The band of Dananites is dead.

—I know.

The large shape of a man stepped to my side. It was Micah.

—Enoch has returned, he said. He is here.

I pivoted then. The Seer was wrapped in a heavy coat of skins, his head and face mostly obscured with fur. I recognized his eyes. When I embraced him, I let myself weep. We both sank to our knees and held each other as we shook.

—When I heard, I came as fast as I could, he said.

—How did you get past the army? I asked.

—The fog and this disguise, he said, opening his coat to reveal the garb of a warrior.

—Clever, I said.

Ishmael and Gensek had mounted the tower and came to us. Their faces were drawn and their brows furrowed.

—Trouble? I asked.

—Two unarmed guards from Nod are approaching the pass, said Ishmael.

—They will want to talk to our leaders, I said.

Micah turned to Enoch and said, Let Ishmael and me go out to meet the guard and receive their message. We will detect if Nod has prepared a trap for you.

—Do you agree with this idea? I asked Enoch.

His eyes focused on what seemed a distant spot; then he looked at Ishmael and Micah.

—There seems to be a distant purpose, he said softly. I will stay here with you and Gensek. We will see what these guards of Nod have to say.

—I should go with them as far as the wall, said Gensek.

—As you wish, said Enoch.

After they had left, Enoch said, You ought to go to your family.

—You should go to yours, I countered.

He smiled.

—You have a point, he said. The weight of leadership can be heavy at times.

—Yes.

—Where is your family? he asked.

—In the City. Benjamin has taken charge of affairs there.

—He's a good man—capable.

—Loyal, I added.

—Like his father.

I smiled this time.

We stood for a while in silence, watching day come to the valley. For the first time I could see the extent of the damage. The Dananite camp was leveled. All we had worked for was gone. Bodies lay where they had fallen. No attempt had been made to bury them or offer them dignity in death. Smoke from last night's fires drifted into the clear morning air like the slim branches of a willow. The fog had burned off in the sun. The clouds had withdrawn. Blue sky. Colder, I thought.

—I can't bear to look at the sight, I said.

Enoch did not answer. I expected that he had none. I felt the numbness return, the emptiness that a parent feels when he knows he has done all that he can and yet a child chooses disobedience.

—We could have forced them to come into the City, I said.

—No, we couldn't.

We stared out over the awful scene for another long time. As though he were reaching for a peaceful subject to cut through the tension, Enoch asked, While Benjamin takes charge of the City, who watches out for your family? Is your family safe while you're here with me?

—Yes. Enos, Joshua—they will watch out over the family. And yours?

—Anna and Melca have struck up a nice friendship with Baruch and Esther.

—Baruch and Esther?

—They've fallen in love. I was to marry them.

—I didn't know. I've been so preoccupied—

—It's alright, he said. No one knew. They are very private people and wanted to keep it that way.

—I would have thought Joshua, Baruch's own son, would have known. If he did, he said nothing.

—Joshua may have known, said Enoch, I don't know. But Joshua's had his own concerns.

—You mean the baby, I said. Eve should deliver any day.

—Do they want a boy or girl?

—One of each.

We both laughed. It felt good.

—I thought Melca was a boy for sure, said Enoch. But Anna knew she was a girl.

—Mothers have an intuition, I said.

He nodded.

—Were you disappointed? I asked.

—That she was a girl? No. But what a handful!

—Enos was like that, I said. Jerel, too.

As I said Jerel's name, I felt a flood of emotion, and the difficulty of the moment returned to weigh down upon me. I turned my face to again gaze out over the valley. Saad stood in the distance, ominous, rich, more dangerous than we had ever given her credit for being. The enemy that we supposed she could not harbor was vast. The number of the army now closing in on us eclipsed all those of the City of Enoch, including the Dananites who had fled here for refuge. In the face of such a company, I forced myself to summon recollections of the power God that had preserved us in times past. I hoped by some miracle he would deliver us now.

—I wish Miriam had waited to be married at your hand, I said, changing the subject.

—She is like a daughter to you, isn't she?

—Yes. Since Shum, I have never thought of her as my niece. I love her every bit as much as my Eve. And I love her daughter, Rachel, like my granddaughter.

—And you love Micah.

It wasn't a question.

—Like a brother, I said, softly.

—They have some hard decisions before them, said Enoch.

I shot him a questioning look.

—She carries his child, I said.

—I know.

—You know?

—Yes. I've been allowed a view of things. Often adversity must precede blessings.

He looked at me then, and I felt my body chill.

—What else do you know? Can you tell me?

—I also know who married them.

—Miriam told me that she and Micah were married by a priest, I said.

Enoch paused and looked off.

—Simeon, he said finally.

My heart sank. Enoch reached out and squeezed my arm. We stood quietly for a long moment.

—I thought I could receive no worse tidings today, I said.

Enoch put his arm around my shoulder.

—I know. I'm sorry I am the one to tell you.

We stood together, the dearest of friends. In my heart I knew that I would not have wanted to receive such news from anyone else. I did not desire to learn what else he had foreseen.

—How deep is your faith, my friend Rabunel? he asked.

—I hope it is enough.

—Would you die for what you believe?

I faced him so that we stood eye to eye.

I said, If they took you in chains and put a sword to your throat, I would take your place and you would live.

His eyes began to tear.

—I know, he said.

—Do you think it will come to that? I asked.

He answered by saying, We say we believe. God has a way to see if we will *live* for what we believe.

We spent the remainder of the morning observing a flurry of activity near the camp of the army of Nod, people coming and going, their guard assembling about the mouth of the pass, our guard tense, pacing. Below and at a distance, Gensek sat on a rock, bundled in a fur wrap, awaiting the return of Ishmael and Micah. Much earlier, we had seen them enter a command area of the army of Nod, retreat with figures, then enter the command area again.

—It looks to be a hard negotiation, I said.

Enoch nodded.

At midday, Ishmael and Micah returned to the wall that closed off the canyon. They were accompanied by the two guards of Nod. Gensek stood as Ishmael and Micah approached and followed them. The three left the guards outside the wall and made their way to the watchtower where Enoch and I stood. A chill shot through my body as they climbed the tower. Micah was the first to arrive. When he pulled himself to the top, he straightened and rubbed his hands together as if he was starting a fire.

—Cold, he said.

—Yes, I said. What did you discuss?

He waited for Ishmael and Gensek to arrive. They paced with folded arms, blowing into cupped hands.

—They want a meeting, said Ishmael.

—Here? asked Enoch.

—There, in their camp.

—With me?

—With you and Rabunel. Gensek, Micah, and I are supposed to accompany you.

My stomach began to feel sick.

—Too risky, I said.

—If we don't do as they say, they will attack us before the sun sets, said Gensek.

—What do they want? I asked.

—Tribute, said Micah.

—How much? I asked.

—Half.

—Of everything?

—It's either that or our lives.

I asked Ishmael, What about the Storehouse?

—They want our resources, but since the Dananites came in from the valley there isn't much left.

—So Nod will take supplies from the families, I said. We won't last the winter. Our choices seem to be either death now or a prolonged siege.

—Maybe not, said Micah. There is another alternative. If you and Enoch can appease them, we could organize the people and escape over the high pass above the tabernacle.

Enoch and I looked at each other.

—Risky, I said again. Once they discover our exodus, they will hunt us.

—Do you think they will settle for less? asked Enoch.

—Perhaps, said Micah. But this I know, if you two don't go, there will be a slaughter for sure.

Enoch gazed long into Micah's face, then shifted his eyes to Ishmael's and Gensek's. These three were to be Enoch's and my escorts. When Enoch looked at me, his eyes appeared weary.

—You should go back to your family, he said.

—No. I've made my decision.

—Then you will come with me? he asked.

—Yes.

℘

Two warriors of the army of Nod guarded the entrance of the head-quarters. They stood erect, holding spears. When we arrived, Ishmael put up a hand and said to us, Wait here. I'll go inside first.

When Ishmael stepped into the large, gray tent, Enoch looked at Gensek and softly asked, Is your family well? The children seem to be growing so fast.

Gensek looked surprised at the question. He glanced at Micah, shifted his feet, then answered They're fine.

—That's good, said Enoch. I'm very fond of them.

Gensek looked down and a charge of anxiety shot through me.

Soon, Ishmael pushed back the tent flap and motioned us in. The image of my family flashed through my mind, and, for an instant, I longed to be with them.

—Let's go, said Micah.

Gensek led out. Enoch and I followed with Micah behind us. Upon entering the tent, I felt the point of a spear in my back, and Enoch and I were ushered to the far side of the tent before the seat of a man poised in the shadows. Dim light seeped through the tent's loosely woven seams, revealing specks of dust drifting in the air. A slender beam fell upon the hands of the man who sat in the dark.

—So, you are Enoch! he said.

—I am he, said Enoch.

—The empire builder! the man continued. The *prophet* who would arm the Dananites to conquer this region.

He is a man of peace! I protested.

Enoch placed his hand on my arm. I quieted. From the dark corners of the tent, armed men stepped forward with spears and pointed them at us. Ishmael, Gensek, and Micah moved aside.

Micah said, Here are the prisoners we promised.

I stared at him, stunned. The guards grabbed Enoch, then me. They bound us with cords. We did not resist. I looked up at Micah and asked, Why?

—The *prophet* has fallen, he said. The two of you would have allowed our people to be destroyed before coming to your senses.

—I loved you, I said. Now you are betraying me? You are my family! You married my niece!

—Not by Enoch's pretended authority, came a voice from the shadows.

I knew the tone, the inflections.

—Simeon! You are behind this treachery? I cried.

—I am pleased to see you too, said my grandfather.

He moved his tall, lean frame into the dim light so that I could see him plainly. His face was hard and old. Since I had last seen him, his hair had gone completely white. His clothing was fine. When he stepped forward and kissed me on the cheek, I turned my head.

—My own flesh and blood will not acknowledge me, he said to those who held us.

Low laughter filled the tent. The man who had sat in the darkness stood and walked toward us.

—I've waited a long time for this, he said.

Suddenly, the face of Gad came clear in the dull light. He struck my face with his hand, then struck Enoch. Ishmael took his turn. He grabbed me by the hair, pulled my head back, and brought his face to mine.

—Now I can finally finish what I started at the pit! he breathed.

—You? I trusted you!

—I am of the Mahan, he said. I may have followed you from Shum, but I believe what you teach is a lie.

I shot a look at Gensek. He lowered his head. A terrible realization burst upon my mind: both he and Ishmael had been informing on the City of Enoch, probably since Joshua had started establishing the Dananite camp. And it was these two who had attacked me and dropped me in the pit. How they had come together I could only surmise. Possibly Gensek had reintroduced Ishmael to the Watchers' doctrine that was prevalent in Shum and both had joined the Mahan society. It was Gensek who had spared my life at the pit, but he took no effort to spare me now.

Simeon's voice boomed above my thoughts.

—Did you actually think we would allow you to make a kingdom in these mountains? he said. The Dananites are ours. Saad is ours. Now, the City of Enoch is ours.

—Have you nothing to say, *Prophet?* said Gad.

Enoch was silent.

—I stood by as you destroyed Shum and my Rahaj, but I will have my way with you now.

Then Gad told the guard to take us away. I turned to Micah and pled with my eyes.

—It is out of my hands, he said.

praying for enemies

ଓଃ

Saad's prison was made of stone and was dug into the earth the height of a short man. Two slits in the corners allowed some light. Mostly cold seeped in. Enoch and I were allowed no fire, so the cold settled on the hard earth floor and stayed. A corner was used for waste. For light, we were given a hardened clay oil lamp with a single wick. Hewn logs served as a single crude bed. A small hatch in the ceiling of the underground cell provided guards access to us. Through it, our guards lowered a ladder to bring us food and beat us. The physical abuse continued until the guards said they could no longer abide the stench of our cell. They resorted to dropping off our food, checking to see that we both were still there, then retreating. The verbal abuse continued. The clothes left on our bodies—Enoch's red coat and turban, my white linens and blue coat—were torn, exposing sensitive skin to the harsh chill of winter.

We came to know Omar. He was the leader of the guards, usually a quorum of three—with Omar included—that rotated and was made up of men from both Saad and Nod. Omar was from Nod. When we were first thrown into the prison we heard his commander give him these instructions: Watch Enoch, or we will have your throat. The other one is insignificant. If he dies, he dies.

By listening to the guards, we came to appreciate their different objectives. When Omar was gone, leaving only the guards from Nod, we heard them plot against our lives. We discovered that Nod wanted us dead, but we did not know why. Saad, on the other hand, wanted to keep us, or at least Enoch, alive. I asked Enoch if we should fear for our lives. He answered that we would be dead already if we were not important to one group, probably Saad.

Omar and his guards did not feed us for the first two days of our imprisonment. But they beat us. When I could stand from my beating, I broke away ice that had formed on the walls of the prison, melted it in my hands, and licked up the moisture. Then I pressed ice against Enoch's bruises. He had taken most of the mistreatment. One eye was swollen shut. His face was the color of a rooster's neck feathers. A gash above his right eye would not close. The guards' mercy extended to returning our coats and giving us two blankets. I fashioned a poor bed of the blankets on the cold floor and laid Enoch on it, his coat bundled about him.

We were finally fed midday of the third day. Omar boiled a turnip and called it soup. The skin of it was hot, but its inside was cold. I dripped the broth into Enoch's mouth and dabbed the spillage with my sleeve. Crushing the turnip with a rock, I pinched bits between thumb and forefinger and fed him. That night the guards began loud conversations.

—The Seer's people are dead!

—All?

—Most. Some have run for the hills. But we will catch them.

—Were they burned?

—Yes. We needed to warm ourselves.

The terrible laughter made my stomach turn. Enoch had awakened enough to hear. He squeezed his eyes shut and said nothing. Into the night, we listened to the guards brag of running men through with swords, ravishing women, torching the City. I sat with Enoch, applying pressure to the lesion above his eye, offering him pieces of cold turnip. As I listened to the oaths, I thought of Micah, how he had stood before Simeon, Gad, and others who had pretended to be our judges, who had sworn that Enoch and I were subverting the region and that Enoch had caused the extermination of Shum. They had accused us of making the people of the City of Enoch militant and said that Enoch and I were secretly mobilizing our people to annihilate Saad.

—Will you sing me a song? whispered Enoch.

—I don't sing, I said.

—Please.

My mind seized on a favorite verse, a song of Zion. I said it aloud, talking it instead of making melody.

—The Lord shall establish Zion; the Lord hath redeemed his people according to the election of grace. The Lord shall bring Zion down from above. The heavens have smiled upon her. She is clothed with the glory of her God. He stands in the midst of his people. Glory and honor and power and might be ascribed to our God; for he is full of mercy, justice, grace, and truth, and peace forever and ever.

Enoch lay still, his eyes closed. When I thought he was asleep, I started to move away. But he reached out a hand and took my arm.

—Sing it again, he said.

I would have protested, but the pleading in his expression softened me. I sang the song; then I sang it again. When I had sung it the third time, the guards quieted. We were finally rid of their offensive communication. That night, Enoch and I slept in peaceful silence on the cold floor of the dungeon.

ೞ

I carved a mark for every day we remained in the prison. After five days Enoch was able to sit up and eat on his own. By fifteen days the swelling had gone from his face, leaving a dark smear of blue along one side. The gash over his eye was marked with a weeping scab. We warmed our hands over the flame of the lamp. We paced to keep our legs from freezing. From time to time, especially when the guards changed, we heard of the continuing murders and terrors inflicted on our people. We had received no word from the outside, nothing about our people or our families. I had tried to pray, but the dark ceiling of the prison seemed to trap my words, and I felt as helpless as a sheep in a shearer's noose.

—Do you think our people are dead? I asked Enoch.

He paced and blew into his hands.

—I think the guards would say anything to torment us, he said.

—What about our families?

He stopped and looked off.

—I don't know, he said quietly.

On the thirty-seventh day, the hatch above us cracked open, and bright light shot through. A silhouetted figure descended.

—Baruch! cried Enoch.

The hatched closed as Enoch and I rushed to embrace our friend.

—They captured me by intrigue, he said.

—Are our people safe? I asked.

—Most. The City is under siege. We were attacked twice. The wall and watchtower in the pass fell. The army has surrounded the City, but so far our guards on the high walls have fought off further invasion.

—What about Ishmael and Gensek? I asked.

—If you mean were they the only ones of the Mahan living in the City, the answer is no. After betraying Enoch and me, they remained with the army of Nod, but Benjamin discovered a covey of the Mahan who practiced their secret ways within the confines of the City. Before he could bring them to justice, they escaped to the camp of Nod.

—How are the spirits of our people? asked Enoch.

—Discouraged. Before the siege many deserted for Saad.

An expression of concern filled Baruch's face.

—What? I asked.

He stood.

—You are very thin, he said, seeming to change the subject.

—We are kept alive, that's all, said Enoch. What else can you tell us?

—Your families . . . he began.

I felt my heart begin to pound in my chest.

—Dead? I whispered.

—No. After you both left for the camp of Nod, Micah returned with a list of prominent men and women of the City whom, he claimed, you wanted assembled to meet with the leaders of Nod for negotiations. Most were leery and did not come. Benjamin, for example. Anna and Melca are safe. Enos tried to rescue you both from prison and was beaten and left unconscious. Men from the City found him and took him to recover at Benjamin's home.

My heart grew heavy and tears welled in my eyes.

—How bad is he? I asked.

—Bruises mainly. No broken bones. He had some swelling to the face. He is much improved.

I breathed easily, then my thoughts turned to my wife.

—What about Moriah? I asked.

—She came with me. My son, Joshua, stayed with Eve and the baby.

—Baby? I asked.

—His name is Ebanel, after your father.

My reaction was mixed: joy for a healthy grandson, grief that I had missed his birth.

Baruch continued, We had no idea you had been taken prisoner. Micah opened the gate at the watchtower and walked with us toward the camp of Nod. Suddenly, Ishmael and Gensek approached us with some fifty guards, who rushed us and took us captive. The men who resisted were cut down. We had no choice except to surrender. Ishmael's son, Reuben, was in our group. When he saw what was happening, he begged his father for our release. Then, when it became apparent that he could not help us, he apologized to us as we were carried away.

—Where is my wife? I asked.

Baruch lowered his head.

—Taken, he said.

—By whom?

—She was bound and forced to go with Ishmael. She was among a group of women—slaves, human cargo.

I knew what that meant. My mind reeled.

—I must get out of here! I said.

—How? There is no way.

I broke down and sobbed, big heaving sobs. Enoch came and held me. I could not stop. When I had cried until I could cry no more, I looked up at Baruch and asked, Where was she taken?

—To Jarom, an outpost near Nod where their army trains.

—Who knows what she has had to endure, I said.

Suddenly, my anger surged.

—Micah! Where are Micah and Miriam, my niece?

—After you were taken, he came into the City saying that Enoch had appointed him governor.

—I said no such thing, said Enoch.

—Of course not, said Baruch, and our people, for the most part, did not believe him. Instead, the people upheld Benjamin, and our guards forced Micah from the City. While I was being held, I heard that Ishmael and Gensek had accused Micah of sedition against Nod and that Micah then fled, taking Miriam and Rachel with him. I don't know where they went.

The hatch above us opened and two guards from Nod lowered food. Enoch retrieved it.

—It's not much, he said, halving a potato and offering parts of it to Baruch and me.

I shook my head. Enoch reached out and took my hand.

—I will get out of here, I said. I *will* find my wife.

—I must get to my family, said Enoch.

I bowed my head.

—I will kill Micah, if I can find him, I said.

Baruch gazed at me and softly said, No you won't.

I glanced at Baruch and a thought shot through my mind: might he not also be a traitor? Planted here by Simeon or Ishmael and Gensek to feed us lies and to glean information? I had been betrayed by one trusted friend. Why not another?

—Why is it that *you* have been placed in our prison cell and not others? I asked.

Baruch looked at me with eyes that said he understood my accusation. He turned to Enoch, then looked back at me.

—I can appreciate your mistrust, said Baruch, and I am not offended. I was held in various locations since I was captured. Five days ago they began to beat me and threaten to find and kill Esther. I was supposed to come here and convince you that your families were dead so that you would lose hope and surrender the City. I agreed so that they would stop the beatings. But, as you can see, I have told you nothing of their lies. I have only told you what I know to be true.

Enoch bade me come to my knees with him. Baruch joined us. I looked upon the emaciated figure of the Seer, his face drawn, his limbs bony, shaky. His eyes were round from fatigue. Here was the man who, at his word, had drawn down the powers of heaven in defense of his people. Here was the prophet who had communed with heaven as naturally as one man converses with another. Now, his body beaten, suffering from lack of nourishment, plagued by little rest, freezing, barely able to hold my hand without trembling, he lowered his head and raised his voice to the God he had trusted, somehow finding the strength to trust him once more. I heard him bless his people, bless me, bless Baruch. He pled for our families. He asked for the cries of God's people to be heard, that their afflictions would be tempered and consecrated for their good. He appealed to God for our strength to endure what we yet had to face and that we would be willing to wait upon him until the moment of our deliverance. He expressed gratitude by enumerating the times God had helped us when we been cast out, abused, despised, when people returned our words with anger. He said he knew that God was merciful unto his children when they cry

to him, that God visits them in their afflictions. Then he prayed for
something remarkable—he prayed for our enemies.

—Turn them to us, he prayed, or turn them out of our way.

I had not considered that the prayers of a righteous man could set
in motion a series of events: that God, if the enemy would respond,
will attempt to touch the enemy's heart and turn it back to the
abused. Or, if that enemy should remain hardened, God would move
him out of a righteous man's way.

Enoch concluded with a plea for the Holy Spirit to reveal to us
the will of God. Then he prayed again for deliverance. I knew the
power of Enoch's prayers. I expected a miracle.

by whatever means, a miracle

ങ

One night, after two guards from Nod had delivered us another meager meal, our stomachs started to seize, and we doubled over in pain.
We began to retch, heaving the contents of our bellies onto the
ground. My head began to spin and I went to my knees, bracing a
hand against a wall for support. Baruch and Enoch lay on the floor
reeling, their knees to their chests, pitching back and forth, groaning.
I spit the acrid taste from my mouth and said, What is it?

—Poison, said Baruch.

I staggered toward him and helped him to his knees.

—You must hurry to get it out of your stomach, I said.

Baruch nodded, turned his head, and gagged himself. In the far
corner of the cell, I saw Enoch cough and collapse onto the cold floor.
Baruch had recovered enough to rush to his side.

—Help me with him! he cried.

I tried to answer, but my throat burned so badly from the poison
I could not. When I tried talk again, my words came out as a whisper:
Help me get him to the bed.

I stumbled forward. Baruch took Enoch by the feet and I lifted
him by the shoulders. For a moment, I thought I would faint. We laid
the Seer on the bed and turned him to his side. Enoch clenched
his hands into fists and once more curled up like a fetus, his eyes

closed tightly. Suddenly, the violent cramping attacked both Baruch and me, and we crumpled at Enoch's side, trying to recover. I folded my arms about my knees and tucked my head between them, fighting the fire in my bowels. Baruch fell on his back and rolled side to side.

—I think I'm a dead man! he said.

I could not go to comfort him.

The next thing I remember was Baruch nudging me awake. He held the oil lamp, its flame the single illumination in the dark prison hole.

—Rabunel, Rabunel.

I stirred.

—Rabunel.

—I am here.

—Can you move?

I tried my limbs.

—Yes.

Gingerly, I pushed myself to my knees and waited for my head to clear. I slowly straightened. Baruch offered me his hand and lifted me.

—Look at Enoch, he said, leading me to the Prophet's bed.

Baruch brought the oil lamp close to Enoch's face. His skin was the color of tallow. His eyes were closed and sunken. I kneeled beside him and put an ear to his chest.

—Is he alive? asked Baruch.

—Yes, but very weak. We should bless him.

Baruch took a step back.

—I've participated in many blessings—for health, comfort, counsel—but never one like this, not for a dying man.

—It's only harder for *us*. The power of God is the same.

We knew we should pray. Many times previously, we had witnessed the prayer of faith heal the sick.

—I'll offer it, said Baruch.

I agreed and went to my knees. Of the many prayers I had heard extended in another's behalf, I thought I had never heard one so sincere as Baruch's. He sounded as though he knew the being to whom he directed his petition. There was nothing he said by rote; rather, he measured his words as if each one exacted from him intense mental effort. He began by expressing humility.

—Of ourselves we are nothing. But thou hast allowed us an ordination to minister among thy children in the authority of the Messiah. We do not suppose that we can act in the Messiah's name without permission and direction. We will not use that name in vain. But let us align ourselves with thy will, and if thou wilt, allow us to declare the words of healing and bless this, thy servant.

When he concluded he remained on his knees with his head bowed. I waited for him to move, glanced at him, and could see that he was struggling to regain his composure. At length, Baruch raised himself and I stood with him. We positioned ourselves on either side of Enoch; then Baruch joined me as we laid our hands on Enoch's head. I was the voice. I summoned the words Enoch had spoken in blessing the old dying man in the lepers' infirmary.

—O God, I said, having the authority of the Messiah, we ask thee to apply the atoning blood of the Messiah in behalf of this man.

Baruch and I stepped back. Enoch had lain still, the shadow of death on his face. He stirred. First a hand, then an arm. His chest expanded. He exhaled, took another breath more deeply, then another until his breathing became more rhythmic. His eyes opened.

—What happened? he whispered.

—The poison rendered you unconscious, Baruch said.

—Is it night?

—Yes.

—And you are . . . ?

—Fine, I said, anticipating him. Both Baruch and I are fine.

He gazed at us both; then a look of understanding crossed his face.

—You blessed me? Enoch asked me.

—Yes.

He reached out and took my hand. Then he took Baruch's. His grip was weak.

—Thank you, he whispered.

—Don't talk, said Baruch. Rest and get your strength back.

—I feel very tired, said Enoch.

His eyes began to droop.

—Do you think you can sleep? I asked.

—I think so.

Enoch closed his eyes, but I did not worry. I sat with Enoch into the night. I checked his breathing once and perceived that it was strong. As the night grew deep and cold, I huddled in a blanket and tried to warm myself. My throat still burned and my stomach occasionally cramped. Baruch sat near me, seemingly more concerned about Enoch. Once in a while he stood, walked around Enoch, studied him, then returned to sit beside.

—He will be all right, I said.

Baruch shook his head no.

—They mean to kill us. We can no longer trust what they feed us.

—Why poison? Why not just kill us outright?

—Enoch is the problem. You and I are nothing. He is seen as a threat.

—By whom?

—By Nod, Simeon and Gad mainly. They want Enoch dead.

—How do you know this?

—I had heard the guards talking. I thought it was hearsay. But now I believe it to be real.

—What was said?

—Nod is now the ally of Saad, but it has no intention of remaining so. Saad is too rich. There is an underlying competition for the region, and Nod is set on controlling the land once the situation of the City of Enoch is resolved.

—I don't understand, I said.

—Saad and Nod have divergent goals, said Baruch. Saad would keep the City of Enoch intact for tribute. Keeping Enoch alive is to their advantage. But Nod wants to take control of Saad, and thus the entire region. In Nod's view, the City of Enoch and Enoch himself are

Saad's potential allies. Nod has an aim: to exterminate Enoch and his people.

—Nod is strong, I said. Why not just attack Saad outright?

—Nod would have found itself caught between two potential enemies, Saad on one side and the City of Enoch on the other. From Nod's vantage point, it was better to align themselves with Saad to conquer the City of Enoch, then turn on Saad.

—And Saad agreed because they thought they would grow rich on the future tribute from our people, I said.

—Yes, said Baruch. But the complication in all this is that, even if the City of Enoch should be conquered, we still represent a potential ally to Saad once it is under attack.

—So Nod would rather exterminate Enoch and our people than risk our joining with Saad, I said.

—That is right. And Saad would keep us alive for the opposite reason since they do not totally trust Nod. Of this much I am sure: Nod is positioning itself closer to its goal—undisputed control of the entire region. They needed Saad's resources to lay siege to the City of Enoch, and now that Saad's forces are preoccupied, Nod will watch for an opportunity to attack Saad. But Nod must proceed carefully, otherwise their alliance with Saad will fall apart prematurely.

—I never cease to be amazed at Simeon's genius for wickedness, I said.

I gazed at Enoch sleeping and felt sudden shame for my ancestry—my own flesh and blood was my dearest friend's worst enemy. Simeon did not see Enoch as a man but as an inconvenience.

—Simeon and Gad will gain enormous power in Nod if they can help conquer Saad, said Baruch.

—They already have great power, I said.

—Yes, but their appetite is insatiable. There are more powerful people in Nod to impress.

—Who?

—I've heard a name—Azazel.

—He's a myth.

—I don't think so. I think he's the true power in Nod.

—Have you seen him? I asked.

—I saw an imposing figure at Nod's headquarters. He seemed to demand the attention of the commanders—Simeon and Gad included.

—Those two would defer to few, I noted. Why would Azazel bother to come here?

—I don't know. Maybe he sees the City of Enoch as a capitol of this region. Occupying it and Saad would give him an incredible advantage, not to mention wealth.

We're doomed either way, I said. If Saad keeps us alive it will be for slavery. But, if you are right, Saad will fall to Nod and Nod will annihilate us. Enoch's life is in immediate danger.

—Maybe we can save him, said Baruch.

I took oil lamp and brought it close to Baruch's face. His expression was serious, the lines in his forehead deep.

—You have a plan? I asked.

—If we can get Enoch out of this cell, we can take him back to our people. Once they have hope they can be rallied.

—How can we get him out? I asked.

—The guards of Nod have not returned since they fed us, said Baruch. They might be made to believe that they failed in their attempt to poison us all and that only two of us died.

I understood his meaning.

—They will see two bodies and one person alive—Enoch, I said.

—Yes. As I said before, you and I are nothing to them. They would probably remove our bodies without a thought, and that is how we can get Enoch out without drawing too much attention—by disguising Enoch as one of the dead bodies.

—And one of us pretending to be Enoch, still alive, I said.

We quieted and considered our plan.

—Wouldn't they check us closely? I asked.

—Probably. But the light in the cell has always been dim, and they do little except to drop off our food. I doubt that they know what Enoch looks like, except for his clothing.

—If they find Enoch still alive, why wouldn't they just kill him on the spot? I asked.

—I suspect that this is Nod's plot and that Saad has nothing to do with it. Do you remember that Omar was gone when the guards brought us our food? I think they are trying to kill us and make it seem like natural death. An open murder could cause a division between Saad and Nod.

—Why don't we all pretend to be dead? I said. Let them think they succeeded in killing us all. Then all the bodies will be removed.

—If they think Enoch is among the dead, they will guard his body and check him closely. A leader's body is still of value to his followers who want to reverence him. Nod could use Enoch's dead body as a ransom. No, they must be made to think that he is still alive if we are to get him out.

I looked at Enoch and studied his condition.

—He is very weak, I said. He could pass for dead. The other one of us would have to be a good pretender.

—I will dress in Enoch's clothes, said Baruch. As though I were Enoch, I will call the jailor and have him remove the bodies of my dead companions. Enoch already looks to be dead. You must pretend. You must find a way to escape and get him to our people.

—Risky, I said.

We didn't speak for a long while, contemplating the plan. I looked at Enoch, breathing shallowly, sleeping.

—It might work, I said, except for one thing.

—What?

—You don't look like Enoch. You don't sound like him either.

—I can do it, protested Baruch. You don't look much like him either.

—But I am closer to his size than are you, and I can approximate his voice. If we want to get Enoch out, I must be the one to take his place, and you must get him to the City. When the guards come, I will moan and cry like I am in pain and mourning. That distraction might cause them to not check you two so closely.

Baruch paused, then paced.

—Once you're found out, there is no reason for them to keep you alive, said Baruch.

—I know.

℘

Late in the night, deep in the darkness, Baruch and I disrobed Enoch and dressed him in my clothing. Through it all, he slept. Then Baruch lay beside him and assumed the posture of death. After I had broken ice from the walls to cool their skin, I cried out as if I were in pain, feigning Enoch's voice. I heard stirring above. Soon, the hatch in the ceiling cracked and a guard yelled, Quiet! We're sleeping.

I moaned loudly.

—I am in pain. Why do you torture me? You murder my people and take my companions.

—What are you saying?

—Dead. My companions are dead.

The hatch shut, and I heard muffled conversation and a spate of activity. The hatch opened again, and two guards lowered the ladder and descended into the cell. Omar was not among them. I hid my face, doubled up on the ground, reeled, and pretended to cry and shout out in agony.

—Shut him up! said one of the guards to the other. Stick a knife in him.

—We would be found out, said the other. It has to look natural.

—You're a fool! said the first. You've killed two but not the right one.

—What do you mean?

—Look at his clothes. The Seer still lives. Who will answer for this? Not me.

—You prepared the food, said the second.

As he said it, he tried to turn me with his foot. I held my stomach and crawled quickly to the corner and pretended to retch.

—But *you* put in the poison, said the first. I told you to put in enough.

One of the guards ran the light of an oil lamp over the bodies, studying them.

—Don't touch them! I shouted. Haven't you done enough?

—Quiet, *prophet*, or you'll feel the back of my hand, said the first.

—Are you sure they're dead? asked the second.

—I think so. If not, they will be soon. I can't stand the stench down here. Help me get them out. Omar will have to answer for this.

I grabbed the hem of a guard's tunic.

—Where are you taking them?

—What's it to you? To the refuse pile. They don't deserve a burial. Let the dogs have them.

He kicked at me to free his garment, grumbled, then turned back to the bodies. He set down an oil lamp next to the bed and hefted Enoch's body onto his shoulder. His companion lifted Baruch. When they had climbed the ladder and pulled it up, they closed the hatch and a gust of wind blew out the light. I lay alone on the floor of the cold cell in darkness.

the time of deliverance

⁊

The terror of twice facing one's worst fear can bring the strongest of men to his knees.

I sat alone in the darkness of the cell. All was deathly still. The thick blackness seemed to pinch out the last flicker of light from the oil lamp. Then, all the horrors of the pit returned to haunt me. Everything above in the guards' chamber was quiet. As yet, they had not returned from disposing of Enoch and Baruch. I would have welcomed a sound, any sound: the scurrying of a rat, cold wind whistling across the window slits, even the foul language of the jailors. I would have called out for food, a blanket, but no one was there, and even if there were, I dared not draw undo attention to myself. I would be found out soon enough, and the early discovery of my true identity could jeopardize my friends' lives and likely my own.

I lay on the bed of blankets where Enoch had lain—now cold. He and Baruch had been gone a long time. I looked in the direction of the window slits but perceived only black. My eyes soon tired and I closed them. I imagined Enoch's and Baruch's bodies being thrown onto the refuse pile. Maybe the guards had thrown earth on them. I contemplated their having to remain deathlike while cold, wet dirt covered their faces, cutting off their breath. Perhaps by now, Baruch had burrowed himself free and had started digging Enoch out.

Or perhaps wild dogs had attacked them, thinking to get an easy meal. Or maybe Enoch and Baruch were dead.

—*This was not a good idea!* I told myself. *There must have been another way.*

I began to torture myself with feelings of guilt. *I was too quick to agree with Baruch. We should have taken more time to develop a plan. We were gambling with the life of a holy man.*

I remembered Baruch's recounting the situations of my family. Moriah. I shuddered to think of my wife's situation. Slavers were a vile sort, without regard for human life, brutal, especially so to women. I found myself wishing that she could die rather than suffer. I thought about Enos, beaten. I wondered if I would recognize him: his face, his personality. I imagined his face broken, possibly never looking the same again. I wondered if the experience would strengthen him or if he would become afraid of life. Would he lose his natural enthusiasm and drive? I wondered if Naomi had stood by him during his trial. I thought about Benjamin, trying to carry the weight of a city under siege—calming the terrorized, tempering the impatient, soothing the enemy's wrath. I imagined Sarah's worry for him, how she would need to wear a brave face for the people, all the while anguishing. Joshua would be strong, I thought. He would be grief stricken over the capture of his father, but he would not let his feelings surface. His place would be by Eve and her newborn, little Fathers Council. How would Eve be recovering? This was the time a young mother needed her own mother. My thoughts returned to Moriah. At the thought of my wife in the hands of depraved men, I envisioned those who had delivered her: Ishmael, Gensek—they had eaten at my table, enjoyed the trust of their own people, all the while living the secret life of the Mahan. They had thrown me into the pit to die. Then, my thoughts turned to Micah, and I squeezed my eyes shut more tightly. If I had the capacity to hate, it was directed at Micah. He had taken away my Miriam without my consent to marry. He had betrayed both Enoch and me, incarcerating us. His treachery had opened the gates of the City and let our adversaries in. Because of Micah, my dear

Moriah was delivered into the hands of Ishmael and Gensek who sold her to slavers. Maybe I would never see her again. Micah had hurt me more than I imagined anyone could. He had hurt us all, every person in the City of Enoch and Danan. We had trusted him, and he had betrayed us, every one.

I lay back and tried to sleep, but the visions that entered my mind haunted me, demonic apparitions attacking my consciousness, torturing me with the horrors of Moriah's condition, my family's suffering, and of Ishmael's, Gensek's, and Micah's laughing. I wanted to scream, but did not. I wanted to stand and walk off the torture, but I could not see. The cold of the cell seeped into my bones. I wrapped the blanket about me, tucked it up under my chin, and shook. I tried to *think* a prayer. I could not fight off the evil phantoms that burned my brain with their railing accusations.

The long, dark night yielded to a dim blue light that penetrated the east window of the jail and stuck to the western wall in the hazy shape of the slit. As I lay on my back, I folded my arms over my chest, and blew white breath into the frigid air. My feet were numb. This was the time of morning we prisoners had typically risen to walk warmth into our freezing extremities. This morning I did not. As the beam grew brighter, I turned my head from it and decided to die. Mine, I thought, was a certain fate. When the guard came to check on me he would find an impostor in the place of Enoch. Then, after attempting to beat the truth from me, I would be killed, and Enoch and Baruch would be hunted. Better to die now and be done with this world. Besides, what could life possibly hold for me without Moriah?

ⅎ

The prod of a dull stick jarred me awake.

—Your food, said a gruff voice.

I recognized it as Omar's. Two carrots fell near my head. A cup of water was placed on the earth.

—Thank you, I said, trying to approximate Enoch's voice.

I turned my face from him.

—You lazy fool, sleeping all day. Lucky for me you were not one of the dead ones.

I grunted an agreement and tightened into a ball on the bed. Omar kicked me. I grabbed my leg and cried out in pain.

—Don't turn away from me when I talk to you! he said.

—Sorry.

I rolled part way toward him. He kicked me again.

—Prophesy, *prophet*. Prophesy who just kicked you.

I lay still. Omar paced, seemingly impatient.

—Eat your food, *prophet*, he said.

—I will.

—You're more trouble than you're worth. When my commander finds out that two of you died in the night, I will be the one who gets the beating.

I reached for a carrot in the dirt and bit off a piece. My teeth ached when I chewed. In recent days my mouth had begun to bleed when I ate.

—You're a pig, Omar said with a tone of disgust.

I did not answer, but tried to eat so he would leave me be.

—A pig. Say it. Say *I'm a pig*.

—I'm not well, I said. Please let me rest.

He knelt beside me and took me by the nape of the neck.

—You'll never get out of here. Your companions are dead. You'll never . . .

He paused, stared at me. A look of puzzlement crossed his face, then anger, then terror.

—You're not . . .

I tried to hide my face.

—Where is he?

—Who?

Omar brought a lamp close to my face, and his went ashen.

—Where is Enoch? he said.

Omar did not wait for my answer. His attitude surprised me. I expected to be killed. He stood and began wringing his hands, pacing.

—I'm a dead man. I'm a dead man, he began repeating to himself.

I sat up. As Omar paced and mumbled, he kept shifting his gaze between the hatch and me. Finally, he stopped, dropped to his knees beside me, and took me by the throat.

—Say nothing! he said.

I reached up with both hands and pulled at his grip. When he released me, he began to shake.

—*Please* say nothing, he begged, kneeling before me.

The first feeling I experienced was pity; then a stroke of intelligence shot through my brain as if to say, *This is your deliverance.*

A plan began to develop in my mind. I carefully considered my words.

—I am ready to die, I said in a loud voice. I will shout out my identity, and you will take the blame for Enoch's escape.

—No! Say nothing. I will do anything you say.

—Then give me your clothing and sword, I said.

—You are going to kill me?

—You would have killed me.

—No! I was ordered to just guard and harass you.

—It doesn't matter, I said. Give me your sword and exchange clothing with me. If you do exactly what I say, I will not kill you.

Omar glanced again in the direction of the hatch, drew his sword, lay it on the ground at my feet, and began to disrobe. I took up the sword and held it at him until he stood naked before me. I motioned him to sit as I removed my clothing and donned his.

—Now, put on my clothes, I said, motioning with the tip of the sword.

He did as he was told, ever watching the sword.

—Exchanging places will do neither of us any good, he said cautiously.

—Why?

—When you go up, my companions will recognize you. They know me, and they will kill you. On the other hand, once it is known that Enoch has escaped, I will be blamed and lose my life.

—Why you? I asked.

—I am in charge. I am a dead man.

—You sound like a man who can come up with a plan, I said, raising the lamp to see his eyes.

—There may be a way out for both of us, he said.

I looked into Omar's eyes and could not determine his intentions. I glanced at the hatch and heard vague activity.

—They will come soon if I do not return, said Omar.

—What do you have in mind? I asked.

—Bind and gag me while I lie on the bed. The two guards from Nod are stationed above us. Blow out the lamp and make the sounds of disturbance. When they investigate, come at them from behind. When they are unconscious, you escape. Later, when they awake and find me bound, I will tell them Enoch overpowered me.

—They still may kill you for allowing this to happen, I said.

—I'll likely have to endure a beating, but not death. If you also knock me out, it will appear that Enoch was powerful and cunning enough to disable us three. It's my best chance, and yours, too.

—I don't like trusting an enemy, I said.

—Nor I.

A voice from above called out Omar's name.

—You haven't much time to decide, he said.

—Lie down on the bed, I said.

I ripped strips of blanket to secure Omar. Suddenly, a light breached the darkness of the prison, and I heard the creaking sound of the hatch opening. I extinguished the lamp and slipped behind the ladder that led from the cell to the hatch.

—Omar? came a voice.

At the silence the man on the ladder called back, No answer. Something is wrong.

Soon, both men were descending into the cell, the first holding a lamp in one hand. A tingling sensation rushed through my body, and my stomach tightened. I crouched in the corner and waited.

—Omar? called the second man.

I jumped out of the shadows at the first man, struck his head with the hilt of the sword, then thrust the blade into his shoulder. He screamed and dropped the lamp, extinguishing it. As he fell, I pulled the second man from the ladder and wrestled him to the ground. With a doubled- up fist I struck him in the face. He reeled and tried to fight back. I hit him again and again. When he went limp, I rolled off him and groped for the lamp. Lighting it, I held it over the two unconscious guards, the first bleeding at the shoulder, the other bruised about the face. I pulled the gag from Omar's mouth.

—By the grace of God I am saved, I said.

—Curse you and your God! Do what you must and be away with you!

—As you wish.

I stuffed the gag back into his mouth, stepped behind him, and struck him hard on the crown of the head.

into the gaping jaws of hell

ҩ

Only the open air of freedom made my journey to Jarom bearable. The weather was bitterly cold—snow covered the frozen ground and dark clouds brought a new layer each day. At night the winds came. I had previously dressed myself in Omar's clothing. His garb stunk of his sweat. The clothes, however, would serve as a camouflage when the time came to rescue Moriah. Over the clothing, I had donned the guard's thick, beaver pelt coat that had a hood that I could draw tightly about my ears and head. Because my hands were bare, I kept them inside the coat as much as possible. Another guard had worn warm, doe-hide sandals, which I now wore on my feet. Since I expected to find Moriah in a destitute and deprived condition, and imagining that she would not survive a cold escape, I scrounged what warm clothing and provisions I could and strapped them to my back. Then, as I set my face northward toward the borders of Nod, I knelt in the snow and pled to God that he would protect me. I commended my life into his hands, knowing that only he had the power to deliver me and to save Moriah.

A journey that should have taken seven days dragged on to fourteen. My weakened condition, coupled with battling the adverse climate, slowed my trek. Each night when I prepared a camp, I cursed my frailty and worried that I would arrive too late to free Moriah.

Sleep fled me. Only when exhaustion enveloped me did I yield, and then it was to a fitful sleep. Vivid dreams of my wife's circumstance haunted me until I awoke screaming. My one consolation was imagining finding Micah, seizing him by the throat, and choking the breath out of him. When I tried to remind myself that I was a man of God, the bitterness only intensified, and I soon became as flint—cold, dark-spirited, hard.

—It is beneath you to harbor thoughts of revenge, I said to myself. But who would not? If any man had cause to hate, it was I.

I had prayed for help in rooting out the anger, but sharp feelings afflicted me, materializing as if they had a life of their own. I found myself yielding to those feelings, leveling accusations on Micah as if I were demanding justice at the bar of God.

As I trod through the snow toward Nod, I recounted the years of friendship I'd had with Micah, how we had traveled together to distant cities to preach, how we had worked together on the temple, how we had laughed in happy times and cried in sad. Systematically, I discounted each good memory of the man and replaced it with thoughts such as, *he was always wicked and was deceitful enough to hide his true character.* Even when he had saved me from the pit, I imagined he had done it to divert attention from his relationship with Ishmael and Gensek. Then, adding insult, he had stolen my Miriam. As I journeyed to Jarom, I rehearsed every word Micah had spoken at Enoch's as he betrayed us to our enemies. I remembered how he had pointed his finger, accusing me of being part of Enoch's plan to mobilize the City of Enoch and the Dananites in an effort to overthrow Saad. When I had tried to counter the charges, a guard struck me and Micah turned away. By his treachery, Enoch and I had suffered in a cold prison while our families and people had huddled in fear for their lives, and my dear wife had been delivered into the hands of vile men. Yes, I hated Micah, and I dedicated my prayers to his condemnation. I wished for God to yield to my will and become Micah's executioner, to carry out the sentence I wanted to impose upon him.

Late on the fourteenth day of my journey, I arrived at Jarom. Just as Omar had described it, Jarom was a soldiers' camp that lay on the south border of Nod. The region about it was flat and open on three sides, with a mounded, sparsely wooded area on the north, closest to Nod. A clutch of small tents defined the perimeter. A large tent that I guessed to be the commander's stood at the center of Jarom with a weather-beaten wood house adjacent to it. Night had brought a cold, harsh wind. Most of the tents were dark inside except for the commander's, which glowed from an internal fire. Three vague figures were silhouetted on the tent's skin. From my observation, I supposed no more than one hundred men made up the population of Jarom. Between the commander's tent and the wooden house was an outside fire where two guards, a big man and an adolescent, sat cross-legged, warming themselves while throwing food into a simmering pot. A plan settled on my brain. I ventured toward them.

—Cold night, I said as I approached the guards.

They both started, and the big man reached for his sword.

—Sorry to alarm you, I said. I've just come to warm myself.

—You didn't give the signal, said the boy.

—I don't know the signal, I said. I just arrived.

—Arrived? asked the big man. From where?

—Saad.

—How goes the campaign?

—When I left, the Dananites in the valley were destroyed and the City of Enoch is under siege.

—Wish I were there, said the boy.

—You haven't been? I asked.

—No. We're stuck here cooking stew.

—Bad luck.

—Yes, said the big man. Jarom is a dismal place.

—Only one consolation, said the boy, tipping his head toward the wood house.

—Who'd want them? said the big man. They're filthy.

—You keep women in there? I asked.

—Captives from many places, said the big man. We feed them. That's our job.

—The job has its benefits, said the boy, a corner of his mouth turning up.

—You're obsessed, said the big man.

The boy turned to me and asked, Are you interested?

—Me? I said. No. I just came to get warm by the fire.

We spoke about the war. The boy said he was from a family in Nod. The big man was from the north, but had joined Nod's army to share in the spoils. Now he doubted he would get any or see any action. The campaign in Saad would be over soon, and he would still be here cooking stew.

—How many do you cook for? I asked.

—Commanders: three. Women: twelve, said the boy.

I studied the stew—carrots and potatoes in a broth.

—No meat? I asked.

—Only for the commanders. This is for the women. It's about done, I'd say.

The boy stood and lifted the pot from the fire with two sticks.

—Need some help? I asked.

He glanced at the big man as if seeking permission.

The big man nodded and said, Go on ahead, I get sick from the stink in there.

The boy handed me a stick, and together we carried the pot to the house. As he fiddled with the latch, I looked back at the big man, his back to us, crouched over the fire, a blanket pulled up over his shoulders, his sword lying unsheathed beside him.

—Come on, said the boy, pushing open the door. They're supposed to be for the commanders, but I won't tell if you take a fancy to one.

I nodded and tried to smile.

Inside the dark house, the boy and I set down the pot, and the boy lit an oil lamp.

—Time to eat, pigs! he shouted.

Slowly, timid figures emerged from the shadows and moved toward the stew. Each shot an anxious glance at the boy, quickly dipped her bowl into the stew, and backed away. As they passed me, I was overwhelmed by the odor. Obviously, the inmates had not been allowed bathing water or a change of clothing. A repulsive stench permeated a back corner that I expected was used for waste. As every woman approached the pot, I studied her face, searching for Moriah. They mostly kept their eyes down. Their look was hollow, their faces bony and drawn, their lips pale and cracked, their hair matted and dirty. Some had bruises. All appeared painfully thin.

—You said twelve, I said to the boy. I count nine.

—What about it? the boy asked the last woman.

He grabbed her by the arm, and her bowl fell into the dirt.

—One died during the day; two are sick, she said, her voice emotionless.

The boy let her go and motioned me to help him pick up the pot.

—You don't want to see for yourself? I asked.

—Why?

I searched my mind for a quick answer.

—Maybe she's lying. Maybe they've escaped.

The boy hesitated.

—There is no escape, he said.

—It's nothing to me, I said, But you'll be to blame if they are gone.

He seemed to ponder my words, frowned, blew into his hands.

—I got no time for this, he said, handing me the lamp. Look around if you want, but be quick about it. I want to get back to the fire.

I turned to the woman who had answered the boy and said, Where are the three?

The woman led me to a far wall. A dead body was shrouded under a blanket. My heart pounded as I knelt beside it and pulled back the covering from the face. Cold, skin the color of paste, dark eyes open and glassy, lips parted—I didn't recognize her. Relief washed over me, but I was ashamed. I was suddenly struck with profound sadness when I realized that she was someone's wife or mother or sister. I could only imagine what agony her family was feeling and how they would likely never know what had happened to her.

—Where are the sick ones? I asked the woman who was my guide.

She pointed to a far corner. I raised the lamp and let the light fall on two blankets that had been made into tents. I stood and followed her. She motioned, and I bent down beside them. Then my guide said, Give them at least the dignity to die in peace.

—I don't intend on hurting them, I said.

—Hurry! shouted the boy.

I looked into the imploring face of my guide, then faced the blanket tents. I hesitated, then pulled back the cover.

Moriah!

I gasped. Quickly, I pulled the hood of my coat about my face so she could not recognize me, but she seemed to be incoherent, hovering between unconsciousness and awareness. I gazed at her—emaciated, eyes sunken, face bruised. Her hair had been chopped short and was totally white. She opened her eyes a crack and moaned. My mind raced.

—Boy! I called out. Come over here.

—I'm cold. Let's go! he called back.

—Come and look at this one.

The boy shuffled toward me.

—What?

When he came close, I grabbed him, put a dagger to his throat, and said, Breathe a word and you're dead.

His eyes went wide and he offered a tiny nod.

I looked at my startled guide, who stood above me.

—Take the cord from my pack, I said.

She fumbled about the pack until she produced a long, white rope.

—Bind his hands behind him and gag him.

As she obeyed, the other women came close.

—What are you doing? one asked.

—I'm taking this woman with me, I said, gesturing to Moriah.

—You're escaping?

—Yes.

—Help us.

—I can't, I said. We will be traveling fast. Too many tracks in the snow.

—You can't leave us here, said the woman. There is no hell worse than this.

I thought hard.

—We are going to the City of Enoch, I said.

—You're a fool! she said. The whole army of Nod is there, and the City is under attack. Why would we escape from here only to go anywhere near Nod's forces?

—Where will you go? I asked.

—To our homelands. Haner and Hannanihah, mostly.

—The boy has a knife, I said. I have two more in my pack. Take them to defend yourselves, and use the boy as a hostage. He will give you little trouble bound as he is. But before you attempt anything, allow me some time to get away with *this* woman.

—Who cares about the boy? said one woman. Of all the guards, he's been the worst.

—It might work to use him as a hostage, said another woman. I've overheard that one of the commanders is his uncle.

—You'll be on your own when you escape, I said. Hannanihah is the closest city. It will be risky, and some of you will die.

—We are dead already, said a woman. At least you've given us hope.

—The boy has heard everything, I said. You'll have to take him with you, at least to Hannanihah. Then, you'll have to decide what to do with him.

The room became quiet as if each woman were contemplating her answer. The woman who had guided me to Moriah knelt beside me and asked, Who is this woman to you?

—My wife, I said.

the last leaf of winter

ೞ

I dressed Moriah in the clothes and coat I had brought for her, then set her on the ground at the back of the prisoner house. Stepping to the corner, I called out for the big man who yet sat by the fire.

—There's been an accident! Come help me!

The big man jerked his head toward my voice, rose to his feet, and came running. I hid outside, at the corner of the prison near the entrance. When the big man neared, I leapt at him, throwing my body crossways at his legs. He fell back, ramming his shoulder into the side of the house. Before he could recover, I rushed behind him, grabbed him by the hair, yanked it back, and stuck the point of my dagger at his throat.

—Move inside, I said.

He stood, carefully. I kicked open the door, and the guide woman met us with more cord and another gag.

—Now we have two prisoners, she said.

—This one has never bothered us, said another woman.

—It doesn't matter, said the first. He's a guard from Nod.

—Do with them as you will, I said. I must take my wife and escape before we are discovered.

I left the big man and boy bound and gagged with the women. Then, gathering all the food I could confiscate from the two guards, I lifted Moriah and asked, Can you walk?

She answered me with glassy eyes and a small nod. Supporting her at the waist, I made for the protection of the woods. A stiff, contrary wind blew snow in our faces. At first I cursed it. But when I looked behind me and saw that our tracks were covered, I considered it a blessing. I checked the sky. Dark clouds had rolled in, and I expected that our journey would soon be hampered by a hard storm. My goal was to backtrack through the woods to an open area on the fringe of Jarom, then make a hard dash for the mountains that would lead back to the City of Enoch. I hoped that the contingent of guards camped at Jarom would not realize we had escaped until morning. I planned to make the best use of the night and the following day to put distance between us and them.

During our flight from Jarom, Moriah had said nothing. I supported her weight by draping one of her arms around my neck and holding her up at the waist. She walked more than ran, stumbled more than walked. When we had traveled halfway through the night, the weighty clouds began to dump their snow. Slowly at first, then harder as the night deepened. The wind at our backs drove the snow at an angle. Exhausted, Moriah collapsed, and I picked her up in my arms to carry her. Even in my weakened condition, I had little trouble, for she had become so thin that lifting her was like hefting a child. I fought off fatigue, knowing that our lives depended on my stamina.

Morning came as cold as the night. As I carried Moriah, I looked up and located the sun, a brown circle silhouetted behind white clouds. The snow fell softly now, and the wind had ceased. My eyebrows and the beard on my face, which I had acquired during my own prison days, caked with ice. I swathed Moriah's head with the hood of the coat and pressed her face into my chest to keep her from breathing too much frigid air. When she occasionally moaned and stirred, I knew she was yet alive.

I ran as long as I could with Moriah in my arms, rested, supported her as I tried to help her walk, carried her again. The hazy orange sun rose ever higher. My stomach burned more than my arms ached. If I was hungry, I could only imagine what my wife felt. I searched for shelter, a place to stop, but we were still in the stark openness of the valley. I did not dare to stop. Because of the snow, I could not see the mountains, which were my goal, and I knew the army of Nod. They were trained to track. Whether they were hunting us, I did not know, but I was sure they could make better time than we. My only hope was to continue to make haste and find shelter in the mountains.

My thoughts drifted back to my visit to the world of spirits, how my father and Jerel had said they had often been near me in times of trouble. I wondered if they were at my side now.

By midday the clouds had dissipated, and the sun broke upon the sea of white that I had traveled with Moriah. For the first time, I could view the expanse of the valley. We stopped, and I set Moriah down. Her complexion was pale, her eyes partly closed. As I had carried her, I sensed how light she felt, her bony ribs, her willowy fingers. Her clothing was a patchwork of rags held together by thin threads. I scanned each direction, before us, behind, to the sides. I saw no evidence of pursuit—only two distant bull elk on my left and, at an equal distance, two wolves on my right. None of the animals seemed to notice us. Moriah's and my tracks feathered back the length of a pine, then became part of the blanket of snow. When I looked forward, I spied the mountains—another day's journey, I calculated. That we would not arrive until tomorrow worried me. We had made worse time than I thought. From where I stood, I judged that Moriah and I were alone in an open valley. Without immediate signs of pursuit, however, I allowed myself to feel cautiously safe. I knelt down beside my wife.

—I think we're out of danger, I said.

I pulled some bread from my pack and offered it to her. She stared at me through round, hollow eyes. Her look was no longer one of fear, but maybe shock. She fixed her eyes on the bread and put out a shaky hand to take it, but failed.

—It's alright, I said. Let me help you.

I pinched a piece from the loaf and put it to her lips.

—Eat, I said. You need your strength.

Moriah opened her mouth to receive the bread and slowly chewed it.

—You're safe now, I said. I'm taking you back to the family.

Moriah gazed at me without blinking, a hint of puzzlement in her face. I gave her more bread and kissed her on the forehead. She moaned and turned away.

—Don't you recognize me? I said. I am your husband, Rabunel.

Moriah closed her eyes and began to tremble. All I could do was hold her. She either would not or could not speak. I wept as I pulled back the hood from her head and regarded her short, white hair. Her face was bony, the skin drawn tight. Her lips were pale, cracked, sore looking at the corners. I took snow in my hands and pressed it to a bruise on her cheek. Then I lifted my eyes to heaven and silently pled for the life of my wife. But the image of Micah formed in my mind. How I hated him! How I wished that God would strike him—not quickly, but in such a way that his death would be long and painful.

At length, I looked at my wife, sleeping now, and I whispered to her, Rest for a while. I will carry you. We still have a ways to go.

Then I stood on my feet, lifted her into my arms, and pointed us toward the mountains. We would make camp in the open of the valley tonight, without a fire.

As the sun disappeared in the western sky, we stopped. The sky burned the color of ripe pumpkin, and the now near mountains were blue, as cold looking as a hard-frozen lake. During the afternoon, I headed toward a distant object that came into focus as a lone tree standing in the valley, its stark, bare branches reaching out like bony arms and gaunt fingers to the chill sky. At its trunk I made camp by spreading a blanket on the snowy ground and draping our coats about us. I leaned back against the trunk, drawing Moriah to me, determined to only allow myself quick naps so as to remain close to consciousness. I lay Moriah's head on my lap, stroked her cheek, and tried to feed her bits of bread. She would not take them, but rolled over and slept.

She's dying, I thought, *and there is nothing I can do to stop it.*

Beyond my feet, I saw the still body of a bird lying in the snow, its beak slightly parted, one wing spread open, the other tucked up tight.

No dignity, even in death, I thought. *It lies there dead and who knows? Who cares?*

I lifted my eyes and searched the tree, its bare limbs trembling in the wind. I bundled my coat more tightly around me and recinched the hood of Moriah's coat about her head.

Useless tree, I thought. *Unable to save anything. Just like me.*

As the night progressed, the wind grew fierce and blew great drifts of snow upon us. I lay down flat on the blanket, covered myself and Moriah in our coats, and pulled her close to me. Her cheek was cold. I perceived no movement. I pressed a hand against her chest but could not detect a heartbeat.

—Moriah?

Nothing.

I positioned my ear close to her nose and listened for air. Again, I sensed nothing.

—O God! I cried. Don't take her from me!

From a distance, I heard the howl of wolves. They called to each other with long, lamenting baying. I remembered the night Jerel died, how wolves had unearthed his body from his grave and carried it off. These that now prowled the prairie were hungry, I expected. That would make them fearless. I lay still, dreading that they might discover us.

I cannot live without her. I continued my prayer in my thoughts. *Don't leave me here alone. Take me, too.*

Once more, my attention turned to Micah.

No! I thought. *I will not let you in my mind. Not now. Leave me alone to mourn.*

I forced the image of Micah from my mind and tried to replace it with the image of God. What was he like? All-powerful? All-knowing? Did he know where I was? Did he know what was happening to me? Could he hear my cries, even when I called out in my thoughts? Did he care? I found myself thinking, *What do I believe? How deeply do I believe it?* Was it possible that the God of heaven had no comprehension of my trouble? Could I believe in a God who had blind spots? Did I truly believe in him as my creator and father? Could a creator create within me an attribute that he did not personally possess? Emotions, for example? Did he have the capacity to experience great happiness or extreme sadness? Could he feel compassion? If so, did he have the ability to help? Would he? Enoch had taught that God visits his children in their afflictions. *Put your trust in God, not man, not the things of this world, not even in yourself.* He said those who trusted something other than God would be disappointed by and by. *There is no security in this world,* he said. *Security is a feeling that comes from only one source.*

Without warning, a deep feeling of despair overwhelmed me, and I began to weep uncontrollably. When Jerel had died, when I was cast into the pit, I thought I had felt exquisite pain, but never had I experienced anguish of soul such as that night in the dead of winter, holding the still form of my beloved wife. The heavy weight of guilt began to press down upon me. Perhaps I could have averted this disaster. I had had a choice. I could have gone to my family, as Enoch had offered, instead of remaining with him to face trial and imprisonment. I would have been there to protect my family. Maybe I could have prevented Moriah's ordeal. I recalled Micah's treachery, and I hated him out loud. My brain burned with rage.

—Let me die! I implored God. Let me die or give me peace!

I suddenly sensed a presence and felt a voice speak to my mind.

—*Peace comes from the same source as trust.*

The thought startled me. I stopped my pleading and considered what had happened. *I am imagining this,* I thought.

—*We promised to help you,* I felt the thoughts communicate to me.

—Father? Jerel?

—*Do you have the faith to hear?*

I did not know. The conversation seemed so quiet that I wrestled with belief and doubt. I looked at my wife, and a wave of despair washed over me. In an attempt at faith, I cried, Can there be mercy for my wife and me?

—*Yes. But we put to you another question: do you have the courage to accept mercy in any form?*

The statement came with such clarity that all doubt vanished. I stopped to consider, *If what I am experiencing is spiritual communication, then God is aware of me.*

—The load is too heavy, I said out loud. I beg you to lift this burden from me.

Suddenly, a memory of Enoch's teaching burst upon my mind: how the Messiah rescues his people, how the Messiah delivers those who believe him, how the Messiah saves those who call upon his name. I sensed a stirring of hope within me, as though a seed had been planted and was sprouting. I forced myself to shut out all circumstance of the world and focus my mind on the Messiah, struggling with all my being to reach out to him and draw upon his power to save.

—Deliver us, I cried, raising my eyes to heaven. Have mercy on my wife and me. Our situation is hopeless. I cannot carry the weight of it. I entreat thee to apply thy power and provide a means of deliverance.

—*We will guide you in how to pray and what to pray for.*

I prayed into the night, all night. Whereas I had been wild with grief, my heart now felt calm. A warmth filled me, and I was gently enveloped by a sense of peace. The sounds of the wolves ceased.

When the morning sun breached the eastern horizon, I pushed back the hood of my coat and brushed off the snow that covered us.

A glassy coating covered each limb above us, and frost sifted down from the snowy top, each filigreed branch shimmering in the sunlight. Then I glimpsed it, a single red leaf still clinging stubbornly to a stark branch as if to say, I will not fall; I will not die.

A stirring on my lap drew my attention. As I pulled back the coat, Moriah's eyes fixed upon me.

—Time to go, she said in a weak voice.

I was consumed with gratitude, but was too fatigued to express it. I was too emotionally spent to be surprised. Somewhere in the night, I had received an assurance that all would be well, regardless of the outcome. In a less urgent moment, I might have succumbed to tears, possibly a shout of elation. For now, I looked to heaven and whispered, *thank you.* I would feel joy and rejoice later. What I did feel was relief. I looked at my wife, alive, her strength returning, and I said, You are right, it is time to go home.

I stood on my feet and helped her up. She teetered, grabbed my arm, and said, Wait a moment while I steady myself.

—Are you alright?

—I will be.

—Can you walk?

—I think so.

As I bent down to pick up our belongings, I paused. Moriah asked what was I doing.

—What I can, I said, tearing off a fragment of my coat.

—I don't understand, she said.

—I know, I said. I'm not sure I understand either. But right now I can't stand the thought that one of God's creatures has fallen and no one knows or cares. It's important to me to offer some dignity to one of God's creatures that could easily be forgotten.

My wife did not question my action. We left the tree, its single red leaf still clinging stubbornly to a high branch, while below, there lay the shrouded body of a small, brown bird. We never looked back. By evening, we ascended the mountain and found shelter in a cave where we built a warm fire and ate bread. We counted sixty days between two complete cycles of the moon that came and went while we stayed in the cave and healed. Moriah's recovery was slow, but, together at last, we had plenty of time. When the snow began to melt, we departed the cave and started through the mountains toward our home and family. For the rest of her life, Moriah would walk with a slight limp. We did not discuss her ordeal. For me it was enough that she was still with me and that spring was coming.

a season of healing

℘

—Father! Mother!

Eve's voice breached the calm of morning as Moriah and I entered the City of Enoch. In order to escape the notice of Nod's army, we had braved the river that flowed beneath the western wall of the City, the one place that remained unguarded. When Eve saw us, she dropped her load of wash, hefted a small bundle into her arms, and ran toward us. We hugged each other in a three-way knot of arms and sobbed, unable to talk. We had all wondered if we would see each other again. Amidst our sobbing, I heard a baby cry.

—He's hungry, said Eve.

—Oh, your baby! exclaimed Moriah, her eyes brimming. Look how he's grown! Let me see him!

Eve drew back the blanket from the bundle she held in her arms, revealing a round-headed child with light brown hair and blue eyes.

—He's a boy! Eve said, proudly.

—He has Joshua's coloring, said Moriah, reaching out with a finger and stroking the child's cheek.

—He has his mother's lungs, I added.

Eve laughed.

—May I hold him? I asked.

—Just for a moment. I have to feed him.

The child quieted when I took him from Eve.

—Support his head in the crook of your arm, said Moriah.

—I know. I've held a baby before.

I touched the child's tiny hand, and he grasped my finger.

—He's beautiful, I said.

—His name is Ebanel, said Eve.

—I'm sure that makes his great-grandfather very proud, I said.

Moriah took the baby from my arms. Eve's eyes became teary.

—I cry too much these days, she said.

—Where is the rest of the family? I asked.

—In Benjamin's home. Since the Dananites poured in from the valley and the subsequent siege, we have all had to double up. It's difficult, but nice to be together. Enos and Naomi married. Benjamin performed the ceremony. Enoch was still quite ill at the time.

—Where is he?

—At his home with his family. He is much improved, but still weak.

—Our family would be complete, said Moriah, if only . . .

—If only Miriam were with us, said Eve, completing the thought.

We three looked at each other, the sadness showing in our eyes.

—Her child will be due this summer, Moriah said. Little Rachel will be so excited.

We became quiet. No one mentioned Micah.

—We think Naomi might be expecting! said Eve, suddenly, changing the subject. She has been spending the mornings sick in bed.

—A sure sign, said Moriah. Oh! I've wanted so badly to see her! I want to see my entire family!

As we started for Benjamin's home, I noticed Eve staring at her mother's short, white hair and eyeing her overall appearance. When she shot me a questioning glance, I shook my head. She nodded and remained silent. I supposed Eve had come to the same conclusion I had reached: she was content to have her mother back where she could heal in the company of those who loved her.

Our reunion had exhausted me emotionally. The recent months' experiences had urged tender feelings to the surface. I found myself unable to hold back tears for the smallest of reasons. Seeing Eve, holding her, holding her child, watching Moriah brighten at the sight of our new grandchild evoked emotions in me challenged in intensity and range only by the memory of visiting my father, mother, and son in the paradisiacal world of spirits. When Moriah and I entered Benjamin's home, the reunion was so sweet, I felt my strength would fail me.

—Grandfather! Grandmother! cried Nathaniel. You are alive!

Benjamin's little boy jumped into my arms and squeezed me about the neck. His little brother, Dan, climbed into his grandmother's arms and cuddled against her shoulder. Sarah reached for him, but Moriah said, It's alright! Let me hold him a moment.

Little Deborah began to cry at the attention being given to her brothers, and I reached down and picked her up in my other arm.

—I won't be able to do this if you have any more! I said to Benjamin.

He wrapped his arms about me, and the children and wept. Sarah came to him and held him at the waist. Then, looking at Moriah, she said, We have spent so many days and nights in fasting and prayer for you both.

Enos reached out to embrace his mother, and Naomi took Deborah. Enos had prided himself in being a *man* and seldom had allowed his feelings to show. But holding his mother, he broke down and could not talk for a very long time. She rocked him like a child and stroked his hair.

When Baruch arrived with Esther, his bride, our family was all red eyed. Esther took the baby from Eve, and Joshua said to his father, It's a reunion we hoped for but wondered if we would ever experience.

Baruch understood. He waited until we had regained our composure, then embraced me like a brother and began to cry. Without a word, I knew what his tears meant: he, too, had not expected to see me again.

Enoch arrived with his wife, Anna, and their daughter, Melca. When he embraced me, he said, Thank you. Thank you for my life.

—You would have done the same for me, I said.

—Don't discount what you did, he said. You were willing to take my place and die for me. There can be no greater demonstration of love and courage.

Unlike me, Enoch had always worn his emotions close to the surface. As he expressed his love for me, his voice broke and his eyes overflowed. Soon, we both were quietly crying and holding each other. *I would do it again,* I thought. *I would offer to die for you again.*

That night, Enoch, Baruch, Benjamin, Enos, Joshua, and I sat around a fire.

—How did you escape? I asked Baruch.

—The guards took us a short distance from the prison and dumped us on the refuse heap, just as they had threatened.

—They never became acclimated to bad odors, said Enoch, raising a smile. They dropped us off and ran. I was barely conscious. Baruch waited until they had left, then carried me to the back side of the City. We had no choice, so we braved the cold water and slipped under the wall to the safety of the City.

—How about you, Rabunel? asked Baruch.

I rehearsed the story of my escape.

—Another blessing from God, said Enoch.

We all nodded our agreement.

—The army seems to be divided, said Benjamin, bringing us back to the present. The captains of Nod seem very aggressive, while Saad has actually invited us to be part of their community.

—Their offer is linked to our paying tribute, said Baruch. It is becoming more evident that Saad and Nod have divergent goals for our people. Nod would have us dead, since we are seen as Saad's potential ally; Saad sees us as an ongoing source of free labor and wealth. I think the time is coming when we can expect Nod to move against Saad.

—But Nod will attack us first, said Enoch.

—Have we seen such movement? I asked.

—We have spies, said Benjamin.

—Who? I asked.

—Reuben, for one, said Enos.

—Ishmael's son? You would trust him? I said.

—As much as I trust Naomi.

I felt my face go hot at the thought of Reuben's and Naomi's fathers, Ishmael and Gensek.

Enos said, Both Reuben and Naomi know they are children of fathers who have disgraced their families. For her part, Naomi labors among the sick of our people, taking up where Miriam left off. She thinks of her work as a kind of penance.

—Why? I asked. She has done nothing wrong.

—No. But it is her way of trying to right a wrong perpetrated by her parents. Reuben's motives are similar. He risks his life by spying on Nod's army, and the information he had gathered has been invaluable. He thinks that Nod will strike us within days and then turn on Saad.

—We are no longer safe in these mountains, said Enoch. We must make preparations to leave.

—How? asked Benjamin. Their army is so large and we are so closely guarded. Even if we could escape, how could we move women and children as quickly as their trained forces can pursue?

—We must turn their attention away from us, said Joshua.

All eyes shifted to my son-in-law. Enos seemed to understand his meaning.

—We have two things in our favor, he said, their greed for our lands and their hating each other. If we can escape and leave the City and its wealth intact, they might be content to revel in their spoils. Then, we must find a way to turn them against each other so that they will fight amongst themselves and not against us.

Enoch stood and paced. He stopped, his face brightening with the look of understanding.

—We will have to move quickly, he said. We will only be able to take a little with us.

—You have a plan? I asked.

—God has presented it to my mind. I can see it clearly.

—We are guarded on three sides, said Joshua. How will we escape?

—Through the fourth side, said Enoch.

—How? The river runs under the wall.

—It runs under the wall slowly, said Enoch, and at this time of year the flow is weak. Rabunel and Moriah forged it with little difficulty and without being seen. Where the river flows under the wall, we can dam off a portion with rocks and dirt to allow us a dry passage. On the day of our escape, we will crawl under the wall. From there, it is a straight climb to the tabernacle on the mountainside. We will enter the forest and head southeast toward the sea.

—We will be seen, said Baruch. We cannot hide such numbers.

—Timing and surprise are crucial. We must escape quickly as Nod makes ready to invade, said Enoch. Once inside the gates, they will see we are gone. We will count on their being astonished at our absence and their being anxious to loot the City to buy us time to make for the safety of the mountains. Perhaps they will not immediately pursue us.

—Where will we go? asked Benjamin.

—To my homeland of Cainan, said Enoch. We will be safe there. Cainan lies in a defensible place. It has not been attacked for generations. Adding our numbers to theirs will make an enemy think twice.

—But will we be welcomed there? asked Joshua.

—All your fathers save Adam and Seth live in Cainan, said Enoch. They are family.

Having agreed to the general plan for our escape, we fleshed out the details into the night, making and revising a list of scaled-back provisions that we would need to take. For speed, we would have to travel lightly. We would take with us one part in ten, a *tithe*, Enoch called it, promising that God would multiply our obedience a hundredfold. The Shepherds were to quietly prepare the people.

Baruch said, Our major obstacle is neither Saad nor Nod. It is our own people.

Besides Ishmael and Gensek, others of the City of Enoch had deserted us to embrace Saad's invitation to become part of their society. Of those who remained, many still resented having to open their homes to the Dananites.

Baruch continued, Our people are weary of the siege. We cannot be sure of their reaction to sacrifice more. If we ask them to risk their lives in an escape attempt, I fear they will not go, or worse, some might defect and endanger us all.

—Can they have forgotten the many times God has saved us from similar difficulties? I asked.

—They are slow to remember, said Enoch, but we must offer them the choice.

—With Micah, Ishmael, and Gensek gone, I said, we stand a better chance of success.

—Ishmael and Gensek are dead, said Enos.

I stopped and stared at him.

—They are dead?

—Yes. When Enoch and Baruch escaped from the prison, Simeon and Gad blamed Ishmael and Gensek, who were responsible for the prison guards. Ishmael and Gensek suffered death by fire in view of the entire army—as an example, I suppose.

The news upset me. I put my hand on my head and tried to think.

—Reuben witnessed his father's death? I asked.

—Yes. But, he could not make himself known. To reveal himself would have put his own life in danger and have exposed him as a spy. As for Naomi, she has mourned deeply for her father, and she has redoubled her efforts among the sick of our people.

—Do you know the fate of Micah and Miriam? I asked.

—We haven't seen them since Micah tried to usurp control of the City.

A long moment of silence ensued. For my part, I considered man's vain ambitions, how those ambitions turn on him when he seeks to fight against God and his people. I remembered my father's and Enoch's words, *Pride is the universal sin, the great vice, the stumbling block of Zion.*

—I have a plan, said Joshua, standing suddenly.

We all turned toward him, wondering what he meant.

—I know how we can keep our intention to leave secret and our plans from those who might betray us. We will instruct the Shepherds to tithe the people—food, clothing, things they can carry, herds they can move quickly—and bring it to the temple. The Shepherds will say that the provisions are to be given to the poor—a truthful statement since the provisions will be kept for the people themselves.

—I am still concerned that we will be leaving almost everything behind, said Benjamin. We might be able to survive only three or four days in the wilderness.

—Yes, said Joshua. We will have to rely on God to provide, just as we have done before.

—This is the plan endorsed for us by God, said Enoch. We have his promise that he will multiply our sacrifice, and we will never be found wanting. When we gather at the temple, we will present the people with this plan; then we will immediately embark. By leaving most everything behind, we will ensure that our enemies have plenty to gorge themselves on and a reason to fight among themselves.

—For our people, it could be a time of division, I said.

Enoch said, Such a decision comes to every person. I am sorry we have to impose this difficulty on them. But in order to save them, there is no other way. Still, we must understand the risks: some may be angry with us; some may rebel; others may defect out of fear. Regardless, we must depart. We cannot look back, even knowing that those who waver might be destroyed.

A sudden rush of sadness filled me. As I gazed upon the faces of those in the room, I sensed that their sentiments were similar. It was one thing to make a plan; it was another to execute it. None of us would have chosen to lose a soul, but we all knew that casualties accompanied the making of an important choice. Our people were about to be tested, individually and collectively. How they chose would have far-reaching consequences. We, who were planning the exodus, had experienced many hardships and had resolved to side with God. For us, the journey would be inconvenient, but to our people, especially those who struggled with their commitments, the adversity might seem overwhelming. We were bound to lose some. How many, no one could guess.

༄

We received daily reports from Reuben. On the twelfth day, our spies informed us that they detected a movement to congregate the troops at the front gate of the City. We quickly summoned the Shepherds to call the people to the temple. We had blocked off at the section of the river that flowed under the western wall, creating a gap big enough for a large man to negotiate.

Reuben and Enos had implemented a plan to pit Saad and Nod against each other. Counting on the two armies' greed, Reuben and Enos planned on displaying the wealth of the City in obvious locations so that the Saad's and Nod's appetite for pillaging would win out over their desire to pursue us. The hope was to create a frenzy of competition between the two factions.

The morning of the assembly arrived cold and wet. Night rains had left the ground wet and the air cold. A haze had settled on the valley, obscuring the view. *This could work to our favor,* I remembered thinking. Still, I wished to have one more unobstructed look at our beautiful city.

As the people gathered to the temple, there were many questions. The Shepherds offered vague answers. The temple itself, yet unfinished, had fallen into disrepair. As I regarded it, I mourned the fact that it had never been used for its intended purpose. Once the hope and symbol of our faith, the incomplete edifice where we had hoped to walk and talk with God now stood an empty shell, not the house of God, but the home of birds and vermin. Somewhere along the way, we had become distracted. Now, we would have to wait for Cainan to experience such blessings. Long years lay between us and the opportunity to once again undertake such a holy work.

When the Shepherds had seated their flocks by families and had sent word that all were in attendance, Enoch stood before the people and offered a prayer to God. He asked that we would be courageous, that we would remember our covenants with God and each other, that we could recall the times past when God had delivered us. Then he prayed for protection as we journeyed. When he ended, a low murmur rolled through the congregation. Heads popped up; questioning looks were exchanged. I noted expressions of both fear and excitement. Enoch stood on his feet.

—We have been a people these many years, he began. We, who fled from Shum, remember how God preserved us. You, who were rescued from Danan, remember your miraculous deliverance by God's direct intervention. We all have been preserved to this point by the grace of God, but not because of our worthiness. In our poverty and our humility, we were blessed. When we had no choice but to turn to God, he was merciful and heard our pleas. Then we came into this valley, became rich, and began to shift our allegiance and dependence to our possessions. Now we see the precarious situation of the man who seeks to find security elsewhere than God. He commanded us to build a house where we could receive of his power and counsel with him, a place of worship. The temple was to be a blessing to us, not to satisfy any need of the Almighty. Because we were not obedient in completing this task, and because we failed to show charity to our brethren, the Dananites, we now find ourselves subject to our enemies. But God is ever merciful and will yet free us if we now humble ourselves before him. He has heard our cries. He knows that many among us are brokenhearted for past misdeeds. For these, God extends a reprieve from your sorrows. He offers a deliverance.

Enoch paused then and scanned the temple grounds. His countenance saddened as he seemed to contemplate the beauty of the place and his love for it. As he stood silently gazing on the scene, we in the congregation looked toward our homes. Although our view was clouded, one could imagine the panorama. No more beautiful and peaceful place had existed on earth. Our City had been a land of promise like the garden place of creation. The human effort that had gone into establishing the City of Enoch exceeded my ability to measure. The quantity of living and loving that the place had housed, the drama that had been played out in its borders from the time we entered this valley were sums I could not fathom. Around me, I saw people wipe their eyes as arms were placed about neighbors' shoulders. I had been so caught up in the plans for leaving that I had not considered the emotions that would attend our departure. Enoch's voice turned us back to him.

—Another home lies before us, he said. God has shown it to me. There, we will build up the kingdom of God. As we learn to serve one another selflessly, then by and by, that new home will become God's home, for we are his home and he is ours. We will be Zion. But first we must leave this, our beautiful city, and journey to Cainan, where we will unite with our family there and find rest for a season.

—When shall we go? cried out a man.

Suddenly, sounds of activity began at the City gates. The entire assembly turned toward the commotion. Reuben and Enos came running.

—It has begun, cried Enos. The armies of Saad and Nod are gathering to attack.

Enoch raised his hands and quieted the assembly.

—Now, he said. The time to go is now.

Baruch stood and shouted out to the Shepherds, Pull your people together and follow us!

Enoch took Anna's and Melca's hands and turned toward the far wall of the City. Baruch followed with Esther. I motioned to my family. Some of the people stood as if frozen in place, frightened, confused. The Shepherds urged their flocks forward and to not delay. Some people stopped to debate. The Shepherds warned them and moved along quickly. Within moments of Enoch's command, the people began to divide: some stood paralyzed; others began to walk back toward their homes; the remainder, which was most of the population of the City, followed Enoch. At the wall, where the river had been dammed, leaving the ground dry, was a gap half the height of a man. Enoch and his wife and daughter ducked beneath it. Others followed his lead, slipping underneath the wall through the gap, past the barricaded river, and out toward freedom. Eve looked back and began to weep for those who were remaining behind. Joshua took her hand and said, Keep your eyes forward. There is nothing to be done. We must move on.

From the wall, we climbed to the tabernacle. At the summit, we heard the commotion in the City like the sound of war. With the fog we could see nothing, but assumed the armies of Nod and Saad had begun to clash over the spoils of the City. By afternoon, we who had chosen to follow Enoch had all crossed over the mountains and had angled southeastward toward Cainan.

Rest was not a part of our itinerary. We traveled from early morning into late evening. We never looked back. We would not stop until we had reached the threshold of summer. Our journey was to be a time of reflection, repentance, recommitment to covenants. Once again, hardship forced unity. I saw people shouldering others' loads, mothers carrying other mothers' babies, children helping push carts that carried the infirm, the old placed on litters and pulled by men and boys, adolescents driving cattle, goats, sheep.

Enos and Reuben were the last to leave the City. When they caught up to us, they reported to a Fathers Council.

—The fog held back the army for some time, said Enos. We supposed they didn't want to attack for fear that we could easily defend ourselves in the mist. We saw the army of Nod triple in size, with many new soldiers coming in from the pass. We had heard that Azazel himself had arrived to personally oversee the invasion. We later found that it was true. When the sun emerged, the army came forward—to open gates. As Enoch had instructed, we had lit torches on the walls and had opened the gates wide as if to welcome wanted guests. Reuben and I tried to convince those who had stayed behind to escape while they had a chance. When they saw the army approaching the open gates, they huddled in a far corner of the City until they were found and begged for mercy. We do not know their fate. Reuben and I watched as the army entered, only a small contingent at first. Certainly, with the gates open, they suspected a trap. By morning the torches had died out and an eerie quiet had settled on the City, no people, no noise, empty except for riches left behind. They paused then, the whole of them having walked inside, and stood staring at our beautiful buildings of white stone. Then, finding the City abandoned, they began to pillage and claim property. We had placed valuables in strategic spots that they couldn't miss. Their greed was insatiable. As the infighting began, they raided our Storehouse, built fires in the streets, and roasted lamb and beef. Some buildings were torched, but most were seized by the strongest of the armies, who marked homes as theirs and stood guard to protect their claims. They competed with each other for the spoils. Then Azazel arrived in great ceremony and declared the City renamed after him and the temple a sanctuary of the Watchers.

Having heard Reuben's and Enos's report, I was once more astonished by the remarkable ability of God to save those who love him. It was a miracle that I would always keep close to my heart. An equally astonishing miracle was that three out of every four people who had followed Enoch were of the people of Danan.

THE WRITINGS OF RABUNEL

As we neared Cainan, I finally allowed to feel safe, and I made a decision to pray for the purpose of instruction. I had felt a spiritual emptiness because, over the last months, my prayers had mostly centered on pleas for deliverance, even revenge on those who had betrayed me. I wanted to relax from urgencies. I longed for the sweet experience of receiving new information. One morning, I slipped away from camp to a secluded area to commune with God.

Most of the ambitions of man are vain. Man is ever learning but seldom able to come to a knowledge of the truth. How great would be man's happiness if he would make this discovery: this present world is not his home. It is neither his origin nor his destiny. He is a stranger here. The seed of his existence was sown countless ages past, in realms of glory. Divinity is planted in his being, for God is his parent. Thus, the future of man is a grand view. But man tends to content himself by setting up camp in this temporary world, unwilling to look up toward a glorious horizon. He puts his effort into building his kingdom and mansion here in a world that was intended to be transitory, a place of journey, not destination. Here, man should prepare for eternity. Here, man should gain experience. Here, man should realize that rewards are earned but seldom delivered. Here, man must work, but the greatest work he can perform is bringing souls to the Messiah—first himself, next his family, then those of his associates. Is not this the work of God—to save man? Can man have a greater work than that of his God?

I asked, *How shall I know if I am doing the work of God?*

When a man selflessly serves another he does the work of God.

I asked, *How shall I know my God?*

Look into the face of the one you have served, and you will see the face of God.

mercy, not judgment

 CB

—Nod has gathered an army to pursue us, said Enos. Their hatred for Enoch is insatiable.

My son and Reuben had been following Nod's movements Nod since our escaped. Because of our numbers, we had left ample evidence of our route and direction. We had feared Nod's attention would turn to us once they had spoiled our city and defeated Saad, even while hoping they would be satisfied with their conquests and remain with their newly gotten lands. It was not meant to be.

—How large is their force? I asked my son. How much time do we have?

—Two thousand armed men. They could overtake us by tomorrow night.

Enos and Reuben delivered their report to Enoch and me as we stood on a precipice overlooking our camp. Enoch gazed out upon the people with a look of concern.

—After three days' running they are very tired and nearly out of food, I said.

—It is me Nod wants, said Enoch. If I give myself up to them, they may leave our people alone.

—Every man in the City would fight to protect you, I said. They have already risked their lives to follow you. They would not let you give yourself up.

Enoch put his hand on mine.

—We have some time, he said. Tell the people to sleep tonight, and we will gather them together in the morning.

I did not sleep that night. I doubted that Enoch did either. Instead, I tossed and turned until Moriah asked me to leave and take a walk. Wrapping myself in a blanket, I lit a torch and strode to the fringe of the camp and back up to the precipice. Enoch was there.

—I couldn't sleep, I said as I approached him.

—Nor I, he said. Do you want to sit down?

I nodded and folded my legs beneath me as I took a place at his side. I planted the torch in the ground, and we warmed our hands on it. We sat silently. We had known each other for so long and loved each other so much that quiet communication was often enough. I admired this man of God. Enoch had the ability to plant in men's hearts an ideal, to give them a vision of their potential. To urge a man to change, Enoch depended on persuasion, love, and the power of ideas. After introducing a concept to the mind of another, he trusted in the power of that concept and the mind of the individual to produce positive results. He inspired men to greatness and to embrace a cause. He had the ability to start men on a path and leave them running as if on their own power. To Enoch, the one thing of supreme importance was the unique human personality. To perfect that personality, or to make it like God's, Enoch felt that every external influence had to contribute to the process of progression—the earth, governments, educational institutions, philosophies, other people—everything had to be made to reflect the attributes, character, life, and society of God.

To his followers, Enoch's attraction lay partly in his dynamic personality. He preached ceaselessly the Messiah's concept of the abundant life that he had incorporated as a fundamental principle in the Zion community. The abundant life came by the regeneration of mankind one person at a time. His method was to patiently work with people until the spiritual powers within them were released to converge with the spiritual forces without.

He was a complete man. His mind embraced the entirety of the human experience, practical and theoretical. Nothing was too trivial or too large to not occupy his thoughts, from the minutia of the elements that make up the earth to the complex revolutions of the heavens. Things of man and God—he could discuss them all.

Enoch possessed an inordinate zeal for education and a strict belief that a Zion society could not be achieved without both the training of the intellect and the teachings of the Messiah. He believed that man was created to dress the earth, cultivate his mind, and glorify his God. Man was saved no faster than he acquired knowledge, and that the man who did not get knowledge would be brought into captivity. He stated that belief in God without education quickly degenerates into superstition, and that education without belief in God becomes a monstrous tool.

Enoch never dissipated his energies in focusing on misfortunes of the past. He lived in the present with his eyes on the future. In solving problems, he followed four steps: he identified a vital need, worked through the problem in his own mind, consulted the written words of God, then prayed for inspiration.

His mind was fertile ground for God to plant the vision of Zion. In that ideal society, Enoch first foresaw that man had no inherent right to own anything, let alone snatch or deal things from others because he was stronger, more far-sighted, or more cunning. Rather, man was a steward and accountable to God for what he had. Enoch believed that every man was entitled to eat, have clothing, live in adequate shelter, provided he was willing to work for these necessities. He believed that the collective system that must displace individualism could not ignore human nature, but must work with it to the extent that it did not interfere with human welfare. He believed that each community that comprised the society should be an independent unit, having its own Shepherds, management, and a storehouse.

Furthermore, Enoch believed that the entire society must rest upon the secure foundation of the teachings of the Messiah, the primary factor in the development of individual character.

—I love this people, said Enoch.

—They are not afraid to die, I said. In a way it would be easier to die than to continue living in such a wicked world.

—But that is not what will happen. God knows we would die for him. The greater challenge is to live for him.

—What shall we do?

—There is great power in asking, said Enoch. We have asked for deliverance before; we will ask again. God does not change.

—But perhaps we have. Maybe we have moved ourselves beyond his blessings.

—It is true this people made mistakes, but look at them now: contrite of heart, humble, ready to be taught, willing to sacrifice, anxious to change. If one of your children, who had done wrong, came to you, his father, asking for help to solve a difficult problem, would you withhold your love or assistance?

—No, I would just want his assurance that he had learned from his lesson and was trying to improve.

In saying so, I had answered my question. I had too many evidences that God had always loved us and had the interest and power to help. Mercy was what he extended to us, not harsh judgment. If we had learned from our mistakes and desired to change, that would be enough. His help was available for the asking.

—How is Moriah? Enoch asked.

—Much improved. Her limp is not so pronounced, and her hair is growing out. She is even beginning to like the color.

—How about her mental state? Does she talk about her ordeal?

—No. She cries sometimes, but is silent on the subject. I don't ask.

—And you? Do you have feelings?

—Of course. But I try not to show them. I do not want her to relive the experience so that I can feel better. I am trying to keep myself focused on the present. Having her back and seeing that she is healing is enough for now.

—But someday you will have to heal, too.

—That will have to come later. My efforts are for Moriah, now.

ಬ

As the people gathered to the center of the camp, Reuben ran toward me with his report.

—The army of Nod will be upon us by midafternoon.

Enoch received the news solemnly and raised his hands.

—God has promised us a land of promise. That destination does not lie in the path of death or re-captivity. We will trust his promise as though it had come to pass, and we will place ourselves in the hands of God for our protection.

—Let us take up swords! cried one man.

—Would you use our women and children as shields? said Enoch. No, we will not take up weapons. Rather, let us put our effort into petitioning our God to fight our battle.

Kneeling at an altar of stones that we had constructed, Enoch raised his voice in prayer. All in the assembly quieted and knelt on the ground, our hearts drawn out to God. I was amazed that Enoch spent considerable time giving thanks for blessings received. He acknowledged God as the source of all good gifts: our food, clothing, shelter, health, families, friends. He expressed, in a way I had not considered, our unworthiness—not that we were nothing, but that we were nothing in strength and worthiness compared to God. We were dependent upon God for our lives, everything that sustained us, each breath and step that we took. Our thoughts and ways were not God's, and we were in no position to counsel him; rather, we sought to align ourselves with his will. Enoch said that we would accept God's deliverance and view it as a miracle in any form that God chose. Then he asked for deliverance in the name of the Messiah. He pled for the gift of hope and faith that we could have the courage to wait upon God for the answer. I had never heard such a prayer. Itself, it was an instruction in how to petition heaven—how to ask and receive blessings.

Enoch told us to remain praying, individually and as families, throughout the morning and into the afternoon. Then, he guided a small group of leaders to a precipice that overlooked our camp and the pass through the mountains that led to it. As Reuben had predicted, in the midafternoon, the army of Nod emerged and began its ascent toward us. When they saw us standing waiting for them, they raised their swords and gave out a great cry of battle. We stood firm, silent. The only sounds were those of the advancing host. Enoch stood quietly watching. Then, as though light burst upon his face, he turned and said, God has pronounced his judgment.

He raised a hand as he cried out, By the power of the Messiah I command the elements of the earth to hide the hateful intent of our enemies and to hedge up their way.

At first there was silence, a quiet more deep than I had ever experienced. It was as though heaven and earth stood still and time stopped in its forward march. No movement of air. No noise. No visible motion. The army of Nod had halted. A foreboding thickened the atmosphere like some feel before an earthquake. Then came random laments from the army below. A piercing crack, like lightening rending the air, shattered the silence. We, on the precipice, fell back. The army collapsed as the earth quaked beneath them. Then, in simultaneous motions, the ground on which the army stood and the elements above them exploded, creating a massive chasm into which the mighty of Nod fell and were buried under a wall of rocks and debris.

As if with one voice, the entire assembly of Enoch's people cheered. The sound rivaled that of the quaking earth. Moriah grabbed my arm as we stood stunned at the destruction of our enemy and our people's celebration. Enoch was on his knees and did not immediately move. Soon, the people quieted and the prophet stood. He was weeping. I had witnessed this scene before as Enoch mourned for his defeated enemies of Shum. He had not changed. He loved all men, even those who wronged him, with godly love, and he sorrowed with godly sorrow.

—How can you rejoice, he cried, when so many of God's children have fallen?

ultimate deliverance

Ↄ

Stopping near the eastern sea beneath windswept cliffs, we camped three years before turning south to the land of Cainan. It was a time of regrouping, a season of recommitting to the principles of faith, repentance, covenant-making, obedience, to be taught and sanctified by the Holy Spirit. We called the place Enoch's Camp, harking back to our first settlement in the mountains above Shum. We enjoyed the different environment, for few of us had seen the sea or been acquainted with the fauna and vegetation that thrived there. Most of our company had never tasted salt on their lips or sampled ocean fish. Gulls were a familiar sight, but we had only witnessed them raiding our farms of freshly sown seeds. Now, we marveled at their agility, riding wind currents, diving into foamy waves for surface fish. The sea and its shoreline offered a wealth of life and natural splendor. Each morning I walked with Moriah along the beaches. She loved feeling hot sand on her bare feet and turning her face into the ocean breeze to smell the salt air.

During our three-year stay, Eve and Joshua's son, Ebanel, was joined by a little brother, Seth. He also acquired a cousin named Ruth from Enos and Naomi. As though they would not be outdone, Benjamin and Sarah announced that they would add a fourth child to their family in autumn time. Sarah had entered the queasy stage and was surrounded by mothers who both pitied and envied her plight. I loved being a grandfather. I loved spoiling the grandchildren, then handing them back to their parents. My own children accused me of being too lenient with the grandchildren's bad behavior. *I hadn't been that way with them, they would say, and the reason the grandchildren liked visiting Grandfather was because he fed them honeycomb and let them get away with everything.*

Baruch and Esther had their own surprise, a new baby daughter born at the close of winter, a beautiful, black-eyed, dark-haired girl who looked like her mother. Our family would have been complete had Miriam been with us. That was a sadness none of us could erase.

We remained at Enoch's Camp three years because Enoch said we were not ready to enter Cainan. We were to stay at our seaside camp long enough to recommit to and live the doctrines of the Messiah. In the camp, we established a tabernacle in which Enoch officiated. There, we made our sacrifices and sought to sanctify ourselves so that we could commune with our God. The Dananites among us seemed to possess a natural spirituality that had a leavening effect on our entire community. Over time, they became exemplary teachers to the families in our group. As was once the practice, Shepherds assigned teachers to care for and instruct each family, and soon marvelous progress was made: familial relationships improved, contentions diminished, poverty and ignorance lessened, love of God and mankind increased. We as a people became confident in our faith in God. We were taught that he was aware of us, cared for us, had the power to help us through any circumstance. In our assemblies of the entire population, Enoch taught us to re-prioritize our lives so that only half our days were dedicated to providing for our support and the balance was for education, culture, strengthening family ties, serving friends, and worshiping God. Our lifestyle brought us renewed peace, and that peace had come through simplicity and trying to live as we knew we should.

One afternoon, in the second year of our camp, Enoch called on Moriah and me in our tent. The look on his face was serious.

—What is it? I asked.

—I've had a visitor, he said.

Moriah stood, as if she'd had a premonition. I regarded her, then Enoch.

—Who? I asked him.

—Micah.

I gasped. Moriah stared into the distance.

—I-I don't know what to say, I said, standing myself, pacing.

—Challenges come in unusual packages, said Enoch, thoughtfully, an expression of concern on his face.

—What does he want? I asked.

—To be forgiven. He and his family want to become part of us again.

Enoch gazed at Moriah and me. I looked at my wife, whose face had gone pale.

—How can we trust him? I asked Enoch.

—I had a long talk with him. I'm convinced of his repentance. When you see him, you won't recognize him. He looks very old and frail. He has paid a terrible price, and his path back has been difficult.

—How is Miriam? asked Moriah.

—I haven't seen her, said Enoch. Micah did not want to subject her to any adverse feelings, so she and the children have remained outside the camp.

I pinched the bridge of my nose, closed my eyes, and reached for a question.

—How old would Rachel be? I asked Moriah. Seven? Eight? I must be losing my memory.

—The baby would be three now, Moriah said.

—Her name is Gabrel, said Enoch, and they have two more, twin boys.

I was stunned, unable to speak. Moriah stood motionless. Enoch seemed to wait for us to comment.

—What did they name the boys? asked Moriah, finally.

—They named them Rabunel and Baruch.

I shot a look at Moriah and felt the rage well within me.

—I don't care! I said. It's all too little too late!

Moriah took my hand and looked deeply into my eyes.

—Miriam is our daughter, she said, and Micah is her husband.

She turned to Enoch and said, Of course we will accept them.

Enoch's eyes filled with tears. He looked upon Moriah as if in regarding her, he was revisiting her ordeal. After a long, silent pause, he gave a slight nod and said, I'll bring in Micah now.

—He's here? I asked.

—Yes. Just outside. Micah requested to meet with you first. Tomorrow, he wants to plead forgiveness from all the people. Shall I bring him in?

Moriah and I looked at each other. She turned to Enoch and offered a slight nod.

When Micah stepped into the room, Moriah took my arm and squeezed. My heart pounded and raced in my chest. He offered a small bow. I stood erect and stared at him.

Enoch was correct about Micah's appearance. He seemed half the man I had known. Once tall and strong, he was now bent, thin, his hair gray and sparse. He trembled inside ragged clothing. He glanced at me with black, hollow eyes, then looked down. The first thing he said was, Will you help me regain my soul?

I did not answer. Moriah did not look at me. A hot blade of emotion sliced through my brain at Micah's question. I dropped my eyes. Enoch stood silently, awaiting my response. Moriah reached for my hand and squeezed it. Then she stepped forward, her eyes brimming with tears, and took Micah into her arms as if he were her child. The big man broke down sobbing, went to his knees, and said, I'm so sorry. I'm so sorry.

As I watched the scene, the whole of my experience raced through my mind. I relived each abuse, every betrayal. I remembered every emotion. The memory of holding my dying wife, bruised, malnourished, senseless from abuse, burst upon my brain. I recalled every oath I had made to hate this man. I looked at Enoch, finally, and said, I cannot.

Then I rushed past him, past Moriah, past Micah, out into the evening air, sprinting down the shoreline toward distant cliffs. I climbed, my face streaked with tears, then fell exhausted into the grass. When I could cry no more, I rolled to my side, came to an elbow and determined to remain there to wait out the night.

The sea, red from the setting sun, lapped a cadence of soft waves onto sandy beaches. The sun became a fiery ball that appeared to sink in the deep water on the far horizon. A single osprey hovered overhead, seeking a last meal before darkness came. I made a fire and wrapped myself in my tunic. Alone, consumed by hate, I stared into the flames and sought for answers. I had lived for revenge. Letting the feeling go was like giving up an old companion. Revenge had given me a cause when my life was shattered. It had provided me a reason for living, albeit the least noble to which a man can be dedicated.

Thoughts of revenge can keep a man alive, I thought. *It may be the worst of objectives, but who can deny its power?*

I shuddered when I thought of Micah and of forgiveness and mercy. I recalled a night in the dead of winter when I had lain under a bare tree on a desolate prairie, holding my dying wife and praying over her. It was mercy I wanted then. When the weight had grown too heavy to carry, I sought relief. I had prayed for a miracle, for the Messiah to intervene, lift the burden, heal us every whit. When I knew that Moriah would live, I remembered the profound gratitude I felt for the Messiah, what awe I had for his power to rescue those who trust him. At the time I thought my affliction lay in the deepest abyss and approached the most impossible of circumstances. But mercy had come, and having experienced it, I recalled dedicating myself to knowing the Messiah, to bringing my family and others to him. At that moment, filled with gratitude, I could not endure the idea that anyone should suffer as had my wife and I. But how could I have known then that my desire was finite and conditional? Had I considered the boundaries of my gratitude, I would have found that I wished the Messiah to extend mercy to everyone except Micah.

I began to tremble. I did not want to admit that such duality existed within me, one man inclined to good, another to evil. I suddenly understood that Micah's pain was much worse than my own and that what had happened between Micah and me could be—had to be—turned over to God. In the end, all that mattered was whether I was right with God. And I knew I was not. I fell on my knees and implored God to exterminate the wicked man within me and root him from my soul forever.

—I don't want to be that evil man, I cried. But where can I find peace?

As I pled for help to forgive Micah, I searched myself for a capacity I knew I did not have. I had no power to conjure the feeling of peace. I had no ability to summon the attribute of mercy.

—I am a slave to the nature of my flesh, I said. That which I would choose to do, I cannot, but that which I hate, I do. Where is hope for man when his desire to do good is ever hindered by the weakness of his flesh? Who can quell the war within him—the spirit that would choose right and the body that yields so easily to wrong?

I knew myself; I could not lie. The natural man within me wanted justice—heavy, indifferent, cold justice. That part of me wanted justice to fall upon Micah and bury him so deep that mercy could never find him. Payment, that is what the natural man desired, Micah's long, hard payment. As though that wicked man within me were speaking, I seemed to hear, *Why should I be required to extend mercy? In this world mercy is unnatural. Does not everything in this world migrate to payment? Sin? Sickness? Imposition? Weakness? Payments and pain—these are the order of this world. Why should I give mercy when justice is required?*

Exhausted, I lay on my side and rested my head on an outstretched arm. I drew my tunic up about me and watched the dying glow of embers of my fire while I tried to clear my mind. The salty sea wind flooded my senses. I could taste it, smell it, feel it on my skin.

Above me, the wide, moonless sky was filled with myriad stars as if the entirety of eternity had opened up before me. I rolled onto my back and considered the view, suddenly feeling very small and insignificant.

—Please help me, I prayed.

I remembered the beauty and peace of the world of spirits and longed to be there. I considered the yearning I had expressed to my father: *I wish I could feel that peace always.*

What is stopping you? he had asked. *The primary difference between our two worlds is that we here have chosen to live a better way. It comes down to choice. If we can do it here, you can do it there.*

I now wondered if I believed it as much as I sought it. Then the thought came into my mind, *Is it possible for God to ignore a heartfelt plea or for a father to forget his child? I have not forgotten you. I never have. I know you better than you think, and I understand.*

—I cannot pretend mercy, I said. I would show it if I could, but I do not feel it.

I know. So you must obtain it from a source beyond you. Charity is a gift.

—What shall I do?

You know what to do.

I did know what to do, but I hesitated, pondering whether or not I had the courage to let go of my bitterness and bid it farewell. Had I grown so comfortable with thoughts of revenge that cutting them from my character would be like amputating a member of my body? Did I really desire to espouse the attributes of God more than pamper my pride? Did I truly believe that Micah was worth saving? That, regardless of his actions, we were loved equally by God? That God would reach out to Micah with the same enthusiasm he had to me? By not getting past the anger, I was distancing myself from God. He had extended me mercy when I was not deserving. I would need his mercy again. I knew that ultimate deliverance comes from one's extending charity and mercy. I went to my knees.

—I know how weighty the demands of justice can be, I began my prayer. I know how those demands can crush the soul. But when I have cried out for help, thou hast been merciful and delivered me. I never want to be beyond the Messiah's mercy. I desire instead to rule my life in such a way that I may always be wrapped in the arms of his mercy. I know it is not possible to obtain mercy while withholding it from another. I would give it if I had it, but I cannot lie to God. I cannot pretend mercy. It is a gift. Bless me that I may be filled with *this* love.

Instantly, I had a sensation like warm fluid being poured into my body, filling me, forcing out every resentment, replacing hatred with sincere concern for the welfare of every son and daughter of God. The thought that any person should be caught in the press of justice caused me to tremble. My whole soul was drawn to those who struggled, and suddenly I knew I could never view people in the same way again. Finally, as a woman who has travailed in hard childbirth, I felt relief. I discovered that my whole body was wet with perspiration. I unclinched my hands, sat back, and began to laugh. I was shocked at my reaction. At length, I lay on my back and gazed up into the heavens. The stars appeared so close that I imagined I could reach out and gather them in. The moon appeared round and orange and dipped toward the horizon. I was struck with the idea of my being a part of it all, that somehow everything existed for me. It was not an egotistical thought, just fact, and I was humbled by the unspeakable love of God for his children. I considered it all, tranquil at last, filled with gratitude, and, exhausted, fell asleep.

In the morning Enoch convened a conference of the people. Micah had asked to speak to them. I stood at the fringe of the congregation, hidden. I marveled that the Prophet was so quick to forgive. After Enoch's abuse at the hand of Micah, he had reason to hate. But Enoch had always possessed a vision of people that allowed him to see in them a potential for good, something worth reclaiming. He forgave freely, never counting personal cost in extending mercy. I did not know how he had come by that ability, but I appreciated that it had come at a price.

Enoch lifted his voice to the people, saying, Let us remember how each of us has faltered and fallen short in the eyes of God.

I watched to see how the people would react. All of them, every one, had been betrayed by Micah. They had suffered at his hands, being driven from homes, some beaten, others abused. Would their memory be short like Enoch's or long like mine? Enoch brought Micah forward. A low murmur filled the congregation. Enoch stepped back, and Micah stood alone, gazing out over the assembly.

—The most beautiful sight I have seen, Micah said.

His voice broke. When he composed himself, he continued, I thought I would never make it back. Now, if you will have me, it is my intention to stay and never depart, for the least place among you is greater than the most exalted place this world has to offer. I realize that now. I have done wrong. I know it. You know it. God knows it. I have nothing of value to offer by way of penance except a broken heart. If you decide against me, then I beg you to at least allow my family a home with you, for they have done nothing wrong. The deeds were mine alone. If you desire, I will leave your company forever. But please restore them to your midst.

I had not heard silence as I heard it that day. I sensed each person struggling, as had I, with the bright memories of Micah's treachery. Some stared at him, others gazed at the ground. Then, without warning, my wife climbed the platform where Micah stood, went to him, her limp obvious, and took both his hands in hers. Then she turned to the people. Her hair was snowy white, her eyes wet. She looked small and delicate next to him, but she straightened and said with a strong voice, This is my daughter's husband, my family, my son!

All eyes in the congregation brimmed, but no one spoke out. I felt a charge of apprehension; then, with a deep breath, I bowed my head and made my way to the platform. As I climbed it, I was aware that the attention of the people had fallen upon me. I did not look at Micah until I came near to him. Then, face to face, I fixed my eyes on his. In his face I saw the pain of a long journey. His look was that of a man beaten, wanting to be hopeful but feeling that such hope was out of reach. Without speaking, he seemed to plead with me. I was suddenly filled with my former love for the man. I gave him a slight nod, put my hand on his shoulder, and turning him toward the assembly, I said, Behold, my friend!

The Writings of Rabunel

It had been my constant prayer and the great desire of my heart to hear and see as did Enoch. I spent the night in prayer, seeking to know God and receive a view of our future. We were to enter Cainan on the morrow. When the morning star faded, the sun's rising brought with it a brightness of information. It saturated my mind, and I wrote as fast as my hand could interpret the words.

Rabunel, my son, you will prosper in Cainan and multiply in number. When you leave, your children will have grandchildren. All of you, the people of Cainan included, will follow Enoch southward to a promised land, a warm place of temperate climate and fertile soil. You will settle there with your families and flocks and herds, and you will call the place Zion—the pure in heart. Enoch will be your king and priest. In that same year, he will have a son whom he will name Methuselah. Enoch's son will become a mighty prophet and preach to the people of the world for over nine hundred years, including several hundred years with his grandson Noah.

Over the course of time, Zion will grow in fame and become the envy of the world. That envy will draw the attention of your enemies. They will attack you, but your confidence in God will become strong, and he will fight your battles and preserve you. You will build a temple in Zion, and you, Rabunel, will be in charge. There, at the center of Zion, God will make his abode. You will learn to walk and talk with him. As your population increases, you will build other temples and become a true society of priests.

For nearly four centuries, Zion will exist upon the earth, and many people will come into your borders seeking refuge from an ever more violent and wicked world. You will accept them with a covenant of peace. In addition, you will send emissaries from Zion out into the world to gather in those who desire to know the Messiah and to live according to his laws. Tens of thousands will flock to you, and Zion will extend its boundaries. Beauty, education, harmony, love, peace, righteousness will make up the foundation of Zion. Its pillars will be service and revelation, the arch sanctification, the keystone individual covenant. As Zion grows in righteousness, the world will grow more wicked. *The primary perpetrators will be the Watchers, who will continue to practice their secret ways in an attempt to wage war against God and corrupt the earth. The Watchers' offspring, the giants, will harass good people everywhere and wage war on the nations. In time, the whole world will become violent, and the only place of refuge will be Zion.*

the consummate gift of seeing and hearing

CB

I considered what I had written and thought back on our history. From the time of Shum, through all our trials, during our journeys and the establishment of the City of Enoch, I had been Enoch's right hand. I had supervised the construction of the temple; I had traveled to many lands preaching the words of the Messiah; I had helped manage the City. Through it all, I had never ceased to be amazed at Enoch's extraordinary gifts. In my mind, I caught glimpses of his future. He would become even more energetic than he had been in his younger years. His skills as a writer would become unsurpassed. He would see in vision the entire history of the world. He would found schools for learning sciences, art, and the words of God. He would draw the plans for Zion and oversee its construction. He would travel extensively, raising his voice in defense of his God, warning the world of certain destruction, and making clear the doctrines of the Messiah.

My vision expanded. I heard the words as if they were audible.

Years will become decades, and decades will become centuries. Living in Zion, you will see your family grow to thousands. You will know them all and gain a greater appreciation for the possibilities of eternity. No accomplishment will give you more satisfaction than being a father. A benefit from your way of life will be that you will be granted extended years. You will be blessed with prosperity. Poverty, loneliness, abuse, contention, jealousy will become abhorrent ideas. *Your children will grow up in peace, though the world will fear and hate you.*

I saw in my mind the fulfillment of Enoch's prophecy regarding our coming to know our God and abiding in our midst. I realized that such a concept was incomprehensible to the world, but we would learn to know and love our God to the extent that we would urge him from his celestial abode, and we would truly become a heaven on earth.

I remembered that Enoch had received a promise from God that he would be the father of the entire human race through his son Methuselah and his great-grandson Noah. Furthermore, he was promised that through his descendants, the Messiah would be born. I heard the words, *You, Rabunel, will receive a similar blessing and become the father of many nations. Through Miriam's daughter Rachel, you will have an eighth great-granddaughter who will marry Noah's son Japeth, whose descendants will fill the earth.*

I saw that during Zion's years on the earth, Enoch would spend more and more of his time in the temple, emerging only occasionally to preach to us. As a people, we would come to know that the time would come when Enoch would be taken from us into the eternal dwelling of God, having been promised that he would depart this life without tasting death. That we would be left behind would be a thought that we would not be able to bear. I saw the day when we would gather and beg to go with him. By that time, we would have become so unified that the thought of losing any member, especially our beloved prophet leader, would cause us immeasurable grief.

I heard the words, *When Enoch's day of departure nears, eight hundred thousand men and their families will plead permission to go with him, and the outpouring of love will be so great that God will grant your request. In the same manner that Enoch will leave this world, so will you, and Enoch will lead you. You will retain your city, your flocks, herds, buildings, even the very walls and foundations of Zion—it will all depart with you. Then, your bodies will be changed to a state wherein death will be interrupted. You will become like angels and be assigned to minister for and to* men as long as the world stands. In the last days of this earth's existence, you will return to help establish a new Zion. You will assist a future people to understand the right way of living, for their Zion will come in a day not unlike yours, corrupt and violent. Zion will be once more established in a world that is running headlong into a wall of disaster. All institutions, governments, associations, and possessions that are of a worldly nature are destined to fail, and when they do, that future Zion will be left standing alone.

I remembered Enoch's having related to me his vision of the progress and future of Zion.

—God has said of Zion, Behold mine abode forever. I saw Zion, in process of time, being taken into heaven. I saw generation after generation come upon the earth, for I was lifted high into the bosom of God the Father and the Messiah. I saw angels descending out of heaven bearing record of God and the Messiah. We, of Zion, were among them. The Holy Spirit fell upon many, and they were caught up into Zion. I saw God weep for the wickedness of his children. I saw the Messiah come in the meridian of time to redeem all those who believe on his name. I saw him lifted up and suffer for the transgressions of his people. I saw that the world would reject him. Many generations then passed before my view. I heard the voice of the Messiah say unto me, I will come again in the last days, in the days of wickedness and vengeance. In those days, the heavens shall be darkened and a veil of darkness shall cover the earth, and the heavens shall shake, and the earth also, and great tribulations shall be among the children of men, but my people will I preserve. Then you, my righteous of Zion, will I send down from heaven. I will gather out my elect from the four quarters of the earth unto a place which I shall prepare, and they shall make a holy city that my people may look forward to my coming, for there shall be my tabernacle, and it shall be called Zion. Then shalt thou, Enoch, and all thy city meet them there, and we shall receive them into our bosom, and they shall see us, and we shall fall upon their necks, and they shall fall upon our necks, and we shall kiss each other. There shall be mine abode, and it shall be Zion, which shall come out of all creations, and for the space of a thousand years the earth shall rest.

My vision ended with the voice saying, *It shall be said of your people that God received you up into his bosom, and from thence will go forth the saying, Zion is fled.*

I arose, then, and made my way back to camp. The sun was bright now, a hot, orange ball in a sky the color of robins' eggs. Moriah would have a breakfast waiting for me. She would not have worried for my whereabouts since it had become my custom, of late, to spend great lengths of time communing with my God. Later in the morning, I would gather my family for prayer, and we would walk together into Cainan. I loved my family. Nothing was more important to me. Having learned something about Miriam's daughter Rachel, I began to observe her with great hope and admiration.

I stopped at the edge of camp and considered the view. Here were the best people under heaven, hated by the world, hunted, driven from place to place. I thought, *When Zion is established in latter times, the world will hate them as they have hated us. In our day, the world never knew us. In the future, the world will not know them.*

zion is a choice

Ↄⵌ

The ancient community of Cainan was located a little inland from the east sea and sequestered in a fertile valley. Adam's grandson Enos had established the place hundreds of years earlier. We stopped on a bluff overlooking Cainan and gazed upon our new home. Even from a distance, there was evidence of order—clean streets bisecting the city, well-groomed gardens, ivy-covered houses of wood and stone. We watched children playing safely while fathers labored in nearby fields and mothers kept their homes. At the center of Cainan stood a large temple of white stone, situated within a square, enclosed area. Although the temple's architecture was different from the one we had begun, it was a temple just the same. Seeing it completed and in use evoked high emotions in me. I squeezed Moriah's hand and said, The temple will be our first visit.

The air about Cainan seemed fresh and clear, the norm, I guessed, for a continual gentle breeze brushed over the valley. I noticed Enoch standing at a removed place taking in the view. His demeanor was one filled with feeling. I glanced at Moriah, who nodded her permission to go to him. She kissed me on the cheek and walked off to be with the family. As I walked over to Enoch, he spoke without looking at me.

—I'd forgotten how much I missed this place, he said.

—I had never imagined it being so beautiful, I said.

He pointed at a place near the temple.

—My father, Jared, built that house. As a boy, I played in the nearby field.

—Where was Anna born?

—Over there, he said, pointing at a house near his. We grew up together. She has always been part of my life.

—Your family will be amazed at how much Melca has grown, I said.

—Yes. They won't be prepared for her energy!

We both laughed.

—I've heard the Dananites expressing some worry about our being accepted into the community, I said.

—I can understand their concern, but they will have no problems here.

As I looked out over Cainan, I considered the destiny of Enoch's people.

—We will live here for a season, said Enoch. There are many things we can learn from the people of Cainan. The time will come when we and they will band together and travel to a distant place that God will show us. Our future will be glorious.

For the first time, I understood Enoch's gift of seeing. To a degree, I had cultivated it with the help of God. But I knew I still had a long way to go before I could approach Enoch's capability. For now, I was satisfied with the progress I was making, content in the knowledge that God was with me and would bring me along as quickly as I was able. I felt no urgency. I felt instead overwhelming gratitude for his constant care and mercy. I knew I had plenty of time to accomplish the goals before me.

I scanned the valley of Cainan. I sensed it would be a place of rest and peace for us. I looked back at my family and watched my grandchildren running and playing on the hillside. Moriah was sitting with Miriam and Micah, cooing at the twins. After their return, they had requested that Enoch remarry them in the tabernacle. They were as happy a couple as I had known, and Micah's recent service to our community had exceeded his best efforts of the past. He was as good as his word in every regard.

—Micah's countenance has changed, said Enoch. He begins to reflect whom he loves, the Messiah.

—He is trying very hard, I said. He pours over the Book of Remembrance that contains the writings of the prophets and patriarchs, and he tries to incorporate every principle in his life.

—For Micah it is a rebirth, said Enoch. His whole being is dedicated to bringing people to the Messiah. He can no longer stand to see anyone suffer.

—In Cainan, will we re-institute the covenant of consecration? I asked.

—Yes, said Enoch. It is an eternal law, but we will no longer focus on mandating its implementation. That has only succeeded in varying degrees. Properly taught, the covenant has the power to change people and communities. The burden rests on us leaders to thoroughly teach the covenant, to instruct the people of the Messiah and how to perfect the basics of his teachings. We must completely step away from the world and *choose* to live what we have been given. There is no greater power than choice. Zion is a choice.

His statement amazed me. I had imagined the Prophet's standing before the people and revealing some grand secret for the establishment of Zion. It had never occurred to me that we had been taught all we needed to know. What was lacking was commitment! In the end, Zion would be built by simply *doing* what we knew to be right. Of course we could not mandate that people live that way. No organizational plan could take the place of an individual's change of heart and devotion to God. For such a person or group of people, there would be no poor, no ignorant, no forgotten, no afflicted. In such a society, its converted, sanctified people would not be able to witness another's pain without a call to action. Enoch was right. We had been taught all that was needed for the ultimate establishment of Zion. It all came down to choice.

—Do you think we can do it? I asked. Do you think we can create a heaven on earth?

—We can. We will.

afterword

In the first book of this *ZION* series, the primary theme was the individual decision to separate one's self from the evils of a corrupt world. Sometimes heartrending, often violent, this separation, we suggest, is more easily accomplished by working with others of like aspirations. Still, history has demonstrated that collectivism can result in disaster. Therefore, in this volume we suggest that a society's success in achieving Zion is in proportion to the depth of the spiritual commitment of its individuals. A flock of sheep can be led to the shearers but is unlikely to create a lasting, progressive community.

Enoch was a leader who focused on individual potential and choice. He taught his followers to know God for themselves and not to rely totally on him, a man. Once they were empowered with this knowledge, Enoch knew his people would not be dissuaded or succumb to fear. They would live together, without coercion, in love and peace by informed choice.

To understand what Enoch did and how he did it, we consulted many sources, including the Holy Bible, apocryphal books and other Christian writings, the pseudepigrapha collections, Jewish texts, multicultural reference materials, commentaries by trusted researchers, and oral histories and interviews (see Bibliography). For the purposes of creating a fictional work, we invented detail and characters, although we attempted to write as accurately as possible. Where sources were in disagreement about facts or specifics, we used our best judgment.

Regarding Fact and Fiction

The places and people of both Danan and Saad were fabricated for literary reasons. In describing ancient marriage customs, clothing, architecture, etc., we relied on the writings of biblical historians and established sources.

Temples and temple worship are historical facts. Temples were also called Mountains of the Lord. They were seen as representing great altars lifted up off the earth, separate from the world, knots that bound earth to heaven. The Zion society was described as one in which God lived in the people's midst, meaning *middle*, in the central point, in other words, in the temple at the center of Zion. There, God walked and talked with his people, and the people were reminded of their covenants and relationship to him though the ordinances that they received and the rituals that they practiced. To the question that we pose in this book, *Can there be heaven on earth?* we suggest that the people of Zion apparently achieved such a status partly due to their devout temple worship and the care they gave to one another.

Priesthood is an equally historical certainty; in fact, Zion was called a society of priests. Priesthood was received by calling and ordination and was believed to be the power and authority of God on earth. Ceremonial cleansing, sacrifices, rituals, ordinances, covenant-making, and special clothing were all part of the temple experience.

The people of the City of Enoch very much believed in a future savior named the Holy One, or the Messiah, a deliverer who would come in the meridian of time to redeem his people from the conditions and consequences of a precarious and wicked world. They also believed in a future resurrection.

Although we do not know with certainty how or where the people of Zion lived, we do know that their society was built upon covenants with each other and with their God. They were called a covenant people. By living those covenants with a determination to bear one another's burdens, they collectively and individually became Zion—*the pure in heart.* We believe the people actively sought individual and communal sanctification. We also believe that a key mechanism implemented to achieve sanctification was those whom we chose to call Teachers, those who ministered to each family under the direction of local leaders, whom we called Shepherds. The idea of sanctifying a person and a people became one of the key issues in writing this book. The clearest definition of sanctification that we found was "yielding one's heart to God."

In this book, we described Enoch's first attempt at establishing a Zion community as having failed. We chose to explore reasons why people fall away from and resist the truth—the Sower-and-the-Seeds principle as taught by Christ in the New Testament. We propose that Enoch's people thought they were converted and expected that they would be strong in the face of adversity, but, in actuality, they had mainly come together by reason of urgency and tradition with a surface allegiance to Enoch's teachings. In the end, only those who had internalized Enoch's teachings to the point that they were independent in their knowledge were able to withstand the intense opposition and remain firm in their convictions.

Also Noteworthy

The ancient world during the time of Enoch was divided into two contesting groups: the Sons of God ("People of God," in this book) and the Sons of Men, those who actively fought against the God and his followers. The fathers, or leaders, of these two groups were initially Seth, who was Adam's heir, and Cain, who murdered his brother

Abel. Since Cain was denied the birthright of the priesthood, he created his own along with a secret group, the Mahan society. The public face of this secret society was the false priests, also called the Watchers. The various books of Enoch name Azazel, a Watcher, as a leader of a group of some two hundred *fallen angels*, or men who had once attained the true priesthood of God, then rebelled. The Watchers misused their knowledge of God and his priesthood to enlist, subjugate, and corrupt others. Although we do not spend much time discussing the Watchers and the Mahan society, we did want to point out that an underlying factor in the destruction of the ancient world was this: secret lives and societies that combined to steal, murder, and commit whoredoms for the sake of gain, power, and self-gratification. These societies upheld their members' conspiracies through secret oaths and covenants, all parts of their mock priesthoods, sometimes called priestcrafts. Once priestcrafts entered the world and infiltrated religion and government, the seeds were planted for universal destruction. Ancient members of covert societies believed that God was also limited in his power; therefore, he could be defeated. Incredulously, they staged an all-out war on God to pervert or invert every true principle. They truly thought they could conquer God and possess the entire world. Another characteristic of those who belonged to these societies was a belief that God was limited in his knowledge, that he did not know what the members of the secret societies were doing or planning. That arrogance enabled society members to sin and not fear punishment. They became laws unto themselves, an elitist attitude that has plagued the world ever since. We tried to portray an initial stage of this attitude in Micah's making his own sacrifice and calling himself to his own mission, both with total disregard for the will of God. Hence, the question stated in the text: "A man may do a good work, but is it the *right* good work?" In other words, is it the work that God would have a man do? In Micah's case, it was not.

We spend some time discussing councils. An interesting description, and something we adapted and incorporated into this book, is found in council literature of the American Iroquois Indians. The Iroquois were taught their government and lifestyle by the man Deganawidah, who, according to legend, came among them in about 1570 A.D. Deganawidah unified the Iroquois nations and taught them the ways of peace, love, and justice. He was said to have been a holy man from unknown origins who would come again in the last days of the world. Interestingly, Benjamin Franklin was so taken by the incredible organization of the Iroquois that he incorporated it as a model for the new American republic.

This second book in the ZION series also attempts to explore some difficulties associated with divergent peoples assembling to a central spot for protection and saanctification. We take a look at the problems of bigotry and intolerance. Because the reestablishment of Zion (called by various names) in our day is such a prominent theme among Christians, Jews, American Indians, Tibetans, and many other cultures, and because our day so closely parallels that of Enoch, we can expect this future Zion to be built by peace-loving people of all nations. Therefore, the attendant challenge of blending peoples of diverse backgrounds will be an issue.

The near-death experience in chapter four is based upon an actual experience of one of the authors along with accounts of other people. No segment of the book was worked and reworked as much as this. Our motivation for including it was not to sensationalize or to reveal savory bits of information about the next world. Rather, we wanted to demonstrate four important principles: (1) God actually lives; (2) God cares about the lives we lead and is capable of helping us; (3) families exist beyond the grave; (4) the consciousness or spirit of man continues on after death. This last point raises some questions: Everything being equal (i.e., man's spirit, which is the same in life and in death), if Zion exists in Paradise, why does it not presently exist here? Is Zion the result of environment or individual choice? As impossible as it seems, can there be heaven on earth? Our conclusion was this: the responsibility of establishing Zion rests squarely upon the individual. In fact, Zion by definition (*the pure in heart*) is an individual and a family and a society. The environment may help, but Zion is a matter of choice, regardless of it location.

ZION: A WIDELY-SHARED VISION

In Zion literature, two facts are clear:
>1. Zion was an actual city that existed in our ancient past, a society that had no violence or hatred, only peace, love, and enlightenment.
>2. In the future, after great destructions and wars, Zion will be established again through miraculous means.

These two facts are prominent themes in many cultures. Diverse peoples with separate histories from virtually every continent share traditions and prophecies of Zion. Some that we have documented are: Christians, Muslims, Jews, the Shintos of Japan, the Buddhists of Tibet, the Kikuyu of Kenya, the Aztec of Mexico, the Inca of South America, the Maya of Central America, many American Indian tribes such as the Hopi Indians, the Nez Pierce, the Shoshone, the Navajo, the Pueblo, the Iroquois, and the Cherokee. A good tape series on this topic is "They Saw Our Day," by Lance Richardson.

That the reestablishment of Zion, or a holy society of peace, will mark the ushering in of a new era in human history is a vision shared by most peoples of the world. If the vision of Zion compels you to action, you need not wait for the society's return. Zion, as we attempted to point out, begins by choice. Zion is a condition of the heart. Zion is the pure in heart and the pure in heart are those who qualify to see God (see Matthew 5:8).

The ways of peace have been explored by great and wise men. The best of these have seldom been able to duplicate what Enoch achieved. But the hope of Zion has not diminished over the ages.

The power of a single individual who seeks to do right cannot be overstated.

Finally, it is our belief that Zion is a gift from God. It comes after all we can do, but ultimately Zion is his.

biography

 os

(alphabetical by publication or entry title)
Norman L. Heap, *ADAM, ENOCH, AND NOAH*, (Walnut Creek, CA: Family History Publications, 1982)

Hugh Nibley, *APPROACHING ZION* (Salt Lake City, UT: Deseret Book, 1989)

Donna B. Nielsen, *BELOVED BRIDEGROOM*, (U.S.A.: Onyx Press, 1999)

Book of Mormon, (Salt Lake City, UT: Corporation of the President of the Church of Jesus Christ of Latter-day Saints, 1986)

Frank Waters, *BOOK OF THE HOPI*, (New York City, NY: Viking Press, 1963)

Doctrine and Covenants, (Salt Lake City, UT: Corporation of the President of the Church of Jesus Christ of Latter-day Saints, 1986)

Hugh Nibley, *ENOCH THE PROPHET,* (Salt Lake City, UT: Deseret Book, 1986)

Zula C. Brinkerhoff, *GOD'S CHOSEN PEOPLE OF AMERICA,* (Salt Lake City, UT: Publishers Press, 1971)

Half-hallels from rabbinical teachings.

King James Version of the Holy Bible, (Salt Lake City, UT: Corporation of the President of the Church of Jesus Christ of Latter-day Saints, 1986)

Letter from William Wines Phelps from Dayton, Ohio, dated June 1841.

Raymond A. Moody, Jr., M.D., *LIFE AFTER LIFE,* (New York City, NY: Bantam Books, 1975)

Pearl of Great Price, (Salt Lake City, UT: Corporation of the President of the Church of Jesus Christ of Latter-day Saints, 1986)

Personal interviews with Hopi Indian tribal council elders and Hopi leaders in Hopi Land, conducted by Lance Richardson and Ron McMillan, March 1998.

George G. Ritchie, M.D., *RETURN FROM TOMORROW,* (New Jersey: Spire Books, 1978)

Blaine M. Yorgason, *SPIRITUAL PROGRESSION IN THE LAST DAYS,* (Salt Lake City, UT: Deseret Book, 1994)

Matthew B. Brown, *SYMBOLS IN STONE,* (American Fork, UT: Covenant Communications, Inc., 1997)

Donald W. Parry (Editor), *TEMPLES OF THE ANCIENT WORLD*, (Salt Lake City, UT: Deseret Book, 1994)

THE AMERICAN HERITAGE BOOK OF INDIANS, (New York City, NY: Simon and Schuster, 1961)

Matthew Black, *THE BOOK OF ENOCH OR 1 ENOCH*, (Leiden: E.J. Brill, 1985)

Richard Lawrence, *THE BOOK OF ENOCH THE PROPHET*, (London: Kegan Paul, 1883)

The Book of Jasher, 1840 translation, (Muskogee, OK: Artisan Publishers, 1988)

James C. Vanderkam, *THE DEAD SEA SCROLLS TODAY*, (Grand Rapids, MI: William Eerdmans, 1994)

Florentino Garcia Martinez, *THE DEAD SEA SCROLLS TRANSLATED: THE QUMRAN TEXTS IN ENGLISH, 2ND EDITION*, (Grand Rapids, MI: William B. Eerdmans, 1996)

Matthew B. Brown, *THE GATE OF HEAVEN*, (American Fork, UT: Covenant Communications, Inc., 1999)

Thomas E. Mails, *THE HOPI SURVIVAL KIT*, (North America: Welcome Rain, 1997)

Campbell Bonner, *THE LAST CHAPTERS OF ENOCH IN GREEK*, (Darmstadt, Germany: Wissenschaftliche Buchgesellschaft, 1968)

Raymond A. Moody, Jr., M.D., *THE LIGHT BEYOND*, (New York City, NY: Bantam Books, 1988)

James E. Charlesworth, *THE OLD TESTAMENT PSEUDE-PIGRAPHA*, 2 VOLS., (Garden City, NY: Doubleday & Company, 1983-85)

THE WORLD OF THE AMERICAN INDIAN, (Washington D.C.: National Geographic Society, 1979)

Thomas W. Lippman, *UNDERSTANDING ISLAM: AN INTRODUCTION TO THE MUSLIM WORLD*, (New York City, NY: The Penguin Group, 1982)

James W. Lucas and Warner P. Woodworth, *WORKING TOWARD ZION*, (Murray, UT: Aspen Books, 1996)